A New Tune

Jenn Faulk

ISBN: 1499723571
ISBN-13: 9781499723571

CONTENTS

CHAPTER ONE

Marie

Even in the sand, she could outrun him.

Little surprise, though, since she'd first learned to walk on this same sand, had tread more than one path across the shore, and had lived all of her life right here by the ocean. He had always been there, three steps behind her.

"Marie!," he yelled, not as winded as she had figured he might be with the speed she'd been running.

She groaned at the energy still in his voice, knowing the truth that it suggested – that she had always outrun him before because he had let her. That he had been content, all these years, to let her think that she was in charge, that she'd been the strong one, that they were who they were because he loved her as much as she loved him.

But what if it wasn't true? What a horrible thought, especially now, as it was all about to change.

"Eish, man!," he yelled, finally putting his hand to her arm and turning her into him effortlessly. She yanked out of his grasp and shot him an irritated look. "You did not give me a chance to explain myself!"

"Oh, I think I understood just fine," she huffed, punching him in the arm with all of her strength.

He didn't even flinch. Blast it, when had he suddenly become immune to her best efforts? *All* of her best efforts? Marie flushed at the very thought of all those efforts coming to nothing –

"Nee, man," he said, "you are so stubborn."

She scowled at him. "Stubborn?," she spat out. "Just because I don't understand *why* you took their side? Why none of *our* plans seem to matter at all to you now? Why you were *so* eager to kiss my dad's butt this afternoon –"

"I did not kiss his butt," he swore.

"Oh, yes, you did," she said. "You stood there, Piet, and told me that I should listen to him. That I should go away."

It was her worst nightmare. Marie Boyd was an American… in nationality, at least. Apart from a handful of short trips to the US to visit her grandparents when her parents were on missionary furlough, she'd never spent any real time there. Life was Africa. Life was Namibia.

Life was Piet.

His parents were nationals, but they'd been home to Marie. From her first days until now, the Bothas had been as familiar, as welcome, as comforting to her as her own family. She and Piet had grown up alongside one another and had never imagined that it would be any different than it was, spending all of their days together seaside, just as they were.

Standing with him, she let her mind roam back through their days as children by the sea as their parents visited together, when they would stay up at night, long after they were supposed to have gone to sleep,

4

giggling together over the scary stories that they would tell, invariably always ending up in the same sleeping bag together because they were too scared to sleep alone. And then to the day when they were teenagers and their sleepovers were abruptly ended because their parents found them wrapped in one another's arms in the morning, innocently enough for them, but looking suggestively enough like the beginning of something else.

And as it turned out, it was, as Marie soon noticed that Piet stood taller, stronger, and felt almost electric to her as they spent their holidays together. And Piet noticed that Marie had curves, was impossibly soft to the touch, and had a thousand different alarms going off in his mind and body every time she glanced at him.

Then, there were sweet kisses and embraces shared when their parents were in another room, certainly not oblivious to what must be going on between their children. And then, of the times they could never have guessed at, when the kisses turned urgent enough that Marie would go out to visit friends and would end up at the Botha house alone with him. Long nights together, when his parents were up in the north, where Piet and Marie spent hours alone discovering one another, inch by inch, in a way they hadn't before, hands and lips, eyes and breaths, moments collected in a dark room by the sea. And even now, as Piet stared at her, Marie could remember how it felt to look up at his face on those nights, the same face of the boy who had been her childhood, staring down at her as they crossed a line together, truly making her believe all the Afrikaans words he whispered afterward, every time, about how he would never love anyone the way he loved her.

Never.

But here they were, on the edge of a challenge to all those whispered promises. Her parents were insistent that she attend university in the States. It would prepare her for life in either nation, for a future anywhere in the world. She needed to prepare for whatever future the Lord had for her, they had said.

How could they not know that she'd already chosen her future? Her future was her past, her present. Her future was Piet.

She watched him as he struggled for the right words to say. How she had always loved his blue eyes, his dark hair, his calm, easy way... well, most of the time, anyway. Now, as he frowned at her and stared intently into her eyes, he was worked up and bothered. And though he called her stubborn, he was more stubborn than she was, more insistent on having his way, and completely unyielding when it came to deciding what he was going to do, what she was going to do, what they were going to do.

They had already decided it. School was done. They were going to marry. They were going to be together.

She had never had to convince him of this. He had been more than eager to make this their reality. He had promised her forever when they were just children, insistent that they would have their own cottage on the beach when they grew up, where they could eat cereal three times a day, buy a trampoline for the backyard, and build forts in the living room to sleep underneath. He had promised her forever when they were young teenagers, hopeful that their cottage would include a video game room, a brick oven for homemade pizzas, and constant access to the beach for surfing. He had promised her forever just the week before, as they tugged their clothes back on between kisses, swearing that the cottage needed nothing more than her and that he had no intention of ever leaving home as long as she smiled that way at him, over her bare shoulder, biting her lip at him and –

She punched him again and cursed at him in the most vulgar Afrikaans she could manage.

Piet said nothing for a moment, then sighed. "Well," he began in English, "that's mature, Marie."

"You want to talk about maturity, Piet? How about being mature enough to man up and do what you want to do, instead of placating my

6

parents?"

"Hey," he said, raising his voice to match hers, "I do what I want to do. I haven't spent any of the past two years asking for their approval. I think we both know that your father would have me killed if he knew the half of it."

"He sure would," she said. "Which should give you even more reason to just keep on with our plans! I think he'd rather us marry than keep on like we've been, honestly, and —"

"Do you think I can provide for a family right now?," Piet interrupted her.

"Oh, good grief, Piet," she sighed, relieved that they were finally getting to the heart of it. "Is that what this is about? About your need to provide?"

"Ja," he said. "And it's not a bad thing, Marie. I'm eighteen. Do you think I can do anything to provide for you right now, just as I am?"

He wouldn't need to do a thing. Marie wouldn't expect it, wouldn't require it, when all she really wanted was him. Just him. Just as he was right now. It wasn't about being taken care of or having anything — it was about being together.

"I love you, Piet," she said, wrapping her arms around his waist. "That's enough. We'll figure everything else out."

He sighed... and slowly withdrew her arms. "I'm eighteen," he said again, softly.

"And I'm seventeen," she said, her anger bubbling up again at the way he was putting distance between them.

"I think I'm too young for what you want," he said.

"I thought it was what *we* wanted," she managed, blinking back tears.

"Piet, you've been promising me a future together –"

"Someday," he said. "But we're too young right now, Marie. I'm too young."

A pause, as she watched him fight to meet her eyes. "Is there someone else, Piet?"

"No!," he shouted at her, putting his hands to her face, his eyes pleading with her to understand. "And there will *never* be anyone else. Why can't you just go and take a few years, let me figure out what I need to do here, then come home to me, and –"

"A few years?!"

"If you really want to be with me for as long as you say you do," he said hotly to her, "then what are a few years to appease your parents, to get the free education you've got waiting for you, to let me set up a home for us? What is it, Marie? Why does it matter?"

It mattered because she knew it would change things. These few years, removed from one another – they would fundamentally change something. Even now, the mere suggestion of spending half a world apart from one another, his calm demeanor at even the possibility... it was changing things.

She didn't want any of it to change.

"I'm not ready," he pleaded with her. "I'm just not ready."

And there was the truth. He wasn't ready because somewhere in his heart, he wasn't sure. She was certain of it.

"Marie," he insisted, as she fought back tears, as he drew her close, "ek lief is vir jou."

"I had thought so," she said to his declaration of love. "But I –"

He leaned in and covered her mouth with his, silencing whatever protest she had to offer. This was his way, to silence all of her protests, her concerns, her worries, with his lips. Although with Piet? Marie rarely had any protest at all.

And as his kiss drew to a close, Marie had the fleeting, horrifying thought that this would be the last time she kissed Pieter Botha.

"We will talk about it more," he breathed out. "Still a few weeks until you must leave, your father said."

She swallowed the lump in her throat and nodded.

A few weeks.

Oom Willem was having a difficult time understanding her tear-stained declarations thirty minutes later.

"I'm not sure I understand, Marietjie," he said, using the term of endearment that they all used for her. "Little Marie." Which wasn't so apt now, given the rude, explicit, and overall loud way she said her earlier statement again, this time in Afrikaans.

"Shame, man," he said, after a stunned moment of silence. "I understood perfectly." He looked to Aunt Sophie and shrugged. "What do you think, Sophie?"

The beautiful, tall American frowned slightly. "Are you running away from something, Marie?"

"Why do you think that?," Marie asked, wiping her eyes furiously.

"Because you have not wanted anything to do with the States before now!," Willem said, echoing his wife's suspicions. "And today, you storm in here and tell us that you're going to college a few weeks early. And you want us to go with you to get you settled in!"

Marie sighed. "Well, perhaps I'm reconsidering it all now. The scholarship to that... tiny school no one's ever even heard of."

Oh, Marie knew a few things about the tiny college that had called her earlier in the year. It was summer in Namibia but winter in the States, and Marie had been, very literally, in her bikini sitting on top of Piet as he lay on the beach, smiling up at her and whispering about all the ways that he would make her very happy indeed –

And the very remembrance now made her stomach turn with nausea, not unlike the way it had turned back on that day at the beach, when the call came in on her cell phone. Marie had no need for American universities, but this particular small, private school with grants and funds especially for missionary children, had plenty need for her. They were calling not only to offer her that money but an additional scholarship which would cover the entirety of her tuition, living expenses, and book expenses, all because of her audition tape.

Marie had never sent an audition tape. She hadn't even knowingly recorded one. As she sat on Piet and ended the call with great confusion, she told him the news. A series of shadows had passed over his face, even then. By the time she figured out and confirmed what she had guessed – that her parents had been behind it all, had filled out the paperwork, had filmed her during a particularly rowdy music service up north in Oshakati – it had all started to unravel.

Piet had started seeing reason where there was none. He had begun to listen to her parents, and their speculation about the future had changed his heart.

"Marie?," Sophie asked, gently, pulling her back to the present.

"I just... I need to go now," she said simply, trying for a smile that fell woefully short of the goal.

Willem exchanged a look with Sophie and frowned again. "Nee, man, what did Piet do?"

"Piet," Marie hissed, "did *nothing*, Willem. Absolutely *nothing*."

"Then why are you angry at him?," Willem shouted.

"Willem," Sophie sighed. "When she says he did *nothing*, she means he did *something*. Clearly. Have you learned nothing in seventeen years of marriage?"

He thought on this for a second. "I've learned nothing... which means I've learned something, ne?"

Sophie smiled at this. "Quite, Willem."

"Ja, I've learned that women are sometimes passive-aggressive." He smiled at Marie. "Shame, man, I've learned what passive-aggressive means as well. Lovely English phrase for a horrible thing that American women are so skilled at doing. Which is something I've tried to warn my nephew all about, but Piet will not listen to reason when it comes to you. You have rendered him as completely hopeless as Sophie has rendered me, and —"

Marie and Sophie both shot him a look, silencing him.

"Well," Marie said, "the something he did was nothing. Piet just sat by and... let my parents convince him that I need to go to the States."

Sophie shrugged. "It doesn't mean forever. Going now, I mean. And you can take a year maybe, on that scholarship and decide if you want to stay there or come back or... the world is open to you, Marie."

Marie knew it. And she knew, more than that, as she thought of Piet's words, that she wouldn't come back. Not to him, when he couldn't promise forever.

"Exactly," she said.

"But why us?," Willem asked. "Why do you want us to take you?"

"Because you can afford it," she said simply. "And you're fun. I can't take a whole lot of crying from Mom and Dad shooting death glares at everyone because he feels so foreign."

"I am less foreign in the US than your father?," Willem asked, raising his eyebrows.

"Ja, man," Marie said. "En jou Engels is pragtig."

He laughed out loud at this. "It is. It really is. My English has come a long way!"

Marie shrugged. "Things are tense at home. It would be better to go overseas with you guys."

It had been tense in the Boyd home for nearly a year now. Talks of college, suggestions on education, outright demands on what she would do – this had been life. Her father had never been an easy man to reason with, and her mother had been in complete agreement with him on this topic. College in the States. Decided. Done.

So *not* done. She hadn't lived the rest of her life for their approval, and she had no reason to start now. She'd go to college, sure, but she would never come back. College on her terms, to show them, to show Piet, to show everyone.

She knew it would wound her parents, this plan. That made it all the more appealing, since they had wounded her by setting in motion this heartbreak from Piet. Would it have happened anyway? Maybe. Marie didn't want to think about it.

"So, Willem?," Sophie asked, looking to him. "Should I speak with Sara, make plans, and…" She left the question hanging.

"Book a flight, Sophie," he grinned, high-fiving Marie as he did so. "Gaan ons na America!"

Scott

"I love you, Scott. I want to marry you."

The evening was young. The lights were dim. They were all alone.

Yet still, Scott Huntington sighed at this declaration with absolutely no intention of returning the sentiment. The words were sincere, of course... but they probably had more to do with the alcohol than genuine emotion.

Besides, Drew, even as he clung to Scott and gazed up at him with eyes that just wouldn't focus... well, he wasn't Scott's type.

Because he was a dude.

"I'm flattered," Scott said, twice as drunk as his friend but three times better able to function despite this. "But seriously, Drew. It would never work."

Drew groaned. "But you have a good job," he slurred. "You could support me. Be my sugar daddy and all. Then, I wouldn't even have to worry about getting a job or figuring out what I'm going to do! I'd make you so happy, Scott!"

"Okay, this conversation is getting really weird for me," Scott said, pushing his friend away just slightly as he took stock of the cell around them.

Yes. A cell.

This was his first arrest, his first DWI... which sucked, frankly. This would end up costing him. A lawyer, a court date, fees, a ticket, and words, so many words, from all the members of his family, on how he was a total loser. It was all sure to be heading his way soon.

It would suck. But at that moment, Scott didn't waste more than a few seconds thinking about all that. No, right then, he was more concerned about his truck and its whereabouts.

He'd had too much to drink, which was true of most nights, and he'd tried to drive himself home, which was true of most nights. Most nights, though, he made it home. That night? He was pulled over, declared drunk, and driven to jail in the back of a police car.

And his truck was still out there somewhere.

"I should've let you drive," he muttered to Drew, expecting an intelligent response from his cellmate.

But seeing as how Drew was a loud, chatty, stupid drunk who was more concerned about his own future lack of job opportunities than he was about his criminal record, he kept right on moaning and groaning.

So annoying.

"I don't know what I'm going to do with my life," he carried on and on, even as Scott stood and began pacing, willing the buzz away so he could think. "I don't know what I'm going to do. Why am I here? What's the whole point of it all?"

"You're going to help me find my truck once we get out of here," Scott said. "And you're here because you're a lousy friend who wouldn't be my designated driver tonight."

"My parents are missionaries, man," Drew droned on and on, not hearing a word. "I mean, I *know* there's more to life than living like this. There's got to be *more*, Scott. Really! There has to be! Jesus has to want more from me, for me, than this!"

"I think," Scott said, sidestepping all of this talk about Jesus and His expectations, "that you need to shut up, or –"

And the prayer he hadn't even bothered to pray was mercifully answered as Drew passed out in a heap on the floor, just as an officer came around to tell Scott that bail had been posted.

"Hallelujah," Scott muttered. He wasn't much for prayer. He wasn't much for Jesus. His family was, but he was cut from a different mold, rarely giving anything beyond the present day and its pleasures more than a fleeting thought. But when he was arrested, he'd had the good enough sense to thank whatever God was out there that his brother, Sam, was on leave and back in the US. Sam was the best of the five Huntington brothers, the quietest, the one least likely to give him a hard time, and the one least likely to tell their mother about this and break her heart.

Scott was an alcoholic and a loser, sure, but he still didn't want to break his mother's heart. Surely that earned him some good guy points in a good guy book somewhere, right?

Points didn't count for much, he concluded, when he walked out into the foyer where Sam was standing with his arms folded across his chest, staring blankly ahead.

That is, until his eyes met Scott's. And before Scott could comment on the rage present there, Sam grabbed his arm, and dragged him out to—

"Why are you in Seth's truck?," Scott asked, recognizing their youngest brother's mess of a vehicle instantly, what with all of the textbooks on the floor. Biology, animal science, and... good grief, was that a dog's skull?

Maybe Scott was drunker than he thought.

"I live overseas," Sam murmured. "I don't have a car. Seth let me use his."

"Okay," Scott sighed, picking up the skull, slipping his hand inside, and staring it in the eyes. Or lack of eyes. "Do you think this is real?"

Sam didn't even look his direction.

"Helllllooooooo, Samuel," Scott said, working the jaw up and down with his hand. "Do you think this is reeeeeeaaaallll? Or is Scott just that drunk? Hmmmmm???" Then, with a sigh, "I don't guess it matters either way. But Seth needs to clean his truck out. A man should have a little more respect for his vehicle, you know? And speaking of, we should probably figure out what they did with my truck, and..."

His voice trailed off as he noticed the direction they were driving.

"Sam," he started in. "Where are we going?"

Sam didn't even glance over at him. And like that, Scott knew exactly where they were heading.

"Sam," he swore, "you are such a —"

"Shut up," Sam cut him off. "One more word, and I'm opening up your door and throwing you out. Then, I'll put the truck in reverse and run right over your sorry butt. Multiple times, until you're nothing but a bloody pulp I'll have to hose off Seth's tires."

He would do it. Scott knew he would. He wasn't sure what went down in Afghanistan or what exactly the Marine Corps had Sam doing out in the middle of nowhere, but the man could be scary psychotic when he wanted to be. So, though Scott's blood boiled at the thought of being dragged to see his super religious, super irritating, oldest brother, Sean, he kept his mouth shut.

Until they got there, walked into the kitchen, and he counted.

Oh, no. Really? All five brothers, in one kitchen, together again.

Scott was about to scold them all for not including their sister, Savannah, in this fine reunion when Sam pulled out a chair and forced him into it with a heavy hand to his shoulder.

"Oww," he muttered. "Do you mind not —"

"Shut up," Sam answered, going over to the corner and sitting on the stool there while the rest of the brothers sat around the table.

There was Sean, the oldest, with his hipster glasses, his tight tee shirt, and... oh, good grief, skinny jeans. The man, and Scott used the term loosely, was wearing skinny jeans. He had his pastoral face on, where Scott couldn't tell if he was really thinking deeply or if he was just mentally calculating how long he'd have to be here, looking as though he was thinking deeply. Nods and sighs, nods and sighs, and a well-timed "bro" and "man" thrown in once in a while.

Ugh.

Then, there was Stu. Good, old, stodgy Stuart. A pastor as well but not hip. Not at all. Just serious, focused, and probably ready to launch into a dull dissertation about reformation, the elect, and the doctrines of grace. Scott had no idea what any of those things actually were, but they were all Stu blathered on about. And while grace was on his lips more often than not, it was likely the thought of alcohol and Scott's inability to stay sober that made Stu look like wrath was about to spew forth from his mouth.

Ugh. Again.

Next was Seth, who looked like he'd probably been sleeping in that horrifically messy truck of his. He wore scrubs, had circles under his eyes, and... eww. What was that on his pants? Blood, mucus, intestines? Seth didn't seem a bit bothered by the disgusting evidence of his work as he watched Scott with wide-eyed innocence and shock, glancing over to Stu and Sean both as they all continued watching. Seth was totally non-threatening... but he might actually have a horse tranquilizer on hand somewhere, with his vet's license giving him the permission and authority to legally use it at will. It would only take a word from Stu, and Seth would acquiesce and stab Scott with it so that he'd be sedated enough to shut up and listen.

Ugh. That would probably hurt.

And then, there was Sam. Quiet, sensitive, thoughtful Sam. Who looked, as he sat on the stool with his hands clenched on the seat, as if he could break apart in a million pieces at any moment, kill them all, and go on with life as if he wasn't bothered in the least bit. He was trained to do it, probably did it on a normal basis in his covert missions, and was now likely completely insane because of it. Insane enough that Scott moved his chair away from him just a fraction of an inch.

The Huntington brothers. My, my, my. What a great night this was turning out to be.

"Hey, Scott," Sean began, in his concerned pastor's voice. "We just wanted to sit down with you, talk about life, and really help you to discover what it is that you –"

"Oh, great," Scott groaned, his suspicions confirmed. "Is this an intervention?"

Seth cleared his throat uneasily. "You were arrested. A DWI."

"Thank you for stating the obvious, Seth," he muttered. "I was there. I know what happened."

"Well, we're all worried about you."

"That's fine," Scott said, "but can someone other than Sean discuss this because the hip, understanding, 'let's talk about your feelings, bro' pastor routine? Is making me want another drink."

Sean nodded thoughtfully at this (nod and sigh, nod and sigh), then opened his mouth to try perhaps another approach. But Stuart cut him off.

"Fine then, you idiot," he spat out. "How about you let me handle it?"

"That's just fine," Scott hissed. "Especially since I've shared more than a few beers with you, friend, and can recall that you're even wilder than I am afterwards."

His mind went to evenings spent with Stu just a few years back. They'd drink together, they'd drink alone, they'd drink to celebrate, they'd drink just because. Stu was cooler drunk than he was sober, that's for sure, and Scott had watched him in awe more than once as he'd done some crazy, stupid, wonderfully pagan things after a few too many –

"Oh, yeah," Stu said. "You remember all that, huh?"

"With fondness," Scott replied. "First time I felt like I had a real brother."

"We were real all right," Stu said. "Real guys with a very real problem."

"Yeah, until Bible Boy over there got to you," he said, nodding towards Seth. "And now, you're just as religious as all the others. And trying to convince me to be the same."

Seth glanced over at Stu. "I'm not sure that's what he was getting at, Scott," he said.

"Yeah, apart from any spiritual convictions or insights I could offer," Stu continued, "on why your excessive drinking is a poor substitute for filling that void in you that only Christ can fill –"

"Ugh," Scott groaned.

"He speaks the truth, man," Sean cut in.

"Shut up, Sean," Scott muttered.

"But that's not my point," Stu said. "Apart from the spiritual truth, there's this truth, Scott. You have a problem. And I know all about it, because once upon a time? I had it with you. I drank alone. I drank all the time. I drank so much that it was all I could think about."

Scott could relate. And he could see it in Stu's eyes. He understood. It was a need. It wasn't even a choice anymore. He did it because he had to. It was all there was to do. When he was anxious, when he was content, when he was bored, when he was –

"They don't get it like we do," Stu said softly. "And I don't know why it's our problem, just you and me, but I know I had to stop it altogether. I can't even handle it in moderation. And neither can you. So you have to stop. Not another drink. Ever."

"Or what?," Scott said. "I'll ruin my life, huh?"

"Or someone else's," Seth murmured.

"Yeah," Sean said. "What if you'd run your truck into someone tonight? Into another car?"

"I didn't hit anyone!," Scott bellowed.

"No, you ran into a telephone pole," Sean pointed out.

"What?," Scott asked, incredulous. He didn't remember that.

"It could have been worse," Sean nodded.

"You could have killed someone because you can't stop drinking," Seth said. "Could have run your car into someone's family and killed their children, Scott."

"It could've been anyone," Stu said, getting visibly angry at the very thought. "It could've been Abby. And Chance, sitting in the backseat watching his Elmo videos."

"Whoa, whoa, whoa," Scott managed. "Are you serious? I didn't hit anything but a telephone pole! And you're acting like I've murdered your wife and son!"

"While he was watching Elmo videos, too," Seth murmured, a frown on his face. "That's really, really sad."

"Shut up, you idiot," Stu said. "Both of you. Do you see how this affects more than just you now? How it's about more than you, your truck, your stupid friend –"

"Drew *is* stupid," Scott allowed. "But my truck! Is it totaled?!"

"Your truck doesn't matter," Stu interrupted. "You've got to stop drinking."

"Agreed," Sean said. "We have an AA group at the church, some guys who've been there and can talk you through the first step in giving it up, and –"

"This is stupid!," Scott yelled.

Then, everyone was talking at once, with no one listening. And as the brothers' voices raised, talking over one another, Sam, who had been silently watching their conversation, finally stood, strode over to Scott, and grabbed him up out of the chair by the collar so that their faces were only inches apart.

Scott noted that he had his crazy psychotic eyes out and everything. Awesome.

"You listen here, you little snot," Sam said, evenly and dangerously. "I don't give two flyin' flips what you think about the Lord, any of us, or even your own sad pathetic self. But you *will* stop this. And you *will* get help. Because, Scott," he said, great emotion in his voice, "I can't go back overseas to what's waiting for me there and get a call telling me that you've finally killed yourself drinking. I can't do it. And I'll spend every waking moment I'm here making sure you give it up."

And he hugged Scott to himself rather fiercely, dropped him in his chair, then left the room.

Every set of eyes followed him as he slammed the door behind him.

Scott concluded that Sam was mentally imbalanced and would come back and kill them all if he didn't at least give sobriety a chance.

And so, after another two hours of arguing with his brothers over it all...
he did.

CHAPTER TWO

Five Years Later

Marie

The United States? Was a weird, weird place.

Marie never felt the certain truth of this statement more than on those rare occasions when she watched her father navigate social pleasantries with people who were decidedly not African in any way at all. Daniel Boyd had spent more of his life in Namibia than in America, and that, on top of his already strange personality, made him as foreign as Marie herself was here stateside.

"Is it just me," he murmured in her ear, "or does every woman in here have big hair?"

"And big makeup to go along with it," Marie giggled at him, smiling when he frowned.

Her mother turned to them both, shaking her head, her voice lowered as she said, "You two are showing no gratitude for all that it cost the Morales family to fly us out here."

Her father slipped his arms around her mother, prompting her to smile. "Sara, I'm very thankful to them for giving me the opportunity to be with the world's two most beautiful women for the week... and the only two women in all of Texas with normal hair, apparently."

"Daniel," her mother chided again.

"And, Mom," Marie added, "I'm pretty sure Mr. and Mrs. Morales didn't pay for much of any of this. Sadie's husband is... well, loaded. Frankly speaking."

"Loaded," Sara sighed. "I just love these American colloquialisms that have found their way into your vocabulary, Marie. And I'm being entirely sarcastic when I say that."

"Should've never sent me back here to go to college," Marie smiled at her.

That had certainly been Marie's way of thinking all those years ago, when she'd said goodbye to Namibia, stepped on a plane with Willem and Sophie, and literally shaken the dust off her feet. She had refused to let Piet say goodbye, had been flippant with her parents, and had been indifferent to the whole lot of them in her forced and eager enthusiasm for the America life that was ahead of her. Too good for all of them, she'd told herself, never looking back.

Until a few weeks later when Willem and Sophie left to go back, leaving her with... no one. Absolutely no one. Her mother's parents had long since passed away, and her father had no relatives. Apart from a few contacts she had of other missionary colleagues who were now retired, Marie found herself completely alone for the first time in her entire life.

Alone in America, at that, which made it a thousand times more strange.

She would never forget the first week of class at the small school no one had ever heard of, how hopeless she had felt, and how her profound sense of loss – of her home, of her family, of her very self – had forced her into a place of dependency that she'd never experienced. She needed God in a way she had never needed Him before, and for the first time, there in a small group of students from a campus ministry organization, the daughter of missionaries came to a saving faith in Christ.

And He changed everything.

Sara looked over to her even now. "Was it all bad?," she asked, knowing the answer.

None of it. God hadn't wasted one single sad moment from that time. The joy that had come with her changed life had been worth it all. It hadn't been all bad. None of it was hardly worth counting as a loss now, compared to who she was in Christ.

Her parents understood this. One of the biggest changes had been Marie's relationship with them, even with all the miles between the small university and the mission house in Africa. Their relationship went from tense to rich, from guarded to open, and from trying to fulfilling. She learned earlier than most what it meant, as an adult, to consider her parents as friends, not just relatives.

"Not all bad," Marie smiled, squeezing her mother's hand.

"Told you so," her father said, still frowning, even as he tugged on his tie.

"Shame, man," Marie sighed, pushing away her errant thoughts, smiling at her parents. "Big hair and all, it was a nice wedding, huh?"

Sadie, the bride, was the daughter of her mother's longtime, childhood friend. Furlough was a long way off still for her parents, and because Marie couldn't afford the airfare back out to Namibia, they had assumed it would still be another few years before they were together again. But Sadie's mother, Emily, had made arrangements for them all to be back in Fort Worth together, paying for the Boyds to come back stateside, and it was like Christmas in the spring. They'd come in a week before the wedding and had spent the whole time together again.

A whole week. It was the longest they'd been together since Marie was seventeen. There had been so many days spent peering into her life now, so many nights spent talking late past dinner, and so many jet-lagged early dawn moments laughing over shared memories as they sat in their pajamas and planned what they'd do next.

Marie didn't know anyone else in attendance at the wedding, but the two people she sat with knew her better than anyone else in the world. So, she had plenty reason to smile. There would be the next day, of course, when her parents would get back on a plane and fly home... but for now, they were together.

For a moment, at least.

"I'm going to have to leave the two of you for a little while," her mother said, standing and pushing her chair in. "I told Emily and Mel we'd have a piece of cake together." She smiled broadly. "It's a long-standing tradition and all."

"Eating wedding cake?," Marie asked, glancing up at her.

"Yes."

"Back from the days when you were all gossipy teens, chatting and over-involving yourselves in everyone's business," her father noted. "Or so I've been told."

"Older than that," Sara said. "Back from the days we were twenty-somethings coming up with some crazy New Year's resolutions and stuffing our faces full of wedding cake."

"I may have heard that story before," Marie said, smiling.

"Probably so," Sara answered as she scanned the crowd for her friends. Then, in a lower whisper to Marie, as she was walking away, "Make sure your father doesn't weird anyone out."

"I heard that," he muttered.

Marie grinned over at him. He was weird, in the best way possible, in a way that reminded her of home, of Namibia, of all that she'd left behind. As they chatted, she fell into Afrikaans as easily as English, and his eyes sparkled just a little as he talked with her.

"I miss it," she practically whispered in English.

"Homesick?," he asked softly.

"Sometimes," she sighed. "I was glad Sophie and Willem stopped by Houston on their last trip. They visited my church, and Willem gave it his approval."

"For what that's worth," her father noted.

"Worth a lot," she said, thinking of her uncle and how they'd spent the better part of the evening at the piano, singing songs together like two long lost buddies. "As was your own approval. I'm glad you were able to be there last week."

"Me, too," he said, reaching over to take her hand. "It's good… you being here. Living your life, starting your own ministry. But you could always come back, you know."

She did know this. It had been an option when she'd finished college. She'd gotten the education they'd forced her into, and now, she was free to go wherever she wanted. Namibia had, of course, crossed her mind as an option more times than she could count.

At times, she had imagined going through appointment with the mission board, finding a similar place in southern Africa, doing the same kind of work her parents did, maybe even being designated to their team. She had imagined stepping off the plane half a world away, her feet touching African soil for the first time in five years, wiping the sand off her shorts, raising her hand to shield her eyes, and looking to see who waited for her just past the window at immigration.

She hadn't spoken to Piet since that day on the beach. He had stopped trying to contact her a few years ago, gradually ceasing the constant calls and emails begging her to hear him out. Now, with her degree finished and the way open before her, she'd sometimes allowed herself to imagine what would happen if he was the one waiting there. Would they continue on, as they had been?

No. She always came back to no.

She thought often of the years that had passed, how she'd changed, and how going back would be an impossibility. It was home, most definitely, but she'd been someone different then. How could she reconcile who she'd been there with who she was here? Would she find herself in a more profound sense, or would it leave her struggling to feel right anywhere?

It was best to leave it all behind. Namibia, Piet... and herself. Who she'd been.

So, she'd made a life in the US. A good life. And while she was confident that she had made the right decisions, that the security she'd found in Christ was the greatest indication that she was where God intended for her to be, she still found herself thinking about her feet planted firmly on Namibian soil, her eyes raised up, looking to see who looked back.

These were the things she wondered about when she was by herself.

"How are Riaan and Ana Marie?," she asked, shaking her head past the fantasy, thinking of the last time she'd seen them, back when she was seventeen. Ana Marie had cried in her arms while Riaan had whispered to her that she would always be welcome back with them. She could still remember the way they had looked, hurt that Piet's choice had taken her from them as well. Their plans for the two of them had been almost as elaborate as Marie's, and she had counted herself as part of their family already.

She'd missed them so much.

"They're wonderful," her father said. "Riaan is still his calm, assured self, and Ana Marie is still as high-strung as ever. Hennie keeps in touch as well, though he's been gone longer than you."

Marie nodded. "And Piet?"

"Finished up medic school," her father sighed. "Back in Swakop, working from there. He bought a cottage on the beach with the money Sophie left in trust for him."

Marie swallowed at this, a flash of his teenage smile in her mind, his whispered words about the cottage they would have drifting through her thoughts. "A cottage on the beach. Wow."

Her father said nothing for a moment. The pointed silence was great enough that she finally raised her eyes to him, only to find him frowning at her.

"He asks about you," he said simply. "A lot. Enough that I want to slap him sometimes."

She smiled sadly at this. "No more than when I was a teenager."

"Probably should've slapped him around then, too," he noted grimly.

"Him and me both," she added, patting his hand with a smile. "It's strange, you know. How we can be so certain of exactly what we want in life... and how it can change so drastically, in no time at all."

29

He nodded at the truth of this. "What is it that you want now, Marie?"

She swallowed, thinking of what she wanted at her very depths, more than anything. "I want to honor Christ. To live life completely for Him, because He gave Himself so completely for me."

He smiled. "Me, too."

"Sure does look different for each of us, though, doesn't it?," she sighed, watching as all around them people chatted, danced, ate, drank, and carried on with life. Not so different than back in Namibia… but different. Different enough that even now, something in her longed for the home that she'd left behind.

Again, her father stared at her, in deeply contemplative silence. Marie watched him as he held her hand, a frown on his face.

"What are you thinking, Dad?"

"Just wishing that we could convince you to come back with us," he said.

And as Marie thought about life, about Namibia, and about all that she had once felt, she managed a small whisper.

"I kinda wish you could, too."

Scott

Weddings? They were breeding grounds for needy, whiny women.

Scott was sure of it, even as he sat at one of the tables at his cousin Sadie's over-the-top wedding reception and checked out the available women in the room. Slim pickings, especially with most of Trent's friends, rich athletes that they were, narrowing down the chances that any normal man would catch the eye of –

"Why is everyone here so tall?," Thomas Fisher murmured beside Scott, blinking several times, then exhaling with surprise.

Scott nearly spit out the water he'd been drinking. It had been thirty years since the Alzheimer's diagnosis and probably a good ten since his grandfather had much of any clarity at all. Scott was certain he'd never even heard Thomas speak at all in the last five years.

"Grandpa?," he asked, incredulous. "Did you just... what?!"

Thomas fixed him with a look. "Well. I see that you didn't even bother to shave for... whose wedding is this?"

Scott began looking around for his grandmother, his mother, his aunt, anyone who would want to speak with Thomas during these moments of clarity, certain that they would be short. "Sadie, Grandpa," he said, patting his arm and jerking his neck around. Where were all the women in his family when he needed them?!

"Oh, well, that makes sense," Thomas sighed. "There's Josh right there," he said, pointing to a young man in a tuxedo, chatting with the rest of Trent's groomsmen. "He hasn't changed a bit."

"No, Grandpa, that's Jacob," he said. "Not your son-in-law. Your grandson. Emily's son."

"What? If that's Jacob, then –"

Scott pointed. "That's Uncle Josh over there."

Thomas gasped. "Wow. He got old. And fat."

Scott smiled at this. "Well, we all got old, for sure. But we're not all fat."

Thomas looked at his grandson. "Well, you're heading that way, likely."

"Thanks, Grandpa. I appreciate that." Wow, he was sharp tonight. Grammy needed to get over here and –

"Where are the others?"

"Well, they're here," Scott said. "Or most of them, at least. Grandpa, let me go and find Grammy, so –"

"Where's Sean?," he said, ignoring Scott. "He still in the ministry?"

"Yeah, yeah," Scott nodded. "Married with… three kids. Last time I counted. Could be four by now, though, and –"

"And Sam?"

He was even getting them in the right birth order! "Still overseas with the Marines. Doing another tour in Japan right now."

"The rest," he murmured. "What are the rest doing?"

"Stuart is married as well. Also a preacher, though of a much smaller church than Sean's. Seth's a vet. Sadie is a doctor and just… well, just got married, obviously. Jacob is an accountant."

"Savannah?"

"Taking the pictures… somewhere." Where were the women?!

"What about Kenji and Kimmie? Still in Japan?"

"No, Kenji's in New York. Kimmie's still in Okinawa. Has all but forgotten she's half-American herself, likely. Which you'd expect, since she always thought we were weird."

"You boys were weird."

Scott laughed out loud at this, marveling at all that his grandfather was saying. He had to find Grammy…

"And how about you? You still running around, making a fool of yourself?"

This caused Scott to pause. "Well, just tell it like it is, Grandpa."

"I do, and I will," he said, shrugging. "What are you doing with your life?"

"I'm running my own construction company. Have been for a while now, down in Houston."

"Just like your dad did," Thomas nodded. "You're doing well for yourself, then?"

"Yeah," Scott sighed. "Pretty well. I was actually working for Dad... until a few years ago, when I decided that a change of scenery would be good and moved down south and started my own company."

"Good for you, Scott."

A pause. "Now, exactly, how do I make a fool of myself?"

"Living your godless life," Thomas sighed, to which Scott frowned. "Please. Don't tell me you haven't been looking around this whole time trying to figure out what woman you're going to take home tonight. That's the way you were heading the last time I remember... well, anything. Living for women and thrills and not much else. You still an alcoholic?"

Scott was a bit shocked, to put it mildly, to hear these very true words coming from his senile preacher grandfather. Shocked... and just a bit impressed by his boldness. No one else was as bold about pointing out how differently he lived than the others. "Well, as a matter of fact, I stopped drinking entirely about five years ago."

"Got yourself into trouble, huh?"

Well... yeah. After the DWI and the much loathed intervention from his brothers, he'd quit, cold turkey. Five years later, he could still remember the long nights spent while Sam was on leave, going everywhere with him so as to resist the pull back to drinking, knowing that Sam would kick his butt if he relapsed, thankful for his willingness to do so.

Even now, Sam called to check on him.

"I did get in trouble," Scott said quietly. "But no more. I've changed for the better."

His grandfather nodded. "Still chasing around women, though?"

"Well, *they* chase *me*," Scott argued. "And I hardly think enjoying the company of a woman from time to time is worth comparing to a drinking problem –"

"No," Thomas cut him off, "but both point to the real problem."

"Which is what?"

"That you love yourself more than you love Jesus."

Well, of course, he did. Who didn't? The only difference between Scott and all the other hypocrites out there in the world was that he didn't pretend to give Jesus more than a fleeting thought.

"You need to get yourself right," Thomas said, quite succinctly. "You need to love Jesus more than you love yourself. And then, Scott? Then, maybe you'll actually be satisfied with life."

"Well," Scott sighed, ignoring this, "sure wouldn't be satisfied with the women here. Mainly because there aren't any I can even see who aren't already falling all over themselves over those athletes."

"I saw one earlier," Thomas murmured. "A good girl. I know her from somewhere. Just can't remember where..."

Scott began looking around for his grandmother again. Grammy would kill him if she knew she'd missed out on these moments of clarity.

"Grandpa," he said. "I'm going to go find Grammy. You just…" He looked in his eyes. "Stay with us, okay?"

"Not going anywhere," Thomas said. "Lydia took my keys years ago."

And the two men looked at one another, in perfect clarity, and laughed at this.

Marie

As she sat with her father, talking about home, Marie happened to spot a familiar face. He was someone she knew from long, long ago. His warm eyes brightened when they landed on her, a smile blooming on his lips, clear recognition as he watched her. He began waving enthusiastically and motioning her to come to him.

Thomas Fisher. She was eager to speak to him.

Excusing herself from her father's side, she smiled as she approached the older pastor, then knelt down next to his chair, knowing from an earlier chat with her mother that his health wasn't good and that moving was difficult. She reached out and met his welcoming embrace, then released him to look into his eyes.

"Dr. Fisher," she said.

"It's Tommy," he said, smiling at her. "I told you that many years ago, Marie."

"That you did," she laughed. "It's good to see you."

Thomas and Lydia Fisher had come to Namibia years ago on mission with a group from the church Thomas had started as a young man. Marie had been a preteen back when they'd come to Africa, so very young yet still so enthusiastic. She'd gone up north with her parents and the Fishers when they had evangelism meetings to plan out and facilitate, and as the team on the field made arrangements, she and Thomas had gone to invite people, door to door, in Oshakati. Marie had been his translator and had watched in wonder as God worked through his English words, translated in her Oshiwambo ones, and eternity was changed in people's lives. Years later, when Christ had changed her own life in college, she would think back to Thomas Fisher and his gifting and that time they had spent together. He had told her, from door to door, that God had big plans for her life, even beyond what she was doing for Him then. She could thank this godly man's lasting witness from so many years ago that she herself was in ministry now.

"It's good to see you," he said. "My goodness. You turned into a lovely young woman. And so sweet and kind, just like your mother was at your age, back when she and her friends spent half their time gossiping and giggling at my house."

She smiled. "Well, I'm older than that, likely. But I know. I look like I'm twelve."

He laughed. "How old are you now, Marie? I can barely remember how old I myself am."

"Twenty-two," she said. "I've been done with college for a year now."

"My goodness," he murmured. "And are you on your way back to Namibia? A missionary yourself, I'm sure?"

She shook her head. "No, I've decided to stay in the States. I'm in seminary. And I'm working as a children's minister at a church in Houston."

"Seminary and ministry?," he beamed. "Oh, I'm so glad. And in Houston?"

"Yes, sir," she nodded. "The southeast side of the city."

"Really?," he asked. "You need to meet my grandson, Scott. He lives

36

down there!"

Marie refrained from telling him that Sadie and Savannah, his granddaughters, lived there as well. This must be the memory lapse her mother had spoken of. Today must have been a bad day for poor Dr. Fisher.

"Does he?," she asked politely.

"Oh, yeah," Thomas continued on. "Owns his own business. Does really well for himself. Hard working, responsible…. real winner of a guy."

"Sounds like a catch," she laughed.

"He'll get there," Thomas smiled. "And I think you're just the kind of girl he needs to meet."

Marie grinned at this, just imagining what kind of grandson a godly man of faith like Thomas Fisher must have. "Maybe so, huh?"

"You remember that name, okay? Scott. Scott Huntington."

She repeated it. "Scott Huntington. And would you believe that I never, ever forget a name?"

He grinned at her. "Perfect."

She smiled at him again. "It was good talking with you… Tommy."

"You, too, Marie," he said. "I can't remember the last time I had such a great conversation."

Scott

"Grammy," Scott said as Lydia Fisher very nearly sprinted along with him to his grandfather's side five minutes later, "he's *all* there! Telling

37

me I'm leading a godless life, and –"

"All there and speaking the truth," Lydia panted. "Oh, hang on, Tommy, I'm coming!"

"We should get the others," his own mother said, hurrying alongside them. "Scott, you need to get them all, and –"

But by the time they got to Thomas, he had retreated into his dark, silent world again.

"Tommy?," Lydia pleaded, her hand to his cheek, forcing his eyes to look into hers... empty and unseeing. "Oh, Tommy..."

Scott let out a breath as his mother wiped away tears. "Grammy, I'm so sorry. I wish... I wish you could have heard him."

His grandmother kissed her husband and murmured, "Well, it's enough that you heard him, at least," she said. "That someone here... someone heard him, right?"

Marie

She caught an early flight back to Houston the morning after the wedding.

There had been tears. So many tears in the airport as she and her mother cried on one another. These separations were hard. But as her mother had said, even as the tears streamed down her face, "If serving Christ cost us nothing, then we wouldn't bring Him such glory in doing it. And this – being away from you – is what it costs me now. So, even this will bring Him glory, huh, Marie?"

Marie wasn't sure how much glory could come from such heartache. But she'd nodded and affirmed the words all the same, knowing that there was truth there even if she didn't feel it.

Her father had been stoic as usual, telling her to call him when she got back home, so he'd know she had made it safely, then embracing her quickly and standing behind her weeping mother. Marie often wondered if he expressed any emotion over these hard goodbyes, after she'd gone on... and had it on good authority, thanks to her mother, that even he shed a couple of tears over the Atlantic.

The thought of this only made Marie want to cry more. But she settled onto the plane anyway and forced her mind away from her parents and their departure across the world. Just as she was clicking through her phone, checking for messages from work, she looked up and saw... well, a very attractive man. Quirky, cute attractive, not like NBA athletes, which frankly, she had seen enough of this weekend alone to last a lifetime. There was something in the way this guy smiled, even as he surveyed the empty seats, looking for a place to spend the short flight. Marie moved her purse from the seat next to her, hoping he'd take it.

Sure enough, he smiled in her direction, and she smiled back. Just as she opened her mouth to say hi, he nodded over her head, to the row behind her, and said, "That seat taken?"

Marie looked away as a bubbly feminine voice responded that he was welcome to it. And so, for the rest of the flight, Marie Boyd got the best introduction to Scott Huntington that she could have gotten without actually speaking with him face to face and without ever hearing his name, the intercom on the plane beeping just as he said it to the woman behind her. He flirted, he propositioned, and he left the flight with a phone number. Marie couldn't help but smile at the clever, if not totally reprehensible way he'd done it, even as she left the plane, got in her car, and drove home.

Scott

Scott couldn't find his pants.

This was one of the hazards of being him, however, and waking up in a strange woman's apartment, as he was oft accustomed to doing.

And this strange woman? Was stranger than most. That's what he got for soliciting women on an airplane. Fun and games as they had spent the night out together, laughing and flirting, leading up to what he'd been getting at all along... and then, afterwards, she had cried all over him, pouring out all the different, troubling, bothersome worries on her heart, clinging to him so tightly that he thought he might suffocate if he didn't get out of there. Women were messy, and this one? Was catastrophically messy. A cup and a half of crazy, as he would have described her.

Scott needed to escape.

Which is what he was trying to do once she fell asleep. He was thankful that he hadn't given her his last name. He *had* shared that he owned his own construction company, because that always impressed the women enough to get him further along in the process, but he had been smart enough to tell her his name was Sam. So, if *she* was smart enough to track him down, she'd come looking for his older brother. Which would be freakin' hilarious, given the fact that Sam was overseas with the Marine Corps and hadn't been stateside in years.

Win, win. Now, where were his pants?

"Sam?"

He froze in place, taking a moment to compose himself, to prepare his story. Then turning to her, he smiled apologetically.

"Oh, hey..." Oh, wow, what was her name? "Um.... hey. I didn't mean to wake you up."

She pushed her hair out of her face, her red-rimmed eyes locking on his. "Were you about to leave?"

You betcha. "Oh, yeah, I know, I totally hate to do this, but I got a... a call. From work. Emergency. *Huge* emergency at work. I gotta go."

She seemed confused. "I thought you worked in construction."

He paused just for a second. "Yeah. Construction emergency. The worst kind. A house... a house *fell* on a family. I mean, like, mom, dad, brother, sister, cat, dog. Just *fell* on them. And they called me –"

"The people crushed by the house? They called you?," she asked, desperately wanting to believe even this lame, lame excuse.

"No, not them, they're not calling anyone. Obviously," he said. Ah! There were his pants! He picked them up and began to put them on. "The police called, and –"

"*How dare you*!," she screamed, rattling him enough that he fell over, his pants only half on. "I open up to you, Sam, and you run out like you're never going to call and –"

"Hey, hey, hey," Scott managed, getting back up, pulling his pants on, and grabbing his shirt, pulling that over his head as well. "Who said I wasn't going to call?"

She began crying in earnest. "I did, because you're *just* like the rest! Just like *all* the men who have let me down! My ex-husband, my last boyfriend, my father –"

Oh, the daddy issues. Was there a woman alive without daddy issues?

"Well, you don't know me, then," he said, leaning over and kissing her, standing just far enough back so that she couldn't grab him. "I'm not like that."

"Really, Sam?"

And he saw such unbridled hope and trust in her eyes... and regretted, just a little, what he had done. He wasn't a praying man, but at times like this? His mind naturally began to utter many things about the Lord and about his need for some serious divine intervention.

At that moment, his phone rang. Divine intervention? Definitely not. But a good distraction, at least.

Scott picked up his phone. "Hey, this is... Sam," he said.

"Sam? Scott, what are you talking about?," his mother asked.

"Oh, so you're saying that the little girl is *still* stuck under the house, right, officer?"

"What?"

The mystery woman on the bed held her hand to her mouth. "Ohh," she said softly, probably imagining the little girl in great detail.

Scott went with it. "And she's crying... *pleading*... for a big, strong carpenter to just get out there and get that beam off of her, huh?"

"Scott, I have no idea what you're –"

"*I'll be there!*," he shouted, hanging up on his mother, then looking to the woman who was now crying because she had chanced upon such a compassionate, strong, capable man. "Gotta run."

"Okay... be careful, Sam!"

"I always am," he said solemnly, shutting the door behind him and breathing a big sigh of relief.

Marie

Nepotism was alive and well, even in the world of vocational ministry.

Marie had graduated with a degree in elementary education and had plans to go on to seminary to pursue a career in children's ministry. As she was searching for a way to finance this next step, wondering if it would be wiser to put seminary on the back burner for a while and build up the funds to pay for it by teaching, she got a call from the mission board stateside. After thirty years on the field, her father was connected, but after twenty years on the field with him, her mother had made him exceptionally well connected, and they knew people everywhere. One of their contacts stateside knew another grown missionary kid, from South Africa of all places, who was pastoring a church and looking for a fulltime children's minister. The good news was that the job was in Houston, where Marie could start seminary part-time.

And the even better news was that Pastor Drew was like a little piece of home.

"Goeie middag, Drew," Marie chirped as she made her way into the offices that Sunday morning, a million things on her to-do list.

Drew looked up from where he stood by the receptionist's desk. "Goeie middag, Marie. Hoe gaan dit?"

His Afrikaans accent was deplorable. He hadn't been born on the field and hadn't had one of the greatest benefits that Marie had growing up – Piet. As much as she regretted from her past with Piet, she certainly couldn't regret the childhood they'd spent together, and her language skills were a missionary parent's dream come true. She spoke Piet's Afrikaans like her own English. Drew, unfortunately, spoke it like a kid who had learned it in high school. Which he had.

Still, though, hearing even a shoddy version of her heart language was a bright spot most days. She had never known Drew in Africa, given the age difference between them and her parents' inclination to rarely leave Namibia, where they remained the only American missionaries.

When she had heard about the job opportunity and her contact had arranged for her to meet with the elder board of Drew's church, she had fallen in love with his family before she fell in love with the church. His wife, Tracy, and their two children had been like a new American family for Marie, and the connection that she and Drew had to Africa? Was just icing on the cake.

"Baie goed," she sighed, smiling. Then, switching to English, knowing that Drew's vocabulary fell woefully short of her own, "The elder board wants to meet with me after church. Can you give me a heads up about what exactly might be going on?"

He nodded. "Yeah, they've approved plans to build a children's wing onto the church. *Big* plans."

"And they want some input? From me?," she asked doubtfully.

Drew smiled at her. "They want you to lead the project."

She frowned. "Well, I have no idea where to even start."

He laughed at this. "I figured you wouldn't. Which is why I've started the process for you by hiring a contractor. Old fraternity buddy of mine."

She grinned. "Frat brother," she said. "I'll meet him with a beer in hand, to get things going. Lekker brew and all."

"You know," Drew grinned, whispering, "the rest of this church would think you're kidding about that, but I know better."

"You know we have it one hundred percent right, here in our American church culture, though," she said sarcastically. "Because Jesus? Drank grape juice, right?"

He shook his head at her. "You're what they would call counter-cultural in our parents' work."

She sighed. "That's the truth." No matter how long she stayed here, she had a feeling she would always be counter-cultural. Out of place. Not really at home.

Oh, well. This place was still good.

"Here," Drew said, pulling up the number on his phone and handing it to her. "His name is Scott, and this is his number. Might as well get acquainted now because you two are going to be spending a lot of time together with that project."

Marie punched the number into her phone without much thought, and as she made her way to the children's wing, she began to imagine what kind of space she could create.

Scott

Frank, his crew chief, had screwed everything up.

That's what Scott got for letting up just a little on his control of everything in his business. It was an efficient, lucrative operation. Scott had the know-how and the skills, and thanks to the degree his mother insisted he get to help him with the business end, he was doing well.

Every now and then, he had to remind himself to step away just a bit, to not hover over his crew all the time, making an annoyance out of himself.

And more often than not, he came to regret it, given the messes that resulted.

This project at some church was one such mess. He'd let Frank handle it from the initial contact, and now, he was seeing the fruit of that stupid decision.

"Frank," Scott sighed, looking over the plans. "What imbecile even imagined this hideous space?"

Frank paused for a moment. "Well, she's not an imbecile. She's actually a very, very sweet girl. Who said she would pray for my sick grandmother. You know, the one who had the stroke, and –"

"A girl?," Scott raised his eyebrows, taking this tangent as even further proof that his crew chief couldn't be trusted to do anything without supervision. "A praying girl?"

"I know what you're thinking," Frank said, frowning at him. "And Miss Marie is too good for you."

Scott rolled his eyes. "Good grief, man. Do you think I want to hook up with every girl out there?"

"Yes."

Well, that stung a little. "No," Scott brushed it off. "I only meant to say that you let some praying *girl* with probably no expertise or any idea what she was doing put together our plans."

"Well, I helped her."

"Yeah," Scott raised his voice fractionally. "Helped her to make a mess of things!"

He spent the rest of the morning trying to figure it out... and concluded that he would have to go down there himself and settle up things.

So, with much grumbling and great irritation, he headed out to his truck and drove over to Drew's church, striding into the offices, where the secretary walked him down the hall and to an open office...

... where a young woman was lying on the floor, stenciling a map on a giant sheet of paper. She had on headphones, her head bobbing up and down, as she softly sang along in gibberish. Absolute gibberish.

He glanced at the door. Marie Boyd. Oh, good grief, this was the woman who was driving this project. Months of his life, devoted to the whims and directions of a woman who looked too young to be allowed into a PG-13 movie without parents, who was even now singing higher and still not speaking English –

"Marie!," the secretary spoke up, practically shouting and finally catching her attention. Marie took off her headphones and stood to her feet, finally looking over at him.

"This is Mr. Huntington," the secretary said. "He's the contractor for the company doing the expansion."

Marie turned her full attention to him and blinked a few times, her grin building as she did so.

She was an unimpressive woman with a big smile. And scary intense eyes. But altogether plain, unassuming, and not someone Scott would have ever noticed in a crowded room. He watched her curiously, all the same, as she shot her smile at him and said, with just a trace of shock in her voice, "You... it's you."

"Pardon?" He felt a little squirmy under her intense speculation.

"So, you're the contractor?," she asked, grinning even wider.

"Yeah," he said, holding his hand out to her. "And you're the lady in charge?"

"I am," she said, taking his hand. "Marie Boyd."

"Scott Huntington," he said, shaking her hand then releasing it as she continued to stare at him.

"Scott," she said. Then, realization. And what looked suspiciously like recognition. "Scott. Scott Huntington."

"Yeah," he nodded. "Have we met?" Just because he didn't recognize her didn't mean she hadn't been in his bed at some point over the years. She was a church girl, so the odds weren't good, but still. She was looking at him like she knew all of his secrets. Maybe they'd run into one another before somewhere, and –

"Nope," she smiled, then shook her head. "Well, Scott Huntington… okay." She took a deep breath and began speaking again, this time with a laugh in her voice. "You probably already figured this, but I'm the children's minister here, and for some bizarre reason, the elder board has given me clearance to commission you and your guys to build the new children's wing." Her eyes widened at this. "Wacky, huh? Since I know nothing about construction."

"I'll say," Scott said.

"I thought… well, I thought Frank would be by," she said. "He's been my contact this whole time."

"Yes, Frank was the contact, but after looking at the plans, I thought it might be wise if I came by myself to see if any of the fantastical things you've come up with are possible."

"How is Frank's grandmother?"

Scott squinted at her. "What?"

"His grandmother," she said softly. "The one who had the stroke?"

"I have no clue," Scott shrugged.

She shook her head, grinning even at this. "Well, let me go ahead and show you what we were thinking and you can tell me if it's even possible."

Marie

This? This was Thomas Fisher's grandson.

She remembered him instantly from the flight, remembered all the smarmy things he had said to get the woman sitting in the row behind her interested in him... and she marveled that this? This was the grandson of one of the godliest men she'd ever known.

Unbelievable.

Of course, it was a big leap to make. Just because he was on the same flight, just because his first name was right... well, it didn't mean that he was *that* Scott.

But the last name. The last name! What were the odds? Even if they were bad, it didn't change the fact that this Scott Huntington? Looked just exactly like Thomas Fisher must have, years ago.

The resemblance was startling.

After the tour, he shook his head at her.

"Miss Boyd," he said, frustration in his voice.

"It's Marie," she trilled at him gleefully. She knew what he was going to say before he even said it, judging by the way he looked over her plans with no small amount of disdain.

"Marie," he took a breath. "Your plans are like something out of a Dr. Seuss story."

"That's totally what I was going for!," she laughed. "Great minds and all."

"Well, it —"

"It's going to be awesome!"

He frowned. "I'm good at what I do, but I have some concerns that we'll be going against a large number of building codes if I construct

Whoville for you."

She sighed. "Shame, man. It would have been so much fun."

"Yeah, well," he said, "you don't seem to have any concept of functionality when it comes to building a space this large."

She shrugged. "You're right. I don't. Which is why the church hired you. Explain to me what's possible and what isn't. And I can work around what you suggest."

He heaved a giant breath of exasperation. "It's a little too late to sit down and refigure all of this," he said tersely. "You and Frank have wreaked some serious damage to my life with your idiotic plans."

"Hmm," she murmured, not bothered in the least by the meltdown he was close to having. "Serious damage, you say?"

"I spent all morning working through this, retooling some of your ideas, and I've concluded that Frank? Is off the project," he said.

"But I like Frank," she said.

"Tough luck," he answered. "You've got me. Every day, likely, for the next three months. Or, God forbid, longer."

She watched him for a second. "I don't think God would forbid you being here a little longer, Mr. Huntington." A pause. "Can I call you Scott?"

He shrugged. "Sure. We're going to be working together. Might as well be on a first name basis, I guess."

She smiled. "I'm looking forward to it, Scott."

Scott

He'd hurried home that night, his laptop next to him in the truck.

The space this woman had created in her mind was a mess. That went without saying. But at least she'd had the courtesy to walk through the plans with him and stay amendable to some suggestions and changes.

And she'd done so with a huge smile on her face. She'd practically skipped down the hallways, and a few times, she'd clutched her hands to her chest and laughed out loud when he made suggestions, telling him, "That's even better than I could have imagined!"

She was happy. Oddly happy.

The project would still take longer than the original expansion he'd envisioned when Drew got in touch with him, but it could be managed. And with him doing the majority of the work himself, it would be managed as efficiently as possible. He was thinking through the particulars of it all even as he arrived home, to the house he'd built himself, his laptop under his arm.

He'd gotten his dad in on the plans for this house. Nick Huntington had passed his inherent abilities with carpentry and engineering down to Scott and Scott alone, and he'd taken the time, even when Scott's life was a wreck, to teach his son everything he knew. So, when things were better and Scott was in charge of his own business, he'd still called his father and gotten his professional advice every step of the way. Scott had intended to build himself a very different house. Smaller, more modern, more upscale, but Nick had encouraged him towards more rooms, a bigger kitchen, a warmer feel, and a huge family room. "You just never know when you might need the room," he'd said to Scott, smiling over the plans.

Scott knew what that meant. Family. Marriage. Children. None of which Scott had any intention of ever having. His life was his own. He didn't even bring women back here, wanting to keep his life, his real life, far away from them.

No one came around here. And he was fine with that. Fine with the silence. The solidarity.

Which made his eagerness to get his computer turned on completely ironic, he noted, even as he clicked through the familiar prompts and waited.

Sure enough, a few seconds later, the screen filled with Sam's face. Sam's very irritated face.

"Good morning, Sunshine," Scott cooed.

"It's not morning, dimwit," Sam hissed. "How many times do I have to explain the time difference to you?"

"More than you have, obviously," Scott said. "Like you were doing anything important. Probably weren't even sleeping."

Sam blinked at this. "No," he said, very simply.

Scott knew all about it. For all the demons Scott himself had chasing him as it came to alcohol and the way it called him even now, Sam had more. Nightmares, the inability to sleep without seeing some of what he'd seen in classified combat – these were the demons that Sam was battling half a world away. Scott knew about it only because Sam came here on his leave, where there wasn't a house full of people being woken up when he'd start yelling in the middle of the night.

Only his brother. Who understood what it meant to be there for someone, because Sam had been there for him once, too.

"You get any rest at all?," Scott asked.

"A little," he shrugged. "Enough that I might actually be woken up by your ill-timed calls one of these days."

"Not today," Scott said, grinning.

"You doing okay?," Sam asked. "Haven't had a drink, right?"

"Not in five years, three months, two weeks, and one day," he said.

"Good."

"But I *need* one today, Sam," he said.

"Oh," Sam asked, stifling a yawn. "Problems at work. New project?"

"Yes," he said. "A church. Expansion of a whole wing. And a woman running it who doesn't have any idea what she's doing."

Sam raised his eyebrows at this.

"Don't look at me like that," Scott said. "Just because there's a woman involved doesn't mean –"

"Sorry," Sam said. "It wasn't the woman part that got my attention. It was the mention of a church." A pause. "You're working at a church?"

"Old frat brother is the pastor," he said. "Drew. Remember him?"

"Drew..."

"Drew of the DWI night," Scott muttered, thinking of the surprise that had accompanied their reunion over this project. Drew had been a mess back then in more ways than one, and now he was leading a church with a wife and children by his side.

He was totally as lame as he'd been back then, honestly. Just in a new, churchy way.

"Oh, yeah, I remember that guy," Sam said. "Hope for the hopeless if he's a pastor, huh?"

"Maybe," Scott shrugged. "Anyway, it's a mess, and I've committed, probably to my great detriment, the next few months of my life to overseeing it all."

"Sounds fun," Sam said, smiling.

"Not fun," Scott muttered.

"Work rarely is," Sam noted.

"You know it better than me probably," he said, watching his brother.

Sam sighed, visibly older and more exhausted than he'd been even a few months ago. "Maybe we're on the edge of some changes, though," he shrugged. "Me and you both."

"I doubt it," Scott shrugged. "But whatever helps you sleep at night, Sam."

And he said his goodbyes a short while later, shut down his computer, fixed himself a small dinner, and spent the rest of the evening by himself, in front of his television. He thought about any number of women he could call, could meet up with, could enjoy the rest of the night with… and put his phone aside, not interested enough to make the effort, his mind on work.

Marie

Marie's Mondays were spent at the seminary. She couldn't even remember what she had expected before signing up for classes, but she was infinitely pleased by what she got.

Scripture. So much Scripture. Taught, read, discussed, exposited, believed, breathed, lived.

She'd never been a great student. She was great with languages, great with people, and great at thinking problems through to some creative solutions. She was just perfect for children's ministry, and the counsel she'd received from those who knew how she struggled with reading and sitting through lectures, in a traditional academic environment, had encouraged her towards a more practical based masters program in educational ministry.

But her father had lobbied for her to go the theological route. "Your method isn't the thing," he'd told her. "Your theology should be. Let your theology define your method of ministry, because programs fail. But knowing Scripture, knowing the words of Christ, as clearly spoken in God's Word? That won't ever fail to change lives, starting with your own."

She listened to him more now than she ever had as a teenager, and his advice had been good.

She'd entered the same masters program he'd done years ago, where her classmates were all men preparing for careers as pastors, professors, and academic theologians. She knew she'd spend time reading, which was an odious chore for her very active mind. But, as she'd been surprised to find, the content made all the difference. She left the campus every day so thrilled by what she was learning that she got in her car with her head swimming and made the drive across town, singing loud praise songs in Afrikaans and Oshiwambo, stopping only when she got to the church, where she would nearly always pull out her phone and send her father a message about what she'd just learned.

She had her phone out to do just that when she entered the children's side of the building, stopping in surprise when she saw Scott using a sledgehammer on a fifty year old mural on one of the walls.

She hated that mural, but it was like a golden calf in the church. Someone's great-grandmother had painted it three generations ago, and even though it didn't fit the theming she had in the rest of the wing, she knew she'd never be able to get it gone without a fight. She'd secretly rejoiced when Scott said the wall was coming down regardless of what anyone thought.

Not so secretly rejoiced, actually. She'd told him she was thrilled.

He stopped when he saw her. "Hey, Marie," he said, nodding at the wall. "Like it?"

"Love it," she smiled. "You been working at it long?"

"No," he shook his head. "Been in the other part of the room getting the crew going. I've got four other guys in today, working on cutting a hole in that stage in the all-purpose room. Just like your crazy plans required."

"Awesome," she breathed out, dropping her backpack on the floor and slipping her phone inside. "But not as awesome as what you're doing here."

"You hated the mural that much, huh?," he asked, a small grin tugging the corners of his mouth.

"Yessssss," she whispered. "I just want to kick back with a drink and spend the rest of the day watching you demolish the whole thing."

He raised his eyebrows at this. "Checking me out, huh?," he grinned.

"You bet," she said, putting her hand to what was left of the hideous painting. "You're the hottest man in Texas right now, demolishing this thing."

"Ugly painting," he confirmed.

"Yeah," she breathed. "I always thought the animals looked like demons entering the ark. See their evil little eyes? What a great welcome for small children. I mean, seriously. Come on in, kids! Nothing but a bunch of nightmare-inducing elephants and giraffes leading you straight into the depths of Hell!"

He laughed outright at this. Then, glancing around conspiratorially, he lowered his voice. "I shouldn't let you, what with our insurance regulations and all... but, you wanna take a hit?" He held the sledgehammer out to her.

She laughed out loud while doing a little hop on the balls of her feet. "Yes!" And she went to pick up the sledgehammer... and actually struggled under the weight.

This made Scott smile even more. "You need some help?"

"Maybe a little," she said. And she let him help her pick it up, until she felt like she had a good grip. "Okay, I got it. You can let go."

"Nope," he said. "All I need is you dropping it on your foot and getting me in trouble."

"I won't do that," she said, looking back at him. "And if you can manage it, surely I can. I mean, you're not any bigger than I am. In fact, if I put on heels, you'd be shorter."

"Thanks for that, Marie," he said.

"Not a bad thing," she said. "You're just vertically challenged."

He narrowed his eyes at this... then smiled. She knew that these past few weeks spent with him here had given her clearance to joke like this, especially when she did so with such light hearted good will. She'd said enough and talked with him enough to know that the life he led was very different from hers, that he believed very differently, and that he was, in its simplest terms, not in Christ.

She wondered at this, at how he could have had the godly heritage he did and still missed it.

But hadn't she missed it, too?

She could relate to him in this, at least. Plus, he was easy to talk to, was hilarious when he wanted to be, and had the best smile. And he obviously liked to hear her talk, as evidenced by the way he made a point to come by and talk with her every time he showed up at the church.

She suspected that God was doing something with him, with every odd look he gave her as she spoke truth and joy to him, as was her way, coming back from seminary, preparing to teach, talking through the goodness of God with him, even as he listened quietly.

No wonder, though. She'd been praying for him from the first day she'd met him.

"Vertically challenged. Fair enough," he said. "But I don't have deficient girl muscles, so I'm ahead of you."

"Deficient girl muscles," she groaned, trying to lift the sledgehammer on her own.

"I'm going to have to put you on workers' comp," he said. "Let me help you and save us both the trouble."

"Oooooh," she muttered sarcastically, still with a smile, as he came up behind her. "Big, strong man showing the little lady how it's done."

"Only as it pertains to building Whoville," he quipped.

And together, they picked up the sledgehammer and broke down another piece of the wall.

Scott

So, the church job wasn't such a big headache after all.

Drew was no cooler than he'd been the night of the DWI. But he seemed to have his life together now. They'd been talking more than they had in years with this new job, and while Scott couldn't imagine the leap his friend had taken from wild, whiny frat brother to a man of the cloth and all, he knew this kind of life well enough to know how Drew likely did things now.

He was from a church family, after all. He knew church.

There was the elder board to approve things. Scott had presented to them more than once, at Drew's request, and they'd approved it all. Their confidence in him had landed his company a couple of other jobs. One at a business owned by an elder, another remodeling a kitchen in the home of a deacon.

Small jobs compared to the church, though.

There had also been meetings with Drew. Casual, short meetings to discuss how it was going, when the building could be expected to be opened, how they needed it cleared out and prepped before Wednesdays and Sundays. As he talked with Drew, he got to know the other staff members. The associate pastor, the youth minister, the financial treasurer, the secretary...

... and Marie.

Scott had spent his life in church, but he couldn't ever remember meeting anyone like this church girl. She'd come in on Mondays, finding him with little trouble and exclaiming, "Pretty sure my brain is going to explode, Scott!" before launching into a discussion over all that she'd been learning at some preacher school that she went to. She was good for conversation, always laughed at his jokes, and radiated an odd sort of sunshine as she always made a point to see and celebrate what he'd done.

He could appreciate the praise, honestly.

He was beneath the stage a few weeks after she had helped him demolish the wall, working on that stupid puppet hollow, when she wandered into the room. She didn't seem to know he was in there as he watched her go from corner to corner, inspecting the work and making murmurs of appreciation. As she moved past the stage, he couldn't resist, and he reached up and grabbed her ankle, causing her to kick him right in the face.

"Holy –"

"Oh, no!," she gasped, cutting him off and keeping him from yelling any number of inappropriate obscenities. "Are you okay?"

"*No!*," he yelled, holding his open palm to his eye. Or where his eye once was, since he could no longer feel or see if the eye was actually still there –

"Shame, Scott," she said, sitting down on the edge of the puppet hollow and putting her hands on his arms. "Does it hurt?"

He frowned at her. "Does it look like it hurts?"

She frowned back at him. "Well, I can't see it, because you've got your hand over it."

He put his hand down timidly. "Is my eye still there? Or did you knock it completely out?"

"Oh, good grief," she said. "It's not that bad."

"It's not that bad, she says," he muttered, "while all of my eyeball juice is running down my face, and –"

"Eyeball juice," she giggled, pulling him closer to her by his arms, placing her hands on his face. "There is a lot of that."

"Why did you kick me?," he whined.

"You grabbed me!," she exclaimed. "Empty church, dark room, unscrupulous man hiding out of sight –"

"Unscrupulous?"

"Better be glad I didn't have my pepper spray," she said, pointing her finger into his chest.

"I stand warned for next time," he muttered.

"You wear contacts, Scott?"

"Yeah... how can you tell?"

"Because," she said calmly, smiling at him, plucking it right out of the eye he still couldn't see clearly out of, "I thought that's what this was. I managed to turn it upside down when I kicked you."

"How did you do that?"

"By sheer force of my total awesomeness," she laughed, holding it out in her open palm. "Here it is."

"I would say that I can see that," he said, "but I still can't see."

"Why don't you close your eyes for a second?," she said. "Then open them again and see if the... well, the trauma –" and she had the gall to laugh at this "—will be done."

He closed his eyes, sighing. "I appreciate how you find such humor in this."

"Shame, man," she whispered, closer to his face than he thought she was, her hands back on his cheeks, her thumbs running over his eyelids.

"Are you trying to hurt me more?," he managed, as she touched him in her surprisingly wonderful way. It had been a while since anyone had touched him like this, and if he was being honest with himself... well, it was nice. Very nice. He found himself beginning to enjoy it more than he should until he reminded himself with some severity that Marie was a church girl.

A *church* girl.

He frowned at this... even as he let her keep touching him.

"Okay, Mr. Frowny Face," she said, "can you see anything now?"

He opened his eyes warily. "Yeah... it's a little blurry."

"Because I have your contact," she smiled.

"And it stings. Did you kick me with spike heels on or something?"

She kicked out her foot for him to observe. "Nope, ballet slippers."

"Well, they're very nice," he said. And they were. As were the legs attached to them. "All three of them," he muttered. *Church girl*, he reminded himself.

"Seeing double, huh?"

"Double and blurry. And did I mention the stinging?"

She laughed out loud at this. "Maybe we should just go ahead and gouge them out completely. Make you like Samson."

"Mmm," Scott murmured, blinking and trying to see if that would fix the double vision problem. "The guy with all the strength."

"You know that story, huh?"

"Please," he scoffed. "I know all of those kids' stories. Samson with the long hair and the strength, killing the lion with his bare hands –"

"And getting himself in a whole lot of trouble with women," she sighed. "Yes, I can see how you'd remember that story."

Well, this was surprising. Had she been reading his mind earlier? "What?"

"Oh, you heard me," she laughed softly, putting her hand back to his face and peering into his eyes. "I think you're going to have some swelling."

"Likely so... but what did you mean about that comment on women?"

She grinned. "Simply that some women? Are trouble."

"The great majority, I'd figure," he agreed.

"Well, in your experience, which is quite varied and extensive."

He regarded her with some suspicion. "And how would you know about that?"

She leaned forward and whispered to him. "I've been talking to God about you, Scott."

Was this some sort of church girl pick-up line? The more he was around Marie, the better looking she got, oddly enough. And her quirky personality was interesting. And that smile, as she radiated a strange sort of joy...

Before he could give her any kind of response to this, she was on her feet. "I'm going to get you some ice," she said, turning to leave.

"Hey!," he shouted after her. "What do you mean you've been talking to God –"

"I'm just yanking your chain, Scott," she said, still smiling. "And you make it *so* easy!"

"Oh." He looked at her. "But still... how do you know that... well, that I'm..."

"Makes you wonder, doesn't it?," she asked, winking at him before leaving the room.

Marie

Marie was sitting in her office a few days later, working on background checks for the new round of volunteers she'd found for the semester. She hated this part of the job. Administrative demands, sitting in front of a computer, filing papers and double checking things. But it was necessary.

And it was made tolerable when she put on her headphones and cranked her music up.

She was so into the music that she didn't hear Tracy, Drew's wife, come into the office. And she didn't see her until she turned in her chair to pick up another file.

"Tracy!," she yelled, clasping her hand to her chest as the older woman smiled at her and settled into a chair across from her desk.

"You're yelling, Marie," she said calmly.

"What?," Marie asked.

"You're yelling!"

Marie plucked off her headphones. "Sorry," she sighed. "Busy day. Where are my little buddies?"

"With my parents," Tracy said, kicking her feet up on Marie's desk. "Date night tonight. Until tomorrow morning."

"Hmm," Marie murmured, grinning at her friend. "All night date night for you and Drew."

"Yeah, I'm going to go home and sleep for twelve straight hours."

"That's so hot," Marie joked. "Lucky Drew."

"He's gotten lucky plenty," she said. "That's how we ended up with the kids, you know."

"You should come have breakfast with me tomorrow before you get them back," Marie said. "There's this little place I found, over by –"

"Hey, Marie."

Both she and Tracy turned to look at Scott, who stood in her doorway.

"Hey," she said, smiling at him. He'd come in to check the work the crew had been doing and had stayed most of the afternoon. She'd taken drinks down to all of them and had sat around and chatted with Scott thirty minutes past his own break.

He was easy to talk to. They'd been talking a lot.

"Didn't want to interrupt," he said. "Just wanted to give you a heads up on those wires hanging out of the wall in the third grade room. Don't start trying to yank them out or anything, or you'll probably be electrocuted. And I can't live with the guilt of having killed a church girl." He said nothing for a moment. Then, "Better yet, don't even go down there and look at them."

"I won't touch them, then," she said, laughing at this.

"Marie," he warned.

She kept laughing. "Well, I'm going to look. You know I will."

"Yeah, which is why I said what I did. I'm going to fix them tomorrow morning."

"Got it."

He appeared to be thinking for a long moment. "Never mind," he said. "I'll go fix them now."

"Scott, I said I wouldn't touch them –"

"But I know you," he said. "And you'll go down just to look at them and some freak accident will happen, like when you kicked me in the eye."

She smiled at this. "That was your fault, not mine."

"Yeah, yeah, still wearing my glasses, thanks to you and the damage you did," he said. "And I'd just rather not take the chance on the wires. It'll take me an hour, tops."

"So, two hours, then?," she asked.

He pretended to be insulted. "Are you doubting my skills?"

"No," she smiled. "I'm just guessing that it'll take longer because you're a perfectionist. Just like you've been with every other part of the project."

He grinned at this. "You're probably right."

"I appreciate you, Scott," she said, thinking of how much she appreciated what he was doing for their church and for the ministry they had ahead of them.

He shook his head at the praise, the smile still on his lips. "You'll appreciate me even more when you see how great it looks down there."

"I'll be that way after I'm finished up in here, then. I brought myself dinner, enough for two. Want me to bring it along?"

He nodded. "Nothing weird, right?"

"This is me we're talking about," she laughed.

"Yeah, yeah, yeah," he said, even as he was walking away. "Thanks, Marie."

She smiled as she watched him go, even as Tracy swiveled back around in her chair and stared.

"Who was that?"

Marie grinned. "Scott Huntington, contractor extraordinaire. He's building the children's wing."

"Have you been hanging out with him a lot?"

Marie thought on this for a second. Yeah, they'd been hanging out a lot. She'd originally figured he would leave the work to his crew, but as the project had carried on and the plans had grown more elaborate, he'd been there, too. There were always questions he had for her, which turned into more questions from her as she watched… and the questions turned into conversations, long talks as he worked, as they got to know one another better.

He was becoming a friend.

"Yeah," she said. "He's a good guy."

"He's an ugly guy," Tracy said, lowering her voice.

"I think he's cute," Marie murmured, laughing at Tracy's observations. "And hilarious. Funniest guy around here."

Tracy frowned at this. "Didn't sound funny to me."

"I guess you have to get his sense of humor," Marie said. She got it. And she'd laugh louder than she normally laughed at anything over jokes he'd make offhand, so much so that even he'd start laughing.

He was fun.

"How'd you find him?," Tracy asked.

"He went to college with Drew," she said, looking at her friend meaningfully. "Was his big brother in their fraternity. How do I know this story better than you?"

"Ohhhhh," Tracy gasped, sitting back. "I do know that story. Scott. *That* Scott."

"That Scott," Marie nodded. Then, a pause. "What do you mean?"

"I mean, that Scott is a total loser," she said. "Drew was a loser back in college, living this crazy wild lifestyle, shaming his parents and Jesus at every opportunity."

"Hmm," Marie murmured, wondering at this. "That doesn't sound much like Drew."

"Well, God changed him, obviously," she said. "And got him away from guys like that one."

"Scott's a nice guy, Tracy," Marie said. "Just because someone is lost doesn't mean there's nothing redeeming in them. I mean, let's hope so, right? Because we were all lost at one point."

"Whatever," Tracy sighed. Then, sitting back up again, "Marrrrrrrrrieeeeeee...."

"Whaaaaaattttt?," Marie asked, kind of hating the know-it-all tone and overall judgment in her friend's voice.

"You aren't missionary dating on me, are you?"

Missionary dating. A believer embarking on a romance with an unbeliever with the intent of saving them... and having a little fun while doing it.

"No," Marie said very sincerely, looking Tracy in the eyes. "I have no desire to be romantically linked to that man if he doesn't have in mind the things of God. You know me. What would I even have in common with him if he isn't living his whole life for God?"

"Well, you said he was cute," she said.

"Which wasn't a declaration of my intent to marry the man and have his child, Tracy."

"Let's hope not," Tracy said.

"Hey," Marie added. "I appreciate your concern. But I promise you this. The most attractive part of any man is his heart for Christ and his willingness to do anything for Him. So even cute guys like Scott? Aren't catching my attention. Not like that."

"Good," Tracy affirmed.

"Yes, it is," Marie nodded. "And what I'm doing now? In being his friend? Is just that. Just being his friend. And praying that God will let me see his heart change towards Christ. Can I do that? As his friend?"

"You can," Tracy said. "I'm just looking out for you. As *your* friend, Marie."

"I promise you," Marie murmured, "that there's nothing more going on. You can keep me honest about that, okay? I promise not to fall in love with Scott Huntington." She grinned at the absurdity.

Tracy held her hand out, and they shook on it.

"I have your word, then, Marie."

CHAPTER THREE

Scott

Marie was a cool guy. For a church girl, that is.

The project was going more quickly than he had originally thought it would, likely because he'd taken such an active role in it when he saw the challenges Marie's plans had created. He was proud of the work that had been done, mainly because he'd done the majority himself, with his own two hands.

And he'd done most of that with Marie watching him. Which he didn't mind, oddly enough.

She'd told him early on that she hated sitting behind a desk. She wasn't cut out for that kind of work, she said. So when children's ministry – which was mostly active most of the time, she'd said – required her to sit down and study Scripture, she did it in the colorful spaces where the children would be gathering later, sitting on a beanbag chair in the very same room where Scott worked.

She'd ask him what he thought about the passages she was studying. On anyone else, it would have come across as evangelizing, as pressuring, as trying to make him into something he wasn't. But on her, it just came across as curiosity and wonder, as though she herself were just now hearing the stories and honestly wanted to share them with him.

She was different. And he found himself thinking on her children's Bible stories more and more as the days went on.

He'd said he believed back when he was a kid. His parents had watched him carefully as Sean and Sam made decisions to live for Jesus at really young ages and as he continued on obliviously. Well, not totally obliviously. He was sharp enough to pick up on the words they used, the ways they made the stories about Jesus their own, and the subtle relief his parents tried to hide but couldn't when each of their boys walked the aisle and got baptized.

It had been real enough for Sean and Sam, he had supposed at the time, and so he had done the same. He'd said the same words, asked the same questions, made the same profession, and had followed them down the aisle and into the baptistry.

He was secure. They'd said that over his six year old head, telling him that once he asked Jesus in, Jesus was always there. He had believed that much, but it hadn't made much of a difference, quite honestly.

There was Sean, though, who spent more time with their grandfather as he grew into his teenage years, asking to be led through studies of Scripture, then going up and making a general nuisance of himself at church, trying to volunteer and find a place to serve.

And there was Sam, who avoided cliques at school where popularity came down to rules you were willing to break and girls you were willing to have. He chose differently, lived differently, and made everything about following Christ.

Scott could see, even then, that they had meant what they prayed as little boys. But for him? It hadn't meant much of anything, obviously, because it hadn't made any difference in his life. He lived for himself, lived how he wanted, and Jesus was relegated back to a prayer he'd repeated at six because he was supposed to.

He'd said none of this to Marie but figured she could guess it as she heard him give all the right answers to her questions then go on like it was nothing at all.

Except... it was. She had the oddest way of concluding these stories she told by making some tie-in to real life. He supposed that he'd heard them before, surely, and that it had been explained to him like she explained it. So why then, had it never made as much sense as it did now? Was he so dumb that it took hearing Scripture from someone who taught it to children for it to sound feasible to him?

He didn't know. But he thought about the stories, about how she said they were lifechanging, and how he couldn't hear even one of them without wondering what it meant if what she said was true.

He thought about this even as he finished up the morning's work, pulling out his phone to check for messages and updates on other projects and checking the children's rooms for Marie. When he couldn't find her in any of the normal spots, he shrugged off the disappointment and began making his way outside. His path led him right by the sanctuary, where incredible music flowed from the doorway.

Incredibly loud music, actually.

He peeked in, curious as to who was in there and what they were playing, and he felt himself smile when he recognized Marie at the piano, where she didn't even notice when he slipped in and sat on the back pew. He hung back, listening to her as she continued on, no music in front of her, oblivious to his presence. And when she stopped playing, he began applauding, smiling when she jumped.

"Well done," he said, making his way from the back of the church up to where she sat behind the piano.

"You scared me!," she shouted, smiling at him.

She had a great smile. He smiled to see it. "Payback for that puppet hollow," he said, walking over to the piano. "I haven't been able to wear my contacts for weeks."

"You look very distinguished with your glasses," she grinned.

"Yeah, well, I feel like an idiot. Haven't worn glasses since I was a little kid. An asthmatic little kid with brothers who beat him up for fun –"

"Wah, wah, wah," Marie muttered, smiling, and playing him a sad, sad tune on the piano. "I'll bet you started each and every one of those beat downs."

He sat down next to her. "Well, yeah."

They laughed together as she continued to play.

"How do you do that?," he asked. "Play without the music?"

She smiled to herself. "I play by ear. I can read the music and do read the music when I don't know the tune, but... I can play without it. And do."

"Huh. How long have you been able to do that?"

She sighed. "Oh, since I was very little. Sat down at the piano at the guesthouse in Oshakati and played... well, played a very interesting song for my mother. I was four."

"Osha... what?" More gibberish. Osha... something.

She looked at him for a moment. "You don't have any idea who I am, do you? All this time, and you still have no idea who I am."

"Sure, I do," he said. "You're Marie Boyd, the lady who has turned a simple expansion project into three months of hysteria."

73

"Three months of fun," she corrected, still playing. "And I did. I really did. You're so lucky that I'm here."

He knew this, even as she grinned over at him. "No, besides the obvious. You don't know this, Scott Huntington, but you and I are..." She leaned over and whispered to him. "Connected."

He looked back at her and grinned a little more himself. "How so?"

"Well, we never met before all of this. Formally," she sighed with a smile. "But I was at your cousin's wedding."

He frowned. "Which cousin? I have a lot of them."

"Sadie."

Scott looked at her dubiously. "Really?" He was sure he would have noticed her.

"Yeah," she smiled. "And I know your family," she said, studying him. "Your grandparents came and visited us on mission in Namibia."

Scott looked at her blankly. "Still have no idea how that connects us. Or where... Nambia is."

"Namibia."

"What?," he regarded her with an odd look.

"It's a country in Africa," she smiled. "My parents are missionaries there. I grew up there, was born there actually, so I'm... well, more Namibian than American, honestly. Anyway, my mom and your aunt, Emily, were best friends, growing up at Grace together."

Scott paused for a moment. "Really?"

"Yeah," she said. "Shame, man..."

He put his hands next to hers on the keys, prompting a smile from her

74

lips. And he began to play a tune himself, though not as easily or smoothly as Marie had. "I have a feeling," he said, "that there are more than just a few things that I don't know about you, Marie."

"Maybe," she murmured. "Of course, I could say the same for you, playing like this. Lessons?"

"Just a few," he said. "Fine arts requirement in college. Worst semester of my life."

"Well, you probably didn't make an A," she grimaced at the clanking he was doing and scooted his hands gently out of the way as she began to play again. "But you're right. You don't know even a fraction of all the awesomeness that is Marie Boyd."

"You make the Bible stories sound interesting," he noted.

"That I do," she said. "And you haven't even had the opportunity to see me tell them with puppets."

"Hence the need for a puppet hollow."

"Smart man," she nodded at him, playing louder and more forcefully, then easing into something light and cheerful as she smiled down at her hands.

Amazing.

"Get a lot done today?," she asked.

"A little," he said. "I'll take you back and show you."

"I would like that," she said.

"But first, I've gotta eat," he said. "So, tell me something I don't know. Are there any normal foods that you eat?"

She'd brought one odd thing after another back to the church and had laughed uproariously at him as he'd tried everything she offered to him.

Eclectic tastes, she'd told him. And now, it made sense. Missionary kid. All of her was eclectic.

"Normal foods," she murmured, stilling her hands on the keys. "Wings. Are those normal?"

"Those sound great," he said. "Come on. You're going with me."

"Correction," she said, standing with a flourish. "You're going with me. I know just the place."

And after a short drive, she walked him into... a bar.

A bar. It had been five years. He could smell the beer. Oh... he could smell it...

The church girl had taken him to a bar.

"Wow, I love that smell," she sighed.

He regarded her with mild shock.

She must have seen the consternation on his face and mistaken it for something else. "I know," she rolled her eyes with a smile. "Totally un PC to say so in our churchy world here, but honestly, all the men I knew growing up drank it like... well, like water, frankly. So the smell takes me back to men being men, and just... well, it wasn't even like they got drunk. At all. Just enjoyed an adult beverage with practically every meal. Probably like Jesus Himself did, actually. And He was a carpenter, too. Just like you. Just a carpenter having a little brew, you know?"

"Well, yeah," Scott managed, thinking about how much he'd like to have a beer with Jesus. Or anyone. Or no one at all. It had been so long...

"Hey," she said, "my treat. What do you want?"

He didn't say anything for a moment. Then, "You're the strangest church girl I've ever met, Marie."

She turned to him with a smile. "I'll take that as a high, high compliment, Scott. So, what would you like –"

"Oh, man," he said. "I'd like a lot of everything, but... I don't drink. Not anymore. Five years sober, and..."

"Oh," she said, blinking at him. "Oh." Then, gasping. "I'm so sorry. I mean, not that you're sober, but that I brought you here, and –"

"No, you're good," he said, telling himself at the same time, *you're good, Scott. Really. You're good.*

"Well, they have the best wings in the city," she said. "Even without a beer to wash them down."

"Won't be the same," he noted, a little dejected. Wings hadn't tasted right in five years.

"They'll be just fine," she said. "Surely, right?"

"No. No, they won't."

She smiled. "Maybe they'll be even better with the company, though, right? Seriously."

And the sincerity and compassion in her eyes had him thinking that maybe... just maybe, she was right.

Marie

He had been an alcoholic. Clearly.

Marie hadn't imagined that this was part of the "loser profile" that Tracy had alluded to back in her office so long ago. But the way he squirmed and seemed to be giving himself a stern lecture, even as they began to eat together advised her differently.

She'd made it her goal to distract him from whatever war he was waging inside. And distractions came in the form of stories, all of them from her years in Namibia.

"You. Were. *Not*," he said, smiling, after hearing one of her favorite stories.

"I swear it, man," she laughed, licking her fingers and balling up the final napkin. "Miss Swakopmund, three years running. Just strutted myself out onstage in a bikini, did myself a little dance, and won the crown, again and again. And the whole reason? Was the kegger of a party they'd throw afterwards for my friends."

"You don't strike me as a beauty pageant type," he said.

"I'm not," she said. "But it was a really, really good dance. Trust me."

"Weirdest church girl –"

"Ever," she finished for him. "You've said that before." She glanced at her watch and looked over at the door again. Any minute now, they'd be here. It was one of the reasons she'd suggested they come here.

For as much as Marie hadn't known about Scott, she had picked up on a few crucial things. He had been churched, heavily churched, the majority of his young life. She was quite sure that he was your typical church kid – raised, saved, and baptized in due time. But he'd obviously been done with it all since.

Well, good. Being done with doing church was a good thing. Because if you were, like Marie suspected Scott had been, doing church apart from knowing Christ, it was probably better to be a prodigal who wouldn't confuse remembrances of past liturgy and tradition apart from Christ when Jesus showed up and spoke your name.

And Marie was more than certain that Jesus had been shouting Scott's name for a while.

She'd seen it there in his eyes when she'd ask him about the stories she would be teaching the kids, when he'd listen to her conclusions, her applications, her exclamations that God was so good.

She glanced at the door again.

He looked over his shoulder. "Why do you keep doing that?," he asked.

"I'm waiting for the regular crowd," she said. "I come here a lot. I have friends who I see here all the time."

She saw it in Scott's eyes, as he imagined a group of chipper, young sorority types, not unlike Marie herself, giggling over drinks and barely touching their food as they all complained about the jobs they'd taken straight out of school. She was about to correct his assumption when the door opened, and two of them came in.

Jerry and Theo. Two of her favorites. As she smiled their direction, Scott followed her gaze, his eyes widening.

They were big guys. With long facial hair and tattoos. The kind of guys you probably wouldn't want to meet after dark on the streets.

"You!," Theo bellowed at Marie, coming up to the table and getting up in her face. "I gotta talk to you!"

Marie could see Scott stiffen out of the corner of her eye. Before he made what looked to be a valiant attempt to protect her, she raised her voice and got right in Theo's face. "Oh, yeah?!"

"Your little homework made no sense!," he shouted.

"You didn't do it right, then!," she yelled back. "Hey, Jerry! Did Theo read the background passages I gave you guys?"

Scott's brow furrowed.

"He didn't, Marie," Jerry said, glancing over at Scott. He held his hand out. "Jerry Thomas," he said gruffly.

"Scott Huntington," Scott managed.

"Oh, my manners!," Theo continued yelling. "Theo Harris!"

Scott recoiled just slightly, shooting a concerned look at Marie. She suppressed a grin and scooted over to make room for the newcomers.

"Guys, Scott's the contractor who's helping out at the church," she said. "And, Scott, these guys are walking through the book of Ephesians with me."

"Walking through the whole Bible!," Theo continued on, reaching into his back pocket as Marie scooted her trash to the center of the table. He put a pocket New Testament in front of them. "Seriously, you gotta explain it to me," he said in a, finally, normal voice.

Marie smiled at this, even as Jerry sat down as well, as they both opened up the Scripture she'd given to them months ago, when she first started coming here. She was non-threatening and young, likely reminded them of their daughters, or who they wanted their daughters to be, and simple, pleasant conversations about whatever sport was playing on the television above the bar had turned to spiritual matters. That happened a lot with Marie.

She'd never been amazed by her father's ability to do the same in Namibia. She'd never seen it as unusual or out of the ordinary when Daniel Boyd would go into a bar and regal an entire group of people who didn't share his skin color, his heart language, or his nationality, with his words. They were words of life, and she'd seen it countless times – how God had transformed lives through her father's witness. An odd man in a land that wasn't his own... the Gospel made alive.

And she was an odd woman in a land that wasn't her own. And Theo and Jerry were the fruit of seeds she didn't even realize she'd known how to sow as her love for Christ had been shared with them.

"Hey," Theo nodded at Scott. "You know what Ephesians 2 is about?"

Scott shook his head, still looking very shocked by this all. Marie smiled at him reassuringly.

"It's about how we were dead, without hope," she said, "and how He made us alive. And everything changed."

"That's good," Theo said. "And true."

"The truth is always good news," Marie said, smiling over at Scott again.

And she watched him again and again as she explained the Scriptures to the men who had already been changed by its truth.

Scott

He watched with wonder as she shared Christ with these two huge men, giggling along with them as they were hearing the words of life, believing them, and treasuring them.

Amazing.

And she sincerely believed every word she said. He could see it in her eyes, hear it in her voice, feel it as though Christ Himself was sitting next to her. Maybe he'd known people like her before, but he'd never remembered being so moved and affected by what she said.

An hour later, he was well past a normal lunch break, as was Marie. She'd said their good-byes, told Theo and Jerry what to read for next week, and had gone back to the church with Scott, watching him carefully while making small talk.

She must have sensed how crazy his thoughts were now. After he'd shown her what he'd done, he'd told her he needed to get on to some other projects for the afternoon and that he'd see her the next day.

There were no other projects. He needed to talk to Sam.

He got home in record time, set up his laptop, and waited anxiously, drumming his fingers on the kitchen counter.

A minute later, Sam's very irritated face appeared on the screen. He was shirtless, likely still half asleep, and none too happy to see his brother.

"I swear, man," he said lowly. "The next time I'm stateside, I'm buying you a clock and setting it to Japanese time. And then I'm going to somehow wedge it permanently into your butt so that you'll always have it on you and won't ever call me in the middle of the night."

"Well, that sounds pleasant," Scott said. "Good morning to you, too."

"Why are you calling?"

"Because I've just had the most bizarre lunch, and it's gotten me all messed up," he said.

"I told you to take something for heartburn the next time that church girl makes you lunch," he said. "You've already told me all about the weird stuff she forces you to eat, and –"

"It's not heartburn," Scott said. "But it *is* the church girl. Or what she said. Today." Dead. Alive in Christ. Everything changes. The truth is always good news.

"Oh?," Sam asked, yawning, then leaning his head onto his hand and closing his eyes.

"How do you know when God's speaking to you, Sam?"

Sam's eyes popped open at this. "What?"

"How do you know," Scott continued on, "when God's saying something to you?"

"Well," Sam said, taking a deep breath and sitting up straighter, "He uses people, circumstances, His Word."

"But what does it feel like?," Scott asked. "I mean, I was sitting there at that bar, going crazy, and —"

"Bar?," Sam asked. "Is that what this is about? Are you drunk right now? I swear, Scott, I'm —"

"No!," Scott yelled. "I'm sober. Completely sober."

"How long has it been since you've had a drink, Scott?"

"Five years, six months, three weeks, five days. But the church girl took me to a bar —"

"What?"

"And she's like a freakin' evangelist there!," he kept on. "I mean, she's sharing Jesus with men twice her age, twice as big as her, and a thousand times scarier than she'll ever be, right there in that bar. And, you know, I've heard her tell the stories before, about what Jesus did and who He is... and it's more of the same. Feeling like something's not quite right, like God is doing something. And it's... it's making everything different." A pause. "Am I making any sense at all?"

Sam frowned. "A little," he managed. "She's been telling you stories."

"Yeah, and I knew them already, but... they didn't make sense like they're making now." He watched his brother for a moment. "I mean, I made a decision, just like the rest of you did, back when we were kids. And I was there every time the church doors were open. And it..."

"It made no difference," Sam said.

"Made a difference to Sean and you," he said. "I mean, Sean's the pastor of a huge church, and I'm pretty sure you can't even make a simple decision until you've prayed about it and read the whole of Scripture to make sure it's the unmistakable will of God."

Sam frowned further at this. "Thanks for that."

"I'm not making fun of you," he said. "Not this time. I'm just wondering why it's like that, Sam. Why is it like that for you? Why does He matter so much?"

"Because," Sam said softly, "when I gave Him everything, I gave Him every part of me."

"What does that even mean?," Scott asked.

"Every decision, every moment, every thought, every desire, all captured and kept apart for Him," he said. "And it's not easy. But I know my fulfillment, my peace, and now my very self, can't be in anyone but Him or in anything but His grace."

Scott said nothing for a moment. "Was I wrong, Sam? Back when I thought I had it done and went on without my life being any different?"

"Were you wrong to have said you believed?," Sam asked.

"Yeah, was I wrong?"

"I don't know," he said. "Do you believe now?"

And Scott swallowed, thinking on this. "Yeah. I do."

"And will it make any difference?"

This was the key. And Scott thought of his life and the way he lived and the choices he couldn't very well make now, knowing that Christ knew him, and he... well, he knew Him as well. Finally.

"It already has," he said rather weakly.

"Then," Sam smiled softly, "maybe that decision was just part of your story."

"And how does that story end?," Scott said, thinking about the way his life was probably about to change.

"Doesn't matter," Sam said. "What matters now is that your story, Scott? Is just beginning."

Marie

Shame.

She'd scared him.

Theo and Jerry were scary enough as it was. But add in the complexities of the book of Ephesians, and it was no wonder that Scott had left that afternoon with horror in his eyes.

Well, she'd been faithful to say what she had. And she'd be faithful to pray for him now, even when the days passed and his crew showed up without him. Frank came back and was on task, and Marie quelled the sadness over not seeing Scott, who had honestly become her friend through all of this, and put her mind back to the task ahead of them all.

She needed Drew to look over her report for the elder board meeting at the end of the week. Background checks, a new budget for curriculum, an update on the construction, and a request for new crib mattresses for the nursery – standard stuff. She'd typed it all up, printed it out, and held it in her hand as she made her way to his office.

"Goeie more, Drew," she said softly, knocking before slipping inside. "I have the..."

And the words stilled on her lips as her eyes met Scott's, as he sat across from the pastor.

"Hey, Scott," she said, smiling at him in surprise.

"Hey, Marie," he sighed. "How are you?"

"Good," she said. Then, brightly, "Your guys have been doing a great job."

"Took a look at it last night," he said, "right before I went home."

"You were here last night?," she asked.

"Most of the day for the past few days," Drew answered. "Just back here, though."

Marie waited for an explanation for this, chiding herself a moment later because she wasn't owed one. "Uh, Drew," she said, looking back down at the papers she held, "I have this for the elder meeting. Just wanted your okay on it before I submitted it."

"You'll be there at the meeting?," he asked, taking it from her.

"Sure will," she said. Then, smiling over at Scott. "Well, we'll see you."

And she turned and began walking back to her office, wondering over why this all bothered her so much. It was none of her business what they'd been talking about, of course. And he certainly wasn't required to come and see her every time he showed up here, either. He was Drew's friend first, and it only made sense that after she'd totally freaked him out by sharing so much truth with him that –

"Hey," she heard, just as she felt a hand on her elbow.

She turned and faced him.

"Sorry that I haven't come by to say hi to you."

She shrugged. "No big deal," she said. "Is there a problem with the expansion? Is that why you've been talking with Drew?"

He took a breath and bit his lip a little, seeming to search for the right words.

None of her business. *Get a grip, Marie.*

"You know," she said, "it's none of my business anyway. I just wanted to make sure the project is still underway."

"Oh, no," he said, "it's fine. It's better than fine. I should be done next week, actually. And out of your hair."

A sad thought, actually. "Oh. Okay."

He nodded at this.

She had. She had *totally* freaked him out with Ephesians. She could see it. She took a breath to make apologies, not for the truth, not for the Scripture, not for Christ, but for the way she'd sprung it all on him –

But before she could say it, he let out a breath. "This is really hard for me, Marie," he said. "But I need to talk to you."

"About the stuff I said at the bar, right? I didn't mean to bombard you like that. I just get really excited about Jesus, and I –"

"No," he smiled, "that was all good. Better than good. And that's what I wanted to talk to you about. Have you got plans tonight? Can we talk about it over dinner?"

She'd loaded up her car already with leftovers from a volunteer lunch she'd done on Sunday afternoon. And when you were the low man on the pay scale at the church with seminary bills to boot, you didn't let leftovers go to waste. They were dinner. Not another meal out.

"My car's full of leftovers," she said. "I was planning on heading back to my apartment."

"Are they good leftovers?," he asked. "Nothing weird, right?"

She grinned. "They were for a lunch for Americans. So I kept it normal."

"Then follow me out to my house," he said. "We can talk there. And you can share your normal leftovers with me."

She was relieved by this. Relieved that they were still friends. Despite the ineffectiveness of her witness, she still had friendship with him, and God had left the way open for her to share with him still, even while enjoying his company.

"Sure," she said. "That sounds good."

And it was good. Better than good.

She'd gone to his house and heated up dinner. They'd sat down to eat, and he hadn't managed one bite.

He'd been talking. Telling her all about what he'd been thinking, what God was doing in his life.

God had been doing more than she had imagined.

There were questions he still had, assumptions he needed cleared up, and things he wanted to say. She marveled over the words he spoke, wondering at what Drew had spent all those hours talking with him about, and she smiled, even as she pushed her plate away, done for now.

He looked down at her empty plate. "How about you?," he asked. "When did you figure this all out?"

She sighed, thinking about the time when everything about Jesus went from theoretical details she thought she knew to glorious reality that she was living. What a difference He had made.

"Well, you already know that my parents are missionaries," she said. "So you can imagine that I heard all about it early enough, right?"

"Probably from the crib," he muttered around the bite he'd finally taken, "which is something I can relate to, having grown up in my family."

She smiled at this. "Yes, well, the witness of your grandfather and your parents, of course, was probably just like my own parents and their witness. A 24 hour, 7 day week preview of what it meant to live for Jesus. And, you know, I thought I was living it, that I was truly believing it, all the years I grew up in their home. But I had my own things going on, my own secrets, my own choices driving most of what I did. Christ wasn't Lord – I was."

He watched her skeptically. "I have a hard time believing that, you know."

"And why is that?"

"Well," he said, shrugging, "you're oozing Jesus everywhere you go –"

"Oozing Jesus," she laughed.

"And," he smiled, "you're talking about Him all the time. Sharing Him with really scary strangers in a bar. Clearly, He's important."

"He is now," she said. "My first semester of college was... really hard, Scott. And not just because I'm a horrible student."

"Ah-ha!," he yelled. "Something you don't do well!"

She grinned. "Are you celebrating my stupidity?"

"No," he said. Then, "Well, yes. Because you seem to be great at everything else. And I doubt that stupidity really applies to –"

"Oh, yeah, it does," she said. "I hate reading. Absolutely hate it. My favorite subject in school was lunch."

He laughed out loud at this.

"And you think school for someone who hates school is hard normally?," she asked. "Try throwing the whole foreign country thing in there."

"Namibia –"

"You said it right," she responded, gleefully.

"Yeah, well, Namibia is about as foreign as it gets."

"Namibia isn't the foreign country I was talking about. Namibia is home. It was the US that was foreign. I had never spent any real time here. I was homesick for lots of reasons, and I found that there wasn't much of anything that could really help with the hurt I was experiencing. Because it was such a default from all those years of being a missionary kid, I went to church. And I heard the Gospel, not for the first time, of course. But for the first time, it changed my heart. Christ changed my heart."

"How does that happen, though?," Scott asked, sincerely. "How do you hear it all of your life… and only really hear it once you're an old man like me?"

She grinned at this. "Are you saying that it makes sense now?"

"I'm saying that something is different, Marie," he said. "And it just complicates everything and simplifies it, all at the same time."

She smiled. "That's good news then, isn't it?"

"How does it work?," he asked. "I prayed the prayer, walked the aisle, got dunked, did it all as a kid. So what's left to do now?"

"To know Him," she said, breathless at the simplicity and profound way that Christ makes Himself known, in His time and in His way.

"Know Him," Scott said.

"Really know Him," she said. "And live for Him for today, for tomorrow, for the rest of your life."

And she knew Him better than she had before, sitting here with Scott, as he began the first day of living in faith.

Scott

It only seemed right to do it again.

Because he hadn't meant it the first time, he felt even more compelled to do it again, this time with genuine motive. A genuine symbol of a genuine life change.

Making this decision as an adult was wholly different than making it as a child, of course, but he'd still felt compelled to call the family to tell them what was happening. He'd gotten them to refrain from coming down to see him walk another aisle, thankfully, but he couldn't keep them from coming down for the baptism.

It was a big day, after all.

He made his way into the back room, right into the tiny closet where the baptistry stairs would lead him into the water, and paused a little when he saw Marie standing there.

"Well," he smiled, "they said a staff member would be back here to help out, but I didn't think it would be the children's minister. I think I'm insulted by what this says about my intelligence."

"Oh, don't be," she smiled back at him. "I pulled in a couple of favors to be the one back here. Are you good to go? Is there anything you need?"

"I look like a freakin' angel, don't I?," he said, holding up his robed arms.

"That you do," she laughed out loud. "You have on a children's robe."

"But it fits," he said, looking down at his feet.

"Short people problems," she sighed. "I know all about them. Here, take that off. Wait…" She narrowed her eyes at him. "You're wearing something underneath this, right?"

He frowned. "Yes, Marie."

"Good deal," she said, handing him a black shirt. "The adults don't wear robes, you ninny. They wear these."

"Ahh," he said, looking at it. "Much better."

"Yeah," she said. "Take off the robe, and I'll hang it back up."

He glanced at her uncertainly. "You gonna freak out when I'm standing here before you, shirtless?"

She squinted. "Got some huge scary scars or something?"

"No," he managed. "I just… you know. I don't know what the new rules are. Everyone keeps their shirts on in church, right?"

She laughed at this. "I'll keep mine on, for sure."

He glanced away from her quickly, trying not to think about this too much. "Here," he said, handing her the children's robe and pulling the shirt over his head.

"You think you'd know some of these things," she said, hanging the robe back up and putting it on the small rack on the wall. "Growing up where you did and all."

"Yeah, you'd think," he said. "But all the details from my childhood are fuzzy."

"And speaking of your childhood, I saw your brothers and your sister out there."

"Yep. Not all of them. But a few made the trip."

"I was beginning to think you were adopted. You look nothing like the rest of them."

He shook his head. "Nope, I'm actually handsome, whereas all of them are… well, not."

She smiled at this. "Well, and then I saw your mother. And wow. You look just like her." She looked at him for a long moment. "And your grandfather, of course."

"You remember him back from Namibia," he noted as she reached out and pulled a thread off of the shirt he wore.

"Yeah, and from Sadie's wedding," she said.

"You saw him there?," he said, thinking that he'd spent the majority of the night by his grandfather's side, except for those few minutes he was looking for his grandmother. Those few moments of clarity.

He hadn't seen Marie. But she'd been so close…

"Sure did. Had a great conversation with him. About you," she answered.

"A conversation?," he asked, confused.

"He was proud of you," she said. "Told me about your business, about how hard you worked, how responsible you were."

"Did he?," Scott asked softly.

"I'm sure he's saying it even more now," she concluded, smoothing out his sleeves as she smiled. "Probably telling anyone who will listen all about you, and –"

Before she could say another word, he reached out and pulled her into an embrace. She couldn't know what it meant, to hear this about his grandfather today, to know that Thomas had held onto a hope in Christ on Scott's behalf, that he had, in his clarity, likely prayed him closer to this point.

He was remorseful for all the years he'd sat under his grandfather's teaching and had failed to hear him. And he was so thankful that he'd heard Christ eventually, long after Thomas had no words left.

"Hey," Marie said softly, her hands rubbing his back supportively as he continued holding onto her. "Big day. Big moment, you know?"

"Yeah," he managed, backing away just enough to look at her. "Thank you for telling me that he said that. It means a lot." More than she could know.

She smiled, her arms still around him. "I'm glad."

"But yeah," he said, reluctantly letting her go. "Big day. I don't even know when I'm supposed to go out there."

"Right after they play the new tune," she said, leaning against the wall and smiling at him. "Drew has the praise band play it before every baptism, so I guess it's not technically new."

"What is it?"

"A song about new life in Christ, about how everything is changing. A new tune for a new life in Christ."

"New life," he said. "Changed life. And I needed a change."

"Didn't we all?," she said, biting her lip. "I have a confession."

"Confession?," he asked, raising an eyebrow at her.

"Yeah," she whispered. "I thought your grandfather didn't know what he was talking about."

"How so?"

"Well," she said, "when I met you here, I connected you to him right away. He'd given me your name. But there was another connection, before that."

"And that was...?" He had no idea where she was going with this.

"We were on the same flight coming back to Houston after that wedding."

Bizarre. "Really?"

"Oh, yeah," she grinned. "And I remembered you because at the time, well... I mean, I thought you were cute."

Well, this was interesting. "You did?"

"Yeah," she said. "But you totally didn't see me. And no big deal, since you sat behind me and started flirting with the woman next to you."

Oh, yeah. *That* woman. The... the last woman, actually.

Had it been that long? It had been. He could hardly wrap his mind around the improbability of that before Marie was speaking again.

"Such a tool," she sighed. "You were such a tool."

"Thanks, Marie."

"I mean, you were a smooth tool," she said. "And I was sitting there, eavesdropping, smiling because you were saying things that any woman would have wanted to hear. Really smooth, you know."

He sighed. "And not very genuine. No matter how good it sounded."

"Probably not. And I only mention it now," she smiled, "to let you know that it's been in the back of my mind this whole time I've known you. The things you said, the way you acted, who you were... and I've got to tell you, I see you now, and I swear, you've changed. And I can see it better than most because I remember that guy on the plane. And I can't imagine you, with who you are now, ever being that guy again."

He was glad for this. Thankful to hear that someone else out there could give witness to the change Christ had brought in his life.

And then his mind went back to something she'd said. "I'm still cute, though, right?"

"Oh, yeah," she breathed.

He opened his mouth, but she cut him off.

"And you know you are," she said. "Which makes it completely ineffective. Null and void."

He grinned at this. "Null and void."

"Yes," she nodded, grinning back at him. "I only mention that plane ride, Scott, because... I want you to be encouraged. To know that other people can see what God's doing here. That He's taken the same old tune you've been playing all your life and leading you to consider that there are other better tunes to be listening to, feeling, you know, right here," she smiled, placing her hand over her heart.

"A new tune," he said. "Just like that."

"Just like that," she echoed, just as the tune out in the worship center changed. "Oh, and that's your signal to get in the water, cutie."

Marie

Hearing him profess Christ and watching him share it with the church had been a thrill.

The change he'd gone through was a thrill. Marie had been thankful for the opportunities she'd had those last few weeks to walk alongside him as Christ had done His work. She'd celebrated it all with him and couldn't wait to see what God would continue to do in him.

She'd slipped out of the service as soon as he was out of the water and headed back to children's church. This is what she did most Sundays – attended the early service, worked the Sunday school hour, then had a huge kids' service in the new room during the contemporary service. It kept things running, of course, but it kept her from getting very connected to others in the church her age.

It was a job, though. Ministry was. There were other opportunities for knowing people, being known... somewhere.

She thought about Scott and his family back in the worship center, wistfully jealous over the community they were a part of now while she was back in the children's wing, missing out.

She got in this funk every once in a while, even while smiling, even while singing from the piano in children's worship where the best voices in the entire church sang songs about Jesus, in a strangely accented English. Every once in a while, she'd catch her own voice slipping into a more comfortable accent, sounding a little like home, more familiar to her ears.

Here, but foreign still.

Just as she was closing up and sending the kids off to their checkout points, where their parents would pick them up from volunteers, she got a text from Scott.

Come by the house. Big family celebration. Want you here with me.

She smiled at the invite and was about to text that she'd be there when a concerned parent caught her in the hall. A food allergy, an event on the books for the next week, and questions over whether or not the form they'd filled out had indicated this.

It was an administrative problem, but it was one that Marie was happy to catch on this end before the child ate something and ended up in the ER. So, she texted Scott that she'd have to do it another time, as she went to her office to double check that everything was done correctly and every preventative measure was in place.

As she finished an hour later, she looked at her watch, wondering if she could still make it to Scott's house, if the invite was still on the table. Before she could text him to see, her phone buzzed at her.

A text. From Namibia.

From home.

She grinned, wondering why her parents were up so late, thankful that they were no matter what the reason. She opened up her laptop and waited, gasping in delight when Oom Willem's giant nose filled the entire screen.

"Marietjie?!," he yelled.

"Willem," she heard her mother say. "You don't have to yell for her to hear you."

"Eish, man," he said, softer. "Baie dankie, lovey. Ek is..." And then, loud laughter, his nose still the only thing visible. "Marietjie! I can see you, darling!"

"Oom Willem," she cooed, tears automatically springing to her eyes, reaching out to touch the screen as she sighed, "ek het na jou verlang."

And she did. She missed him every day. She missed them all.

"Jy lyk mooi, Marie!," he continued. He was yelling. Again.

"Shame, man!," another voice shrilled. "Beweeg oor!"

"Ana Marie!," Willem frowned.

And after only a moment, there she was. Tante Ana Marie, just as lovely as she had been when Marie had last seen her face years earlier. "Marie!," she practically sang. "You look beautiful!"

"I already said that," Willem noted sourly, pushing his sister out of the way. They were old enough to be grandparents, both of them, and yet they acted like this.

Marie smiled, missing them even more because of this.

"Shame," she said. "Why are we only just chatting now, like this? You two must get online more often, ne?"

Ana Marie rolled her eyes. "Oh, I have no time to be sitting still trying to figure that all out, you know," she said, grinning. "The centers take up all of our time! And Riaan es –"

"An insane man," Willem interrupted. "He has us scheduled for four trips up north this next month, Marietjie!"

"Shame," Marie murmured. "That's a lot. Wish I could join you."

"That's why we're calling you! Well, not because you can join us, obviously, since you are living your lekker life in the States and all," she said.

Lekker life. Not really.

"But why, Tante?," she said, trying not to think about this. "Why did you call tonight?"

"Well, we're working on the plans," Ana Marie said, smiling. "And we got to talking about Oshakati and the big two week trip we all took when you and Piet were fourteen. And I had to call you and see you! Do you remember that trip?"

Oh, yes, she remembered. They'd had a busy summer season, and it had concluded with one last trip up north. They'd sat around a fire in Oshakati talking and laughing with a potjiekos cooking, under blankets to keep from getting bitten by mosquitos, complaining and laughing about how hot it was to do so.

Marie remembered that night. Her father had finally agreed that she could lead out on a team when they went into the neighborhoods, that she was old enough for this responsibility.

It had been a big night.

But even bigger than that had been the way that Piet had laced his fingers through hers under the blanket that night, for the first time ever. And when his parents and her parents went inside and left them to watch the fire flicker out, he'd leaned over and kissed her. They'd learned how to do that together, by the fire, slowly discovering each other through taste and feel while the night sounds in Oshakati hummed around them.

She could remember it all. Every moment.

"Hoe gaan dit, Marie?," Riaan said, smiling at her from the corner of the screen he pushed into for just a moment.

Marie blinked past tears at the sight of him. He had aged, more than the others, but looking at him reminded her of how old they were all getting. Who did they have now, to watch out for them, to be there for them, except Piet? She suddenly had visions of her parents, ailing and sick, or worse yet, and of her complete inability to get back to them quickly enough.

It was a horrible thought that made her homesick dread have some credibility.

"Baie goed," she said, swallowing past this and answering Riaan's question as he continued to look at her.

Ana Marie gasped out loud.

"What?," Marie asked, concerned.

"Jy het n' aksent nie!," Ana Marie hissed. "Sara! Why does Marie sound like that?!"

"She's lived in Texas for five years," Sara sighed from off camera. "She's had it for a while. You've just not heard it. I'm afraid that accent has covered up her Namibian accent."

"Shame," Ana Marie said, looking quite scandalized at this.

"She sounds lovely."

Marie heard the voice and suppressed a gasp.

Piet.

Oh, Piet. But before he could come into the screen, the picture disconnected.

She put her hands to it a second too late, just as Willem and Ana Marie disappeared from sight.

Piet. His voice. Namibia. Just like it had been, all of them gathered around, preparing for another adventure...

... and she was here, all alone, half a world away.

She sat at the computer thinking on this for what seemed like hours, only being prompted out of contemplative silence when her phone buzzed again.

A text from Scott.

Missed you. Wish you could have come by today.

CHAPTER FOUR

Scott

The job at the church was done. Which meant that he didn't get to see Marie as often.

Well, that wasn't true. He was up at the church soaking up all the information and teaching he could every Sunday and Wednesday. She could usually be persuaded (quite easily, actually) to let him take her out to eat afterwards, which was always awesome. And Mondays were football days, and because Marie didn't have cable, she'd always take him up on his open invitation to watch the game at his house. Same with Saturdays and college football.

Come to think of it, he spent most of his time with Marie.

But it wasn't enough. So, he came up with more reasons to see her.

He got past the children's workers that next Sunday by using a construction excuse. Marie and all the time they'd been spending together had been occupying his thoughts a whole lot more as of late, and he was determined to get a word in with her, even if it included being sneaky.

"Have to check and make sure my guys cleaned up all the mess," he said to the woman guarding the desk. "I was supposed to speak with Marie Boyd about it this morning."

The woman pointed him towards the new common room, with the stage they had worked on for so long. He waved his thanks to her and made his way down the hallway, giving casual glances to the walls and the work he had done along the way.

No one heard him enter the room, thanks to all of the loud singing and dancing going on. There were kids on huge African drums and a woman who sat behind the piano, playing powerfully and singing beautifully. Before Scott could wonder where Marie was in the volunteers spread throughout the room, the boisterous song ended, and the pianist stood up and clapped her hands, laughing as the rest of the class applauded as well.

Marie.

She caught his eye and smiled.

"Oh, boys and girls!," she exclaimed. "We have a very, *very* special visitor today." She eagerly gestured for Scott to join her onstage.

Scott made cutting motions on his neck, but she completely ignored him.

"Mr. Scott? Can you come up here to this fabulous stage you built?," she said, motioning to him from the front of the room.

All of children in the huge crowd assembled there turned their eyes to him. *That's a lot of little eyes*, Scott thought to himself, as he made his way up to the front.

"This," Marie said to her class, "is Mr. Scott Huntington, the man who built *all* of this. But you can call him Mr. Scott."

"*Hi, Mr. Scott!*," all the kids chorused together.

"Hey," he managed.

"Hey, Mr. Scott!," a shrill voice sounded behind him.

"Oh, oh, oh!," Marie laughed, as the children began laughing and whispering as well. "I think we've woken up Bolt and Sprocket, our space monkeys!" She moved over to the puppet hollow. "Which one of you boys was talking to Mr. Scott?"

"It was me!," a monkey puppet in a space suit proclaimed, to the applause of the children.

"Sprocket! Back from space so soon?"

"Yeah," he said. "Came back to see this great new place you've built here, Miss Marie! Or, that Mr. *Scott* has built! Let's give Mr. Scott a big cheer!"

The children did so, and Marie winked at him as his face turned red.

"Hey, Mr. Scott," Sprocket said.

"Um... yeah... monkey," Scott said.

"The name's Sprocket," the monkey warned.

"Okay, Sprocket," Scott answered.

"Are you Miss Marie's boyfriend?"

Marie laughed out loud, as did the entire class. "Oh, Sprocket, you are one cheeky monkey!," she giggled. "Asking our guest questions like *that*."

"You have to *kiss* him if he's your *boyfriend*!," one of the boys in the class yelled, delighted by the ick factor of this possibility.

"I would *never* do that," Marie proclaimed, "because boys? Are gross."

The girls cheered, while Marie smiled over at Scott.

"I think *girls* are gross," Scott smiled back, to the cheers of the boys.

"Well, perhaps we should have a little contest between the boys and girls then, huh?" Cheers on all sides. "If the girls win, Mr. Scott gets a pie in his face next week. And if the boys win, Miss Marie gets one in hers, okay? Your Sunday school teachers will tell you all about the contest!"

Thunderous applause all around. Then, Marie dismissed them to their Sunday school classes, and once they were gone, she turned to Scott.

"Shame, man, sorry about the pie in the face," she said, biting her lip.

"I'm not," the teenager crawling out of the puppet hollow managed. "It would've been me, so thanks for taking the bullet, man."

"That's okay... cheeky monkey," Scott said, looking back at Marie. "What does that even mean? Cheeky?"

She laughed. "It means he says some crazy, crazy things, you know?" She linked her arm through his. "Hey, come and check out how well your guys cleaned everything up!"

Marie

She'd been laughing with him outside the offices when Drew and Tracy came back with their boys.

"Mr. Scott's gettin' a *pie* in the *face!*," three year old Max laughed.

Drew raised his eyebrows at this. "You don't say."

"Only if the boys lose the game," Marie said, poking the tiny boy in the tummy. "Which they so totally will!"

"Game?," Tracy asked. "I got a note about that. Fundraising for... what is it again?" She shifted around one year old Ian on her hip to pull the note out of her purse. "Neon orange, so I can't miss it," she murmured.

"That's why I picked that color," Marie said, "for all of you multitasking, brilliant mothers out there."

"Thank you for that," she said. "Okay, so... coins. Spare change. Money for the fall festival." She frowned. "Why don't you just do the fundraiser you did last year?"

"Do you even remember what I did last year?," Marie asked.

Tracy thought for a second. "Nooo..."

"Yeah, no one else does either, and I'm super glad about that," she said. "I was new on staff, and my ideas were awful. The fundraiser was a dismal failure. But this one might work better, since even three year olds can remember to bring change to put a pie in someone's face."

"*Pie!*," Max shouted.

"Exactly," Marie smiled at him.

"You guys want to go to lunch with us?," Drew asked.

"I was going to take Marie out anyway," Scott said, "but she could probably be persuaded to include the four of you."

"Sure could," Marie added, sharing a smile with him. "Max can keep on talking about the pie you're getting next week."

"Here, take these," Tracy said, putting Ian in Drew's arms and putting Max's hand in his. "I need to talk with Marie. We'll meet you boys out by the car."

"Sure," Drew sighed under the weight of his children, as Scott waved goodbye to Marie, who was now being herded down the hallway by a very exuberant Tracy.

Once they were out of earshot, Tracy turned to face her. "You promised. I had your word."

Marie grinned. "On what? That I wouldn't make you take part in another fundraiser?"

"Not that," she groaned. "Him. That *guy*."

"Scott? When did I give you a word on... oooooohhhhh." She smiled even bigger. "No worries."

"Oh, I'm plenty worried."

Marie sighed, a little annoyed by this. "Tracy, there's nothing going on. He is absolutely, one hundred percent, unequivocally *not* attracted to me."

"But are you attracted to *him*?"

Marie thought about this for a second. He was cute. There was that. And he'd been a great friend. She preferred time with him over just about anyone else. They'd only recently discovered a common love for – of all things – American football and now spent even more time together yelling at Scott's big screen television because the Texans just could *not* manage to get it together.

But he wasn't interested. And neither was she. He was new in Christ, and while all that he was learning was exciting and amazing... well, even if he was learning it all so quickly and astounding Marie with the godliness and spiritual maturity the Lord was working in and through him... well...

What was the question?

Tracy heaved an even greater sigh. "Marie!"

"What?," she giggled. "He's not interested. And neither am I." Not really. Well... "And besides, even if I was, he's a new man. He's right with God. There would be nothing wrong with –"

"He was a *loser*," she said.

"We all were, before Christ –"

"You know what I'm saying."

"I do," Marie said simply. "But you don't need to worry about it. Because there's nothing there."

And even as she said it... well, she wondered.

Scott

Monday night football. Which meant that Scott had cleared his schedule for Marie to come over and watch the game at his house.

Actually, his schedule was clear most days now... or filled with Marie. There had been no opportunity in all the time, though, to tell her what he was thinking. To wonder at what she thought of him, to imagine what kind of music they could make together, metaphorically speaking, of course, and –

"Shame, man!," she yelled at the screen, sending a whole bag of chips flying off the couch and all over the floor.

Or maybe there was just no bravery on Scott's part, as he spent most of their time together staring at her, just like he found himself doing now as she frowned at the screen.

"What are they doing out there?!," she huffed.

"Playing football," Scott deadpanned.

"Not playing it very well," she shot back at him. "I think you could do better than some of the pinheads they have out there right now."

He regarded her with a smile. "Oh, I think you're right. I was quite the athlete back in high school."

"Seriously?," she said, eyeing him critically. "You don't look like you could play football."

"This is Texas, Marie. Every boy had to play at least a few seasons of football. It's like a rite of passage."

"Hmm," she murmured, smiling at this. "Like rugby, I'd imagine."

"No, it's not like rugby," he said.

"You're right. Rugby's much manlier and all."

He raised an eyebrow at her. "And what would you know about rugby?"

"Plenty," she laughed. "Played all the time with the guys back home."

"You?," he scoffed. "It's a dangerous sport. Women shouldn't be out there playing."

"Shame, man," she said. "Didn't peg you for a chauvinist."

"Not a chauvinist. Just want ladies to be treated like ladies."

She shrugged. "Well, I always had Hennie out there to look out for me."

"What's a Hennie?," Scott asked.

She smiled at him. "My unofficial Afrikaans brother, Hendrik. Hennie would rough up the guys who got handsy with me and would help me tape down my ears so they wouldn't get ripped off in the scrum –"

Good grief. "Are you serious?"

"Oh, yeah," Marie laughed.

"You're lying," he scoffed. "You aren't nearly that tough."

She smiled at this, knowingly, and stood up. "Get up, Scott."

"Excuse me?"

"Get up."

He sighed and stood up to face her.

"You up for a little wrestling?," she asked, grinning at him. "We'll see who's tough."

"I'm a gentleman," he drawled out, "who knows better than to hurt a girl."

"I'm not a girl," she said. "I'm a woman."

Oh, yeah. He knew this already. "Please," he scoffed. "You're built like a twelve year old. A twelve year old boy."

She laughed out loud. "Oh, no, you didn't..."

"I did," he laughed back. "And I'm not one for hurting twelve year old boys."

"Oh, you won't hurt me, big guy," she laughed, pulling him to middle of the floor, chips crunching underneath her feet. "Get down on all fours," she said with a smile, just as he was attempting to put his hands on her waist.

He looked at her with mock incredulity. "Just what do you intend to do to me, Marie?"

"I plan to kick your butt," she said. "Go on, get down."

"Fine," he sighed, crouching down, then grinning when she got down beside him. "So, what are the rules?"

"No rules," she said. "We can get as dirty as you want."

He laughed at this and glanced back at her with raised eyebrows.

"Get your mind out of the gutter, you pervert," she said. "And just because of that cheeky look, I'm *really* going to hurt you."

"I'm so scared," Scott muttered.

"On the count of three," she said. "One, two, three!"

And she had him on his back a whole second later.

"What –"

"I win," she trilled gleefully.

"Re-match," he swore. "I wasn't ready."

"Fine then," she said, helping him up and getting into position again. "You count this time."

"Okay, okay... one, two three –"

And again, she had him on his back and was – whoa – pinning his arms down with her knees.

"How did you do that?!," he yelled as she laughed. "Okay. One more time. I'm not going to go easy on you this time."

"Fine," she sighed, smiling. "Give me your best."

"Oh, I'm going to," he muttered, getting behind her this time, certain that doing so would give him the edge. "One, two, three!"

And for a moment? They did struggle, until she cried out, "Ow, Scott!"

"Marie," he panted, his touch turning tender in an instant, "are you okay –"

 And she flipped him on his back again and climbed on top of him triumphantly. "Gotcha, buddy," she laughed out loud.

"That's low, Marie," he said. "So low."

"Just using all the resources available to me," she said, smiling her amazing smile down at him. "Demure, helpless, frail girl and all. Playing dirty, you know."

"And how," he laughed. "I guess this means that you won, and I –"

"Lost, buddy," she grinned, leaning forward on his chest. "Which makes you a *loser*." Then, she sat up straighter, her hand to her mouth. "You're not a loser, Scott," she said softly. "You're not. I've never thought that."

He was glad to hear her say it, even if he had no idea why she felt she needed to. He didn't much care for the whys, only that she was here right now with him, like this.

Because Marie with him right now, just like this, smiling at him, even as he reached up and pushed her hair out of her face...

... certainly felt as though he was winning like never before.

Marie

Days turned into weeks. Weeks into another month. Work, school, missing home more poignantly than she could remember having missed it before... and Scott.

They were together a lot. Not *together*, of course, in that sense, but she saw him a lot.

He'd figured out that she had to go to the early service at the church with all of her responsibilities during the regular service, and he began showing up early as well, sitting next to her so that for the first time since she'd come to the States, she had someone to sit next to at worship. He'd talked her into finally joining a small group in the evenings with him, and they went together, staying out late afterwards, talking through all he was learning, all she was learning, all they were learning at the same time.

The time spent with him was so great that she found herself missing him when they were apart. She felt his absence on Mondays especially, when she spent the entire day in classes and had no lunch break to meet up with him from whatever site he was working near. She'd heard his disappointment over this as well just the night before another day of school and had smiled a little to know that he appreciated her as much as she appreciated him.

"You're in a good mood."

She looked up from her notes at the sound of the familiar voice. Chad Harper. A guy she'd gotten to know well enough over the semester, as they'd both opted to do a full day of classes instead of just a handful. Chad was on a fast track to the mission field, likely Africa, and had, as a result, taken a special interest in speaking with her every week. She'd told her mother, who was always asking if she was meeting any young men, about him offhandedly once earlier in the semester, and she'd rightly said that he sounded just like Marie's father.

Marie could see it even as he watched her with a slight smile on his face.

"Yeah, I guess," she said, smiling, thinking of how Scott had brought ice cream to her apartment after he'd hung up the night before, telling her that she needed a study break. She'd spent the rest of the evening talking to him, laughing at his jokes, and not getting back to the studying she had ahead of her.

Great night, though.

"Good day at church?," Chad asked.

"Busy day," she said. "Getting ready for all the holiday events we've got coming up. Children's choir, Christmas pageant... things like that."

He nodded. "Seems kind of silly, huh?"

She had thought it as well. Had even mentioned it to Chad earlier in the semester, how the American church was focused on things that didn't reach people with the Gospel, how the programs were more focused on entertaining the masses, on failing to offer any real discipleship to people in an effort to attract more crowds and keep things low key theologically speaking.

They had been so above it all. Marie had been especially. Until Scott had been there with her previewing scripts for potential children's Christmas productions and had said, with dumbfounded amazement over the Christmas story, "You mean, the manger was a feeding trough? Joseph let his woman give birth to God in a barn? That's just wrong!"

Perhaps there was depth even in the simplest parts of the story. Maybe there was still some Gospel meaning left in a children's pageant.

Marie shrugged. "It's still good work," she said. "Things going well at the apartment complex?"

Chad had moved to an apartment complex on a shady side of town, full of refugees from eastern Africa, and he was making it his goal to share Christ with them all.

"Yeah," he said. "Meeting with five families now."

"Chad," she smiled. "That's incredible."

He smiled back at her. "Would love to have you come join us sometime, Marie. They'd love to meet you."

He'd said things like this before. And like before, she looked down at her notes, wondering at why this invitation wasn't as appealing as it should have been. Why it wasn't as appealing as the thought of another day spent with Scott...

Well, that was weird. Why was she thinking this way?

Chad took her silence for consideration. And he leaned closer to her as he said, in a lower voice, "Actually, I'd love to just meet up with you outside of class sometime to talk about it all."

She looked up, saw what he must surely mean, as evidenced by the look he gave her. And she wondered at her own hesitation, even as she thought about her mother's words, about how this guy was just like her father, someone who was something like the home she'd come from...

"Okay," she said, very simply.

And even as he got her number and told her he'd call her with the details, she wondered why her mind went back to Scott.

Scott

He had been working on a project on the west side of town. Too far away to grab dinner with Marie like he wanted to, but close enough to meet up with his sister, Savannah. She was as godless as he had always been, and they'd bonded in that in their younger adult years. She didn't seem to know how to handle him now that he was living for Christ, but she still met up with him every few weeks for dinner.

On his dime, of course.

"Look at this, Scott," she said, by way of welcome, as he sat down across from her at the restaurant she'd picked. She tapped her fingernail on a check.

"Pay to Savannah Huntington," he read, "in the amount of... good grief, Savannah. Are you doing something illegal?"

She grinned. "Not this time. No, this is a royalty check from Sadie's wedding pictures. Nine months after the fact! I'm *still* getting royalty checks from those pictures! And a national magazine just used them in a spread covering other professional athletes who got married this year, so this is the biggest check yet. It's like having a baby. Nine months and then... the big payoff!"

"Very nice," he said. "I take it this means that you're picking up the tab tonight?"

"And deny you the pleasure of being a gentleman?," she asked, dropping the check into her purse. "No way."

"Hmm," he murmured, picking up his menu.

"You need to marry a celebrity," she said. "Let me do the pictures and keep the money rolling in."

"Don't think that's going to happen," he said.

"Yeah," she said. "Since you don't ever go out twice with the same girl. Not even the new redeemed Scott can keep his interest narrowed down to one woman."

He glanced up at her, smiling with his secret.

"What's that look for?," she asked, putting her own menu down.

"You underestimate the new redeemed Scott," he said.

"Maybe... but probably not." She went right back to her menu. "How's the new Jesus thing working out?"

"Awesome," he said. "Completely and totally awesome. It's like everything we were ever taught as kids makes sense now. You should give it another thought, Savannah –"

"Uh, uh, uh," she warned, holding a finger up at him.

"What?"

"I hear it from Sean. I hear it from Stu. I hear it from Seth. And on the odd occasions when Sam is in the US, I hear it from him."

Scott grinned at this. "They're consistently annoying, aren't they?"

"They are," she said. "Don't join their ranks. Be your Jesus freak self – fine. But keep me out of it."

"For now," he said. She frowned at him and began to speak again, but he cut her off. "Business going well, apart from royalties?"

"Oh, yeah," she said. "I'm booked up solid through next summer. I didn't really want to become a wedding photographer, but I'm going to take the offers while they're coming."

"I would love for you to come out and take some pictures of the church remodel we just finished," he said. "Would be good for some promo material for some projects I have coming up."

"You can't afford me," she said.

"I'm buying your dinner," he said. "Surely you can take a few pictures for me."

"Maybe," she muttered. "In that case, I'm ordering the steak."

"Order away," he said. "And you can meet Marie when you come."

Savannah was so suddenly silent that Scott couldn't help but look up at her. She grinned at him. "Marie, you say?"

"Oh, yeah," he nodded.

"Same girl you kept texting when we all came out for your baptism?," she asked.

"Yeah," he said. "Though she was just a friend back then."

"And she's more now?," Savannah asked.

He shrugged. "Not officially. But I'm going to change that."

"There's the old Scott," Savannah sighed contentedly. "Always a woman waiting in the wings. Easily swayed, easily convinced, easily... well, easy."

"Marie's different," he said. "She's a church girl."

Savannah frowned at this. "A church girl?"

"Missionary kid, children's minister, all about Jesus. Different, Savannah."

Savannah watched him for a long moment. "Why is she hanging out with you?"

Scott looked up at her. "Well, thank you for that vote of confidence."

"I'm just saying," she said, "that you've never been the classiest guy. It's why you're my favorite brother, you know."

"I'm not your favorite," he noted.

"You are tonight," she said. "Steak *and* lobster. That's what I'm getting."

He shook his head at this, thinking about Marie, about how he'd been a bit of a creep... about how he was more than he'd been. "I'm different, seriously," he said to Savannah. "And I'm going to handle this all differently. Do this the right way. Treat Marie with respect. Put her first. Keep things pure and all. You know how it is."

"I don't, actually," she said. "And I'm not sure you know how to do things the right way, either. You've never treated any woman all that well —"

"Thanks a lot, Savannah. How many different ways are you going to say that I'm —"

"But," she interjected, pointing her finger at him again, "you've never been all into Jesus either. Maybe it'll be different."

"This is different," he said. "She's different." And he couldn't stop smiling at this.

And Savannah saw the difference in his expression.

"I think you really *like* her," she said, grinning.

"I think you're right," he said, grinning himself.

Marie

Chad had called her right before she got to the bar.

As he was concluding their conversation about the date they had for the weekend, she told him why she needed to get off the phone, about who was waiting inside to hear more about Ephesians, and about how much Theo and Jerry had been challenged over the past few months.

He'd spoken appreciatively of what she'd done, but he spoke of it like it was a job, a mission assignment, and not just the natural overflow of her heart, of who she was, of her life.

Maybe she was hearing him critically, though, as she wrestled with feeling apprehensive about going out with him. There was nothing wrong with him. He was very nearly perfect for her, after all... wasn't he? She wasn't getting any younger, and it was difficult enough to meet godly, serious men when she spent all of her time in ministry, back in the children's department.

Not like she needed a man anyway. Not like a man would magically make her less lonely or more fulfilled or any of the things that she could only be in Christ anyway, right?

Still, though, someone to walk alongside her in ministry, to love Christ as she did, to understand her need to have someone, somewhere to go home to…

She shook her head free of her confusing thoughts and opened the door to the bar, scanning the booths for Theo and Jerry. Her eyes landed on them quickly enough, and her breath caught to see that they weren't alone.

There was Scott, sitting right there with them.

"Well, Drew said that the real heart of this passage is God's command to wives. But I swear, y'all, Paul says more to men than he does to women in this chapter," he was saying. "Clearly, Drew is wrong. Which you'd expect since he can be a real pinhead."

Marie bit back a smile at this as she watched them silently. They hadn't seen her, and she hoped they wouldn't as she continued to listen.

"Paul keeps talking about a mystery," Theo said in his rough, loud way. "Is this the same mystery that he was talking about two chapters over?"

"You would think," Scott said. "But the first mystery he talks about is how Jesus died, not just for the Jews but for everyone. Which doesn't sound like such a big deal to us, but back then… well, all the research I've done says that it would have been an incredible shock to the people of Jesus' day. I mean, the Jews were the only ones God seemingly cared about… until Christ came. And it all changed. That was the first mystery, how Christ brought peace to both Jews and, well, guys like us."

"That's deep," Jerry said.

"And this mystery," Scott said, "is about Christ and the church. Not like a church building but people who are following Jesus. We're the church. Us. And just as Christ loved us, husbands are commanded to love their wives. As sacrificially and fully as Christ loved the church. And they're to answer for the spiritual health and wellbeing of their wives."

"And that's deep as well," Theo said.

"And it just gets deeper," Scott said, staring down at his Bible. "I mean, it goes deeper than just caring for and loving someone. It means being willing to sacrifice everything for someone else. And leading them well, treasuring them, counting their lives as more valuable than our own."

Theo exhaled. "And I thought it was just about making our women do what we want them to do."

"As Drew explained it, sure," Scott said. "But that's just bad theology, Theo. Submission and sacrifice work together. And it's a higher calling on us as men, isn't it?"

Marie watched them all, dumbfounded, a smile on her face. As Scott and Theo continued on, she thought about slipping back out and leaving them to their own, clearly inspired study, but Jerry saw her.

"Hey, Marie," he called out.

Scott and Theo both looked over to her. "Hey!," Theo yelled.

And Scott stood as she approached their table, moving his stuff out of the way so she could sit in his seat. He smiled at her.

"Hey, guys," she said smiling back at him, standing there for a second too long, looking up at him in wonder. "Ephesians 5, huh?"

"Yeah," he said, watching her as intently as she was watching him. "We don't have a clue."

"Sounds like you know plenty," she said, feeling her heart speed up just a little as he continued looking at her.

"Marie, sit down," Jerry said, forcing her to break the locked gaze she'd held with Scott. "Scott's been coming here on Mondays, and we've just about got it figured out. But we could use some of your seminary smarts."

She sat down, glancing back over at Scott as he sat down next to her. And she found herself staring at him again, even as he raised his eyebrows at her and stared right back with a silly grin on his face.

"Marie?," Theo said. "Aren't you going to explain it?"

"No," she said softly. "I think I'd like to hear Scott explain it again."

Scott

That was it.

Scott was going to tell her how he felt.

They'd left the bar that afternoon with more smiles than normal, more laughter, and more long, lingering looks.

Scott had no idea what interest looked like coming from a church girl... but he sure hoped that was interest in her eyes as they met his.

He was going to tell her everything.

And what better way to seduce... well, no, that wasn't the right word. He was going to be honorable about this, as honorable as his intentions. So what better way to woo... well, that sounded a little old fashioned. And he was going to be honorable about this but still keep it in this century.

Okay. What better way to win (ahh, that worked) a cool guy like Marie than with wings and a night on the couch watching football?

It was a foolproof plan. The game was on network television, so Marie would be able to get it at her place. Scott figured he would arrive there in plenty of time for the pregame, wings in hand, with every intention of telling her how he felt.

"Marie?" He gave just a small knock, as was his custom these days. As it was on that night, his hands were full, so he could only manage a knock with his elbow, which he gave with a smile. "Open up! I've got wings, and I swear, it's—"

The door opened, and an uptight man stood on the other side.

"Oh, hey," Scott said. Then, standing up straighter. "Who are you?"

"Chad Harper." He gave Scott an appraising look.

Scott returned that look, studying this "Chad Harper" character for a moment. Younger than him, likely. Butt ugly, too. And Scott was more than certain that he could beat him up if he needed to.

"Are you..." Chad began, then didn't seem to know how to finish.

"Marie?," Scott called out, confused, inching past Chad and into the apartment.

"Hey, I think you need to..." Chad offered, trying to stop him and thinking better of it.

Just then, Marie came out of her room looking.... well, amazing. She was wearing a little black dress and heels and had obviously spent more than a few minutes getting ready.

He'd never seen her like this. Twelve year old boy nothing...

"Wow," Scott managed. "Look at you." He glanced back over at Chad and frowned, suddenly even more irritated with him.

"Scott, what are you doing here?," Marie asked, smiling. "Chad, this is my... contractor, Scott."

"Oh," Chad said. "A contractor... that delivers wings?"

"Best contractor ever," Marie laughed. "Can you give me a minute?"

"Yeah," Chad nodded. "I'll just go… out there…" He indicated the porch and lamely wandered out there.

"Who's the dweeb?," Scott asked after the door was shut behind Chad.

"My date for the evening," Marie said in a low voice. "And you shouldn't call him a dweeb. He's a seminary student."

Scott looked at him through the window. "You have… a *date*?"

"Well, yeah." She looked at him oddly.

He looked her over again. "Well."

"What?"

"Do you go on many dates, Marie?," he said. Ugh, he hated the way he sounded, even to himself. Like her irritated brother, and –

"From time to time, yeah," she sighed. Then, "What?!" at the look on his face.

"Well, then," he said.

"Look," she reasoned with him. "I'm a woman. I have needs."

His eyes rounded at this, and before he could launch into a speech that would reinforce all those irritated brother stereotypes he knew he was already fulfilling, she interrupted.

"You are such a pervert," she said. "I'm not talking about –"

"Well, good!"

"I'm simply saying that I enjoy, from time to time, going out –"

"I take you out all the time!"

"Having doors opened for me –"

"I always open doors for you!"

"Being told that I'm pretty –"

"You're not pretty!," he hissed.

"Wow," she managed. "Thanks for that –"

"You're not pretty," he said again. "You're beautiful."

And she said nothing for a moment, watching him, post-admission like this.

He hated himself even more. Because he hadn't said it before. And now, she would spend the evening smiling her amazing smile at someone else, telling her quirky jokes to someone else, falling in love with someone else –

"And you lied," he spat out. "You have heels on, and you're *not* taller than me. And I'm just as tall as that guy out there!"

She watched him silently for a moment as he berated himself for saying this much.

"Scott," she said softly.

"I just…. I just wanted to watch the game with you," he huffed. "And I come over and you're all dressed up like I've never even seen you dressed up, and you're going out with *that* guy, and –"

"I wish you had called."

"Didn't think I needed to," he pouted.

"Scott," she said. "Are you mad at me?"

"No, I'm mad at myself," he said. "And after that wonderful introduction with your beloved *Chad* –"

"He's not my beloved anything, and you –"

"I'm your *contractor*," he said. "Yeah, I heard. Thanks."

She looked at him for a moment. "Well... what was I supposed to call you?"

Scott wasn't sure. But standing here with his wings, knowing that Marie had a life apart from him, and that she looked like *this* for other men... well, he wasn't happy with being *just* a contractor to her.

"I don't know," he muttered. "I'm just in a sucky mood because I wanted to watch the game with you, and you're... going to be spending the evening with him."

"Well, you're welcome to park it on the couch and watch while I'm gone. This can't look any stranger to Chad anyway."

"It's not the same without you," Scott shrugged. And that? Was the troubling truth. That even the best parts of life were, without Marie... well, they were just generally sucky.

Oh, good grief. There went the foolproof plan! Here he was, instead of smoothly convincing her that she needed him, acting like a pouty sap. And here was Marie, in her little dress, making his thinking fuzzy and making him want to pound some seminary student in the face –

"Scott," Marie said softly, again.

"What?" He looked at her, certain that all of his conflicting emotions were playing out on his face for her to plainly see.

She shook her head. "I don't understand you sometimes. But I really want to. Will you let me know what's going on when you figure it out?"

He took a deep breath. "Sure."

And he took his wings and left the apartment.

Marie

She'd been distracted the rest of the night.

Chad was a nice guy. A visionary, a man called to difficult circumstances, someone who was already living out God's calling on his life there in that apartment complex, ready and willing to do anything anywhere the Lord called him.

He was like her dad in that, at least. And what was it they said? That women naturally gravitated towards men just like their fathers? That they'd end up with men just like their fathers?

Scott wasn't anything like her dad. Nothing like him.

Yeah. She'd been distracted, trying to focus on Chad, while these thoughts of Scott kept popping up, almost as if he sat at the table with them, turning all of Chad's intense, serious phrases into jokes.

She'd smirked a little imagining some of them. Then, she'd bitten back any smile, afraid she'd hurt Chad's feelings.

And, wow. He'd gone all out for this. A really fancy dinner at a restaurant she couldn't imagine he could afford as a graduate student. And probably on to something else that just wasn't... her.

She'd rather be back at home, eating wings and yelling at the Texans with Scott.

Chad had picked up on it somehow. And he'd mercifully ended the date early without any word about another time, about even seeing her in class.

She came into her apartment, tossed her purse onto the couch, and flopped down beside it, pulling off her heels and thinking about Scott.

What was this? How had things changed? When had they changed?

For her… she couldn't even pinpoint when she'd started thinking of him like this. It had to have been earlier, weeks earlier, as he'd started learning the truth of Scripture beside her, as his own maturity in the faith had deepened… as he continued to be who he'd been before, funny, charming, interesting, just set to a different tune now.

And she put her head in her hands, wondering what Scott was doing right then…

Scott

Five hours later, he finally broke down and called her.

Oh, he had wanted to call much earlier, but his pride had kept him from it. *Let her go on her date. Let her be bored into oblivion by that ugly seminary student. Let her miss him…*

… please, please, please let her be home already, he thought as he called her.

"Hello?," she answered quietly.

"Marie? Are you still out?"

A pause. "Scott? Is that you?"

"Yeah. Are you still out with whatshisface?"

A sigh. "No, I'm trying to sleep. I got home two hours ago."

A three hour date. That was a bad sign, right?

"So," he asked, going for casual disinterest. "How was it?"

"I'm sorry… what?"

He blew out an exasperated breath. "I was asking how your date went."

"Why?"

"Why?"

"That's what I just asked! Why? Why are you suddenly going all big brother on me?"

Oh, well this wasn't what he had in mind. At *all*. "I'm not trying to be your big brother."

"Then why does it even matter?"

"Because I want to know how it went."

A pause. "Do you want me to tell you that it was amazing and that he's everything I've ever wanted in a man?"

Not particularly. But before Scott could say this, she went on.

"Or do you want me to tell you that I spent the whole evening wondering what was going on with us and wishing that I was back home in my sweat pants and a sweatshirt eating wings and watching the game with you?"

He took a breath. "Well, that sounds a lot better. Except I'd rather you wear that dress instead of the sweat pants, if we're being honest."

A long pause. "Are we being honest, Scott?"

"I would sure like for us to be."

"Then what do you want?"

Scott could hear his words before he could even think through them. "I want you to be with me. Not him. Not anyone else."

"For real?"

He sighed, exasperated. "Yes, for real, Marie. I. Like. You."

"Thank you, Scott."

"I. Want. To. Get. It. On. With. *You*."

"Okay, well, that might be taking it too far. But I appreciate the honesty."

"Yeah, well," he sighed. "I don't know how to do this the right way yet."

"I appreciate that you're trying," she said softly.

He took a breath, his heart racing. "Can I come by tomorrow, then? Pick you up, take you out to breakfast?"

"Yeah," she murmured. "I'd like that."

So would he.

It was no different, he told himself that next morning. No different than all the other times he went over to Marie's apartment to hang out or to pick her up to go grab something to eat. This time was *no* different.

Except, it was. He took a shower like normal, then shaved his face, and spent longer than any sane man would making sure his hair looked just right before he dressed. Then he put on cologne, decided it was too much, and had to go through the whole ridiculous process all over again. Another shower. More primping in front of the mirror like a girl. Then, he took his truck to get it detailed. And checked his teeth in the mirror. Three times.

No different. Yeah, right.

Kudos to Marie, though, who managed to open the door for him and shoot him a smile as though this was, honestly, no different for her, even as he was pretty sure his own heart was about to beat out of his chest.

Except, it was entirely different, the way her smile made his knees weak.

And suddenly? Everything was clear to Scott.

Marie

He was freaked out. Oh, wow. He was so freaked out.

She'd noted that early enough that morning. He'd spent the better part of breakfast staring at her with wide-eyed surprise. It had gone from there, with rare silence from him as he watched her, as she talked over the awkwardness.

She suggested they go back to her place and watch some college football. Surely that would alleviate some of the daze Scott seemed to be under. She had just pulled something to drink out of her fridge and handed it to him when she noticed the look on his face. Panic. Pure and simple. She sighed, knowing what this meant, what had been lost between them.

"Scott," she said, walking around the counter, leaning back against it, and looking him in the face. "Clearly, this is not what you thought it would be. And that's okay. I don't want you to feel guilty if this isn't.... just what you thought it might be. Can we at least stay friends, though, and move past –"

And she didn't have a chance to say anything else because Scott put his drink down, pressed against her, and put his mouth on hers.

CHAPTER FIVE

Scott

Well, he'd been wanting to do that all morning.

She'd been a great friend. A cool guy to be around, you know. Then, he'd admitted he was attracted to her, and the night before, he'd stewed over the thought of losing her before he'd even really had her. She'd invited him in that morning, and as soon as he'd seen her… he'd known.

For the rest of his life, it was just going to be Marie.

He couldn't believe the calm certainty that had washed over him as he'd realized this. And he'd probably looked panicked and freaked out that morning. Not because of what he knew about Marie and what he felt, but because this was such a new thing for him, being so certain and hearing God's affirmation so clearly.

A big, resounding yes.

He'd marveled over that, even as she'd given him quite the dejected look back at her apartment. And he hadn't heard what she'd even said because he was warring with himself. She was it; he knew that. But he was going to do things right. He wasn't going to just rush in and be the old Scott. For once in his life, he was going to do things the right way. He was going to take time, be a gentleman, make his intentions clear through his words, not his actions, and –

Oh, who cared? She was his. He knew it. So he went right ahead and did what he wanted to.

And as soon as his lips touched hers, she erased any good-intentioned resolve he'd had by pulling him closer and being so completely right there with him. Maybe even more enthusiastic than he had figured she would be, as she came at him as eagerly as he came at her.

A church girl. Praise. God.

There was wonder even in that, in being able to connect what was going on in Marie's kitchen with the goodness of God. It made Scott smile, even as he held her in his arms.

A long, long, long while later, Marie put her hands to his chest and pushed him back. "Oh, my," she managed.

"Oh, my," Scott breathed, leaning in again and kissing her once more.

"Scott," she murmured. "You're really good at that."

"Oh, I'm good at a lot more than just that," he grinned at her.

She shook her head. "Shame, man. I don't doubt it."

He sighed heavily. "I've got huge regrets now."

Just a tremor of doubt passed over her face, but like Marie was so good at doing, she shrugged it off. Wow, Scott loved how she could do that, so sure of herself. "Regrets?," she asked, running her fingers through his hair.

"Oh, well," he groaned appreciatively as she pulled his face close and kissed him again. "I'm regretting that I've been wasting my time sitting around watching football games with you when I could have been doing this," he said, going straight for her mouth again, then trailing his kisses down to her neck.

"Mmm," she murmured as he kept on. "I love football, though."

"Oh, but I love you more, Marie," he murmured back.

Silence for a long moment, then, "Wow." She shot him a devilish grin. "That's *heavy*. I mean, I know my kisses are intense, but –"

"Marie..."

"Oh, I know you didn't mean to say that, Scott. Don't worry." She pulled his face up to look at her. "Seriously," she smiled at him, her voice softer.

"But I do," he said, so genuinely that the sound of his own voice surprised him. "I love you. I don't say that lightly. I'm sure. I'm completely sure about you."

And she gave him a small smile before leaning over to kiss him again.

Marie

It was... well, heavy, what he'd said.

Marie hadn't known how to take his words, how to process what he meant, and how to move forward. But Scott wasn't looking for her to say it to him. He wasn't looking for much of anything except her answering kisses, as he led her over to her couch and sat with her, telling her how he was sure.

They'd spent the entire morning there, sitting and talking, and Marie concluded during one of many kisses shared that there was certainty in this, at least, in feeling that she wasn't alone half a world away because he was here with her.

She was immersed in memorizing every inch of his mouth with her own when her phone buzzed at her. She was content with letting it go to voicemail, but Scott backed away fractionally and smiled. "It sounds like a text."

"Yeah," she said, putting her hand to her lip and reaching over to see who it could be. Her parents. Wanting to chat.

She looked up at Scott, who watched her with… unabashed devotion. She wasn't sure what she'd done to deserve that, but it rendered her speechless. He smiled at her. "Important?"

"Just my folks," she said. "Nighttime in Namibia. They wanted to chat."

"Oh," he said. "Well, I can leave, or…" He looked to her for direction.

"Stay here," she said, kissing him again. "I'll just take my laptop in the kitchen. Just a few minutes."

And his eyes followed her as she went that way, even as she was thinking through the conversation to come with her parents. So much had changed since their talk a few weeks ago. She wasn't sure where to start, what to tell them, what to omit –

"Hey!," her mother exclaimed as their eyes met an ocean apart. "Daniel, she's home!"

Marie pasted a smile on her face as her father slid in next to her mother, shooting her a knowing grin.

"I know what you've been up to," he said.

Marie's eyes darted over to Scott, sitting on her couch and flipping through one of her textbooks. An exegetical study of Romans. Definitely not light reading.

"Oh?," she asked, feeling very much like she had at seventeen, sneaking home late at night, checking herself in the mirror, pretending like she hadn't spent the entire evening doing any number of things they would have been shocked to learn she was doing.

Her father narrowed his eyes at her.

Was he reading her mind? His scary intense eyes suggested that he could. She gave him the very same eyes.

"What's up with you, Marie?," he asked.

"Nothing," she said. "Why?"

"You seem a little on edge," her mother noted.

"Just... lots going on," Marie managed.

She was a grown woman. And while she was certain that her parents would be none too pleased to hear that she'd spent the better part of her day making out with a man, she comforted herself with her mind's whispered insistence that it was none of their business. She'd gotten in the habit of trying to please them, trying to honor them, knowing that Christ was honored when she continued to acknowledge their authority in her life, something she had resented and fought against as a teenager.

But still. They didn't need to know about Scott. Not that there was anything wrong with him. Just that... well...

She swallowed, confused by her own thoughts. "Just busy," she said again.

"Busy making the best grades of your entire life," her father said, grinning. "That's what you've been up to."

Oh. This. She'd sent him a copy of a research paper she'd done, so proud of the A she'd received. It had been hard work, but she enjoyed the subject matter for once in her life.

"Yeah," she said, relieved. "Thought you might appreciate seeing that. The first A I've ever gotten, I think."

"We'd take you out for a celebration dinner if we were there," her mother said softly. "We'd do so many things if we were there. Or if you were here."

"Well," she sighed, "it's actually morning here, so dinner wouldn't be really fitting anyway." She blinked back tears at this, imagining home again.

"You know what I mean," her mother said, likely blinking back tears herself.

And then the picture on her laptop began to shake. Her parents continued speaking, but she could no longer hear them. Technology was amazing, but the connection didn't always work right.

"I'm losing you guys," she said, hoping they were able to hear her. "I'll call back soon. Okay?"

And they nodded, hearing this, her mother kissing her fingertips and holding them up to the screen, and Marie doing the same, just as their faces disappeared.

She sat for a silent moment, dropping her hand back to her lap, then closing her computer, willing herself not to cry.

And pasting another smile on her face, she made her way to the living room, where Scott held up the textbook and pointed a finger at it.

"This? Sounds like my brother, Stuart, wrote it," he said. "You'll like him when you meet him... if he doesn't bore you to sleep within five seconds of saying hello."

"He sounds exciting," she murmured.

"Hey, are you okay?," he asked, concerned.

"I'm fine," she said, sitting down next to him, reaching out for his hand.

"Heard you mention an A on a paper," he said. "Sounds like something that needs to be celebrated. Can I take you out tonight?"

"You just took me out this morning," she noted, her hand on his face, naturally, like she'd been here with him, just like this, forever.

"Just looking for excuses to spend the whole day with you," he said softly.

"No need to make up excuses," she said. "Just stay." This place wasn't home, but as she'd learned over the last few years, home was what you made of it.

So, even as her heart ached, she felt a fresh wave of appreciation for Scott, who made this place better than it had honestly ever been. She'd never been completely happy in the US, but these last few months with him? She was closer than she'd ever been.

The smile that she gave him as he came close for another kiss was genuine.

Scott

Well, that had been the best day of his life thus far.

All day on Marie's couch, her in his arms, as they talked about everything and nothing all at the same time. She'd asked him about his family, and she'd laughed so hard at his descriptions of his brothers that even he'd seen the humor in who they were.

He wasn't dumb. He knew the phone calls to Namibia were probably hard for her. As uninvolved as his own family was in his life, he had the assurance of having them close by. And he'd grown up nearby, so he couldn't understand entirely what she felt.

You couldn't always fix someone's problems, but you could do your best to distract them from them.

He'd done a good job of that. He had plans to take her out to some fun places he knew around the city to get her mind off of Namibia, to celebrate her A, to revel in the fact that they were together now... but Marie had just wanted to stay on the couch and kiss him.

Well, that worked, too.

They'd said good night before morning came, and Scott headed back home with a smile on his face.

He had thought there might be some awkwardness the next morning at church after the way they'd gone so quickly from friends to more. Not awkwardness on his part, of course. He was planning on playing it smooth and cool, like he always did.

Except... well, he felt kind of queasy.

Attributing it to nerves, because Marie got him nervous in a way no other woman had, Scott went on ahead to church that morning, smooth and cool.

Except... not cool. Kinda feverish. Wow, Marie was really messing him over.

Smooth and cool, Scott, he told himself as he found her at the entrance of the sanctuary, directing parents to the children's wing, shaking hands as she did so. She caught his eye, gave him a shy smile, and said, "Hey, Scott."

"Hey, Marie," he managed, smooth and cool... right before he threw up all over her shoes.

"I'm so sorry," he said ten minutes later as Marie, now barefoot, put a hand to his forehead as he sat on the sofa in her office.

"You're so hot," she said.

"Yeah, I know," he laughed, then groaned at the way his head was pounding.

"You better watch it," she said, smiling at him.

"Oh, I was watching it all right," he managed. "Right before I barfed all over you. Not my best moment."

"I work with children. It happens to me more often than you would think." She moved her hand from his forehead to his face. "The good news is that my shoes took the worst of it, so the mess was minimal. But you, sir, need to go home. Right now. You clearly have a fever. And likely the flu, if your explosion was any indication. You don't need to get everyone else sick."

"Oh, it'll pass," he said, waving her concerns away.

"Did you get a flu shot this year?"

He looked at her and grinned. "Please. I never get sick. So, I don't need one."

She shook her head at him. "You should've gotten one. Think you can drive yourself home, or do I need to hunt someone down?"

"My sister," he groaned, handing Marie his phone. "Call Savannah."

And even as she dialed the number, he closed his eyes and snuggled in closer to her.

Marie

After church that night, Marie arrived at his house, where a beautiful young woman opened the door with great irritation on her face. Even still, she gave Marie an appreciative welcome, scooping her right up into a hug. "You're Marie, aren't you?," she asked, clear relief in her voice.

And Marie couldn't stop the smile that came as she patted Savannah on the back. "Yeah, I am. And you're Savannah, his sister… right?"

"That's me," she said.

"I was glad to get to meet you over the phone, even under these circumstances."

"Circumstances," Savannah scoffed. "Like loads of barf and raging fevers and –"

"The flu," Marie nodded.

She looked Marie over for a second. "You're not the type of girl he usually goes for," she said simply, without hesitation.

"Oh?," Marie asked, wondering at this, smiling still.

"Yeah, but don't get me wrong," Savannah clarified. "The type of girl he usually goes for isn't the type he needs. And goodness knows, he talks about you like he's never talked about any of those skanks he's always bringing –"

"Savannah!," Scott shouted from across the house. "I hear ringing!"

"It was the doorbell, Scott! Shut up!," she shot over her shoulder. Then looking back at Marie, "I'm sorry, what were we talking about?"

"Skanks," Marie added helpfully. "You look tired. You should go home and rest. Leave me to take care of him."

"Seriously?," Savannah asked.

"Very seriously," Marie said. "I don't have anything else to do tonight."

"Hallelujah," Savannah muttered, hugging Marie again. "You're seriously an answer to prayer. Just exactly the kind of woman Scott needs, and —"

"Savannah?" Scott called from his bedroom. "Savannah, the room is spinning."

"Then shut your eyes, you idiot!," she yelled over her shoulder. Then, to Marie, "I swear, if the room isn't spinning, his feet are throbbing, his tongue is spongy, his hair hurts, his fingers are tingling —"

"Shame," Marie managed through her laughter. "He sounds like a bad patient."

"Understatement of the year," Savannah said, searching for her purse. "And you would think being his kid sister would give me some degree of compassion, but with him? It just —"

"Savannah, I think I'm dying!," Scott gasped.

"You bet your boots you're dying because I'm about to come in there and strangle you myself!," Savannah shouted back at him. She took a deep breath and looked to Marie again. "Are you sure you want to help?"

"I just might save Scott's life," she smiled.

Scott

He woke up drenched in his own sweat.

There were only vague memories of what had gone on the past… day? Two days? Images of Marie bringing him medicine filtered in and out of his mind and... a breathing treatment?

He looked over at his bedside clock. 3am. But since, for the first time in who knew how long he felt like doing it, he got up out of bed and went to shower. He got cleaned up, threw on some shorts, and made his way into the kitchen to try and find something to eat, finally hungry again.

After rummaging through the fridge, he looked into the living room, certain that he was seeing things. Because there on his couch? Was Marie, curled up and asleep, looking super hot in one of his shirts and a pair of his boxers, her hair down and her mouth slightly open.

Well, if this was a hallucination because of the fever, he was never more glad to have the flu. And he decided to just go with it, especially if it was just a really, really good dream. He made his way over to her, sat down on the ground next to the couch, and reached out to touch her face softly.

She awoke immediately, fixed her eyes on him, and sighed. "Scott, are you okay?"

"Yeah," he whispered. "Much better, actually. You're still here."

She put her hands to his neck again. "Fever's gone," she smiled. "Finally. And you're not wheezing anymore."

"Wheezing?"

"Yeah," she sighed again, relief on her face. "Savannah neglected to tell me when she left me with you four days ago that you have asthma. Pretty serious asthma, actually."

Scott wasn't sure what part of this to concentrate on first. "Four days ago?!," he said, deciding to start there.

"Yeah," she nodded. "You were really sick."

"And why was the asthma a concern?"

She rubbed her eyes and yawned. "Because you were having trouble breathing. The flu can do that sometimes. I was so scared, Scott. Kept trying to keep you awake because you weren't breathing right. Almost took you to the emergency room, but when I called Savannah, your mother was over there. Came down to be her assistant on a photo shoot, she said."

"And?"

"And," Marie sighed, "since she was in town, she came over and helped me find your inhalers."

"So... you've met my mother?," he asked, just a little weirded out that so much had gone on while he was semi-conscious.

"Yes," Marie closed her eyes and put her hand to his face again. "She's a very sweet woman. Wanted to stay here and take care of you herself when she saw how worried I was, but I told her I had it under control. That I wanted to take care of you myself."

Wow. Not only had she brought him back from the brink of death (thanks for that, Savannah), but she'd also managed to get his mother to leave him alone.

He wasn't sure which feat impressed him more.

He climbed onto the couch next to her, pulled her close, and wondered at this. "So Savannah almost killed me. I actually remember that."

"Yes," she smiled, putting her arms around him, "but I took good care of you. And there was no way I was going to leave you alone after watching you struggle to breathe like that. I mean, I know it's totally inappropriate, me staying here overnight and all. But surely Jesus didn't want me to leave you if were in danger of dying because you couldn't catch your breath, right?"

"I would hope Jesus would want to spare me death by my negligent sister's hands," he said.

"So, I've been here with you."

"Sleeping on the sofa," Scott said. "There are other beds upstairs."

She glanced over that direction. "Didn't even check them out," she murmured. "Wanted to stay here, close by, in case you needed me."

"Will you head that way now?," he asked. "Get some good sleep finally?"

"I should probably head home," she said.

"No," he shook his head, pulling her closer. "Stay with me. You spent all this time here, and I didn't get a chance to enjoy having you with me. Seeing as how I was unconscious the whole time."

"The flu will do that," she murmured, smiling.

So right. Everything about her was so right for him. He knew it more and more acutely, even as she smiled up at him, exhaustion and joy in her eyes.

"I love you," he said. Again.

And she sighed as she put her lips to his. "I love you, too, Scott."

Marie

She'd said it. And meant it.

What she hadn't told him was that her initial intent had been to leave him comfortable, to go back to her own place, and to check up on him that first morning. But he'd pulled her close as she tucked him in, cuddling just her arm in his fever-induced state, and had murmured, "Need you. Forever, Marie."

There had been affection for him. Attraction, most definitely. And just a hint of more to come, with time, so much more time. But when he'd said forever, she'd celebrated it in her heart. To be needed forever, to have someone forever, to have a place to call home forever...

These were wonderful possibilities.

Just when she'd resolved that he would be okay for the night, he'd begun gasping for breath. She didn't know what to do, how to help, and she'd found herself, even as she'd held his face in her hands and told him to stay awake until she could figure it out, she'd felt her heart clench at the thought of losing him. Completely illogical, likely, as she imagined rushing him to the ER, being there as he flat lined with the flu, of all things...

... but she'd fought back tears as she searched the contacts on his phone, holding him close, wondering at the cruelty behind losing someone who felt like home, after only just finding him.

She hadn't realized how much she felt until she felt she was about it lose it all.

Then, she'd figured it out, thanks to Savannah and Jessica, Scott's mother. Jess had seen the concern in her eyes, the near despair as she blinked back tears, and she'd hugged her close, no longer a stranger, whispering, "He's not going anywhere."

And Marie had stayed with him, had taken care of him, resolving that she belonged with him, right here.

And as he smiled back at her, finally better, she decided that it would be him, forever, even as she fell asleep there with him.

Scott

He watched her sleep until the sun came up, then he left her on the couch with a soft kiss, determined to get back to life, starting with some phone calls.

Savannah wasn't too happy about the early morning wake up call, but she did seem relieved to hear that he was still alive. Frank was up next, and he was more up to date than Scott could have imagined he would have been, having gotten the details from Marie, who looked over his work calendar and arranged everything from this end, without even being asked or expected to.

When she said she took care of him, she really meant it. She had taken care of everything. Scott felt immensely thankful and just a little worked up, thinking on what this meant, what it said about her, how amazing she was...

Marie came into the kitchen while he was still on the phone, smiling over at him lazily and walking around to the fridge as though she belonged here. Right here with him.

And she did. She belonged here with him. Forever. She grinned over at him, eating the Trix right out of the box without any reservations at all as he hung up the phone. "Good morning," she said. And he could picture this same scene playing out here for years and years.

Starting now.

He went to her and swept her up into his arms, Trix and all. "You want some?," she smiled up at him. "I could even put yours in a bowl. With milk."

"Mmm... that sounds great, but actually," he said, "I want to know what your plans are for today."

"Today?," Marie asked around a mouthful of cereal. "Well, thanks to you being so sick, I had a reason to do all of my work from home... well, from your home."

"Oh, just go ahead and call it home," he said, kissing her neck.

"Um… okay," she laughed. "Wow, when you kicked the flu, you kicked it, buddy. You're acting like you feel on top of the world."

"That's exactly how I feel," he said, laughing out loud.

"I love you," she said again. Wow. That was the best thing he'd ever heard. She smiled at this. "And I don't care if I get sick. I'm going to kiss you. On your germy lips."

"Please do," he said.

And she did, tossing the box of cereal to the counter before she wrapped her arms around him and went right ahead.

"Well, that involved more than just my germy lips," he murmured a moment later.

"I know," she sighed. "I'm going to be so sick later. Delirious with fever and all."

"Delirious enough to make some crazy decisions, I hope," he said, smiling.

"What?," she asked, laughing at this.

"I hope," he murmured, taking a deep breath.

She regarded him with an odd look. "What's up with you, Scott?"

"I'm just trying to figure out what you have to do today," he said simply.

"Nothing. I'm off of work until Sunday."

"Perfect," he practically sang, kissing her on the lips loudly. "I have a plan. Can you be ready to go shopping with me in a couple of hours?"

She looked at him, confused. "Shopping?"

"Oh, yeah," he smiled. "Shopping."

"Are you sure you're not still feverish?"

"Marie...."

"Okay, yes," she laughed as he began kissing her neck. "You've got to stop that, or I'll never be able to leave and get ready back at my apartment."

"Oh... you've got to leave?," he asked, disappointed.

"All of my clothes are back there!," she said, moving away from him and putting her cereal back in the pantry. "Except for the outfit I was wearing when I came over here four days ago, which is currently in the dryer, *and* which I will gladly change into now and get on the road. To *my* home. I don't live *here*, buddy." She grinned her amazing grin at this, leaned up to kiss him on the lips once more, and then made her way to the laundry room.

"Not yet," he whispered to her retreating back.

Marie

He had picked her up thirty minutes later, and one kiss had turned into more than she could count before he finally proclaimed that they really needed to get some shopping done. Honestly, she was the one who jumped in the truck, then unceremoniously jumped on him, backing him up against the door, more aggressive than she probably should have been.

Even after she pushed away from him and sat on her side of the truck, smiling with just a bit of shame over at him, as he dramatically fanned himself off, she considered just what a temptation this man was to her.

149

And her mind went back to another time, when she hadn't shown any control and had regretted it so sorely. She was intent that this time, she wouldn't make the same mistakes. Especially since Scott seemed so very important, so very special, so very set apart to her. She wouldn't let herself get carried away again.

"Shame, man," she said, touching her lips. "We need to set some ground rules for... well, this. Because I'm having a hard time walking the straight and narrow with you."

Scott glanced over at her with a smile. "I agree. So. Ground rules. But can we wait to set them until tonight?"

She gave him a strange look, wondering at this. "Want to get in one last, 'anything goes' day, huh?"

"Oh, no," he said. "I'll promise now not to touch you again until we've set the ground rules tonight. On my honor and for the Lord's glory. Honest."

"Well, that's admirable," she said. "But maybe just one or two kisses?"

"Agreed," he said, and before too long, they were at their destination.

Marie looked at him, confused. "Why are we at a jewelry store?"

"Because we need some jewelry, Marie," he said, jumping out of the truck and coming to open her door for her.

"What kind of jewelry?," she said, still not understanding him.

"Matching jewelry," he said, drawing her close and lifting her out of the truck. "Well, actually, yours will probably be a whole lot more expensive than mine. But I'm prepared for that."

"Okay, you need to explain what's going on," she said. "I thought you were taking me out to replace the shoes you threw up on –"

And she gasped out loud when he got down on one knee, right there in the parking lot, and said, very simply, "Marry me. Today."

"What?"

"Marie," he said so sincerely, "you know I love you. I meant it when I said it, and this week, with you at home with me, I don't want you to ever *not* be at home with me. I know this is quick, but I'm sure about you and about us and... marry me. Today."

She looked at him, baffled. Then her shock slightly abated as she gave it more thought, and a smile began to take form on her lips.

Surely he was joking.

"Are you for real, Scott?"

"For real as for real can get," he said. "Yes. I'm ready to buy whatever huge ring you want, book whatever flight it takes to get us somewhere that they can legally marry us, and go to sleep tonight as man and wife, forever and always and—"

"Ahh, is that what this is about?," she sighed. "Now, I see what you were thinking by wanting to set some ground rules tonight. But marriage to get a little bit of —" she indicated her body "—this? That's pretty heavy, buddy."

"That's not it," Scott promised. He stood to his feet and took her face in his hands. "I'm seeing things a lot more clearly since coming to Christ, and I'm telling you that everything I see in you, that I love in you, that makes me completely crazy about you, is all that He's done in you. And I know now why I spent so much time chasing after loads of women —"

"Loads of women, Scott," she said. "How wonderful..."

"Mmmm," he consented. "Not so much, huh?"

"Not so much," she smiled.

"Well, that was just the old me, wanting and never finding what I have here, with you. Someone who is a good fit, a good match. I could look for the rest of my life and never find another you. So, why waste any of our time questioning or searching or asking anything when we know that the answer is you and me?" He got back down on his knee.

She considered this for a moment. Considered what she really wanted instead of what she thought would be smart. And him looking at her like that, smiling at her so winningly? Well, he was all she wanted.

Though she'd sworn to her heart that she would never, ever again, picture it in her mind... well, she pictured Piet on the beach on that sad day so long ago, telling her that he wasn't ready. A whole lifetime of knowing her so completely and fully, and he still hadn't been sure. The "ek is lief vir jou" he had proclaimed had been empty, with no commitment, no promise behind it.

And here was Scott. There had been no lifetime, only these few months. Yet, he was sure. And the "I love you" he had proclaimed, was *still* proclaiming, was full of commitment, full of promise.

He was certain. And he felt certain to her. Secure. It had been a hard road, feeling so untethered to anything since coming to the States, and while she had found some semblance of permanence and stability, most days she still felt like she was without a real home, waiting and wondering when something would feel more stable, more secure.

He certainly felt that way. He made her feel secure, like this place, like he could be home.

She'd said she needed more time. Needed to be responsible with these feelings, smart about what came next. But... she'd already decided that this was forever, hadn't she? The thought of life without him, only a few days earlier, had been unbearable.

Why put this off when it was so clearly inevitable?

"Am I completely crazy for wanting to tell you yes?," she asked, over the pounding of her heart.

"You'd be crazy to say anything else," he said confidently.

"Then... yeah. Okay." What was she even saying?! She laughed out loud. "Is that crazy?"

"Yes, it is," he said, hugging her, then pulling her towards the doors to the store. "Now, come on, let's go get some wedding rings."

Scott

She picked out a ring. A tiny little ring. Scott's pride wouldn't stand for any wife of his wearing such a tiny little pebble, so he picked one identical to it, only a whole carat larger. Just as he thought Marie would refuse, he slipped it on her finger, and she was sold. So was he. And they picked up a matching band for her, then one for him, and within fifteen minutes of entering the store, they were back out in his truck, already wearing them. A quick trip back to her apartment, where she packed a bag while Scott made flight arrangements over the phone, then on to his place where she did the same for him – throwing his clothes into the suitcase right alongside hers. A few kisses later, and they were off to the airport. And before they had time to even think through what they were about to do, they were on a plane headed west, then before a justice of the peace, where Scott found himself choked up, promising her forever.

An unredeemed Scott had thought that one woman for a lifetime sounded like a dull prospect indeed. And a redeemed Scott had accepted it as just part of dying to self and living for Christ. But Marie? Had both Scotts rethinking their stance.

Because a whole lifetime with Marie, standing here with him, looking at him as though she honestly believed that he could be the man God was calling him to be... well, a whole lifetime wouldn't be nearly long enough.

CHAPTER SIX

Marie

There was no formal honeymoon. Only a night away, then a flight back to Houston, where he picked her up in his arms and carried her across the threshold of his house. Now her house, too, she supposed.

Even as he put her back on the ground and immersed himself in kissing her thoroughly and fully, her mind was on this.

Home. This was home now... wasn't it?

"Welcome home," he whispered, pulling away and seeming to read her mind. "Home just got a whole lot more exciting." He grinned at this and picked her up again, very nearly lifting her up and over his shoulder as he pointed his feet towards his bedroom, when she put her hands to his chest to stop him.

"Home," she said.

"Yeah," he said right back. "Yours. Mine. Ours."

"So, I'm moving here?," she asked, grinning at the thought.

He put her down on her feet slowly. "Well... yeah. That just makes sense, right? I mean, you're just renting your place."

"I am," she said, turning and looking over the massive kitchen. "I just... we didn't talk about what was going to happen next. I haven't even gotten a chance to really look around here yet."

"You've been over here more than a few times, Marie," he said.

"Yeah, but not as the... lady of the house and all." She blinked at him, a laugh caught in her throat. "That sounds weird, you know."

"Sounds great to me." He grinned at this, reaching out for her hand. "Well, let me give you the grand tour, lady of the house."

"Please do," she said, kissing him softly.

He pulled her close, regarding her very seriously for a moment. "I've never brought a woman here, you know."

"Never?," she asked, feeling a rush of pleasure at this.

"Never," he said. "And for what it's worth, Marie, there hasn't been anyone, anywhere, since I met you."

Overwhelming pleasure at this. "Well," she said, "that's because I kept you so busy with the church renovation. You didn't have time for anything."

He smiled. "I have time now, though." And he picked her up and had her over his shoulder again, heading her towards his room.

"Scott!," she scolded. "The tour? Remember?"

"The tour," he nodded, groaning and letting her down slowly. "Where do you want to start?"

"Umm… upstairs?," she asked, looking around. "I didn't even check up there when you were so sick."

"There are four bedrooms upstairs," he began, leading her that way.

"Four?"

"Seems a bit excessive, huh?," he said. "My dad helped me with the plans and suggested it. The only thing it's been good for is housing all my siblings when they come through town."

"And you have five?," she asked. "Sean, Sam, Stuart, Seth, and Savannah."

"Yep."

She sighed at the thought of so many new people. New family now. Wow. "I guess I'll get to meet the rest of them… at some point, right?"

He smiled at this. "They're going to love you. All of them."

Marie was thrilled by the excitement in his eyes… thrilled and anxious about her own family hearing this news. At least Scott's family knew she was in the picture. She'd never even mentioned him to her own family.

"What?," he asked, seeing the apprehension on her face. "What's wrong?"

"Just thinking about telling everyone what we've done," she murmured.

"I think my parents are going to be cool with it," Scott said diplomatically.

"Really?"

"Yeah," he said. "I mean, they were starting to think I wasn't ever going to get married, so this will be a good surprise. And my mother already loves you, I'm sure, which makes it a *great* surprise."

"Really?," she said. "Why did they think you'd never get married?"

"Oh, my mom thinks any man over thirty has a harder time finding a wife because she got married so –"

"Over thirty?," Marie looked at him, confused.

"Yeah," he said, looking over at her. "I just turned thirty-one. How old did you think I was?"

She blew out a breath, shocked by this. "Closer to my age, I guess."

He kept looking at her. "Which is..."

"Twenty-two."

"What?!"

"Please," she said. "That's not that young."

"Well, no, but... wow. How did I not know that?"

"I don't know," she regarded him oddly, wondering at how surprised they both were. "I guess we just... never talked about that."

"Oh, well," he shrugged. "Not that it matters, right?"

"Not at all," she confirmed. "And it won't make a difference to my parents either way."

"They're going to love me, right?," he said, now confidently moving his arms around her again.

"Eventually. Maybe."

He stopped what he was doing. "Maybe?"

"I'm an only child," Marie said. "And I've never even mentioned you to them. It's going to be a… surprise." She bit her lip as he watched her.

"Are you worried?"

"A little," she admitted, imagining her father's reaction to this. "My dad is… well, he might be upset. A little. Maybe."

No maybe about it. She could almost feel him now, glaring at her from across the Atlantic, somehow sensing that something wasn't quite right with his Marietjie.

Scott took a breath at this. "Do you have daddy issues, Marie?"

She couldn't help but grin at this. "What?"

"I only ask," he said, "because I'm convinced that there's not a woman out there without at least some kind of daddy issues, and we really need to figure yours out early on if –"

"Scott," she laughed, suddenly not caring nearly as much about what anyone thought as she leaned up to kiss him on the lips. "I don't have daddy issues. But my dad? He has issues."

"Like what?," he asked, genuine concern on his face. Marie went for the joke, just to ease his worry.

"Well, he's a pioneer missionary to a wild, wild country in Africa," she sighed. "Killing wild animals with his bare hands, putting on war paint like the natives, driving out demons, you know."

Scott stared at her. He really thought that Namibia was like this. She felt a twinge of disbelief that he could know so little about her, about home…

… well, home was here with him now, wasn't it?

It would have to be. She wanted it to be.

"Demons?," Scott asked, weakly.

"Oh, good grief, Scott," she said. "I was kidding. He lives in a city. In a house. With running water. And while he's a little overprotective sometimes, I don't honestly think he would kill anything or anyone." She paused. "Or at least, he hasn't so far."

"That's reassuring," he managed. "But, hey. It's going to be fine. We'll tell them, and it'll all be fine. Okay?" He kissed her again. "And now, for your tour..."

"Forget the tour," she said, pulling him closer, wanting to think about him and him alone for now, forgetting what was ahead, and all of the troubling thoughts she was having about home and what it all meant now. "Take me to your room. Excuse me, *our* room."

He needed no further invitation than this and was happy to oblige, even as she smiled against his lips and he carried her that way.

Scott

It had been a whole week, and they still hadn't called the family.

Scott had managed a few calls to his crew and to Frank to make sure things were going as they should. And Marie had called the church to finally cash in on her long since saved vacation days. He should have taken her somewhere special, somewhere meaningful. But every time he brought it up, she just pulled him back down into the bed, telling him that this was perfect.

So perfect.

While she slept in one morning, he left a note telling her that he was going to pick up some food. Halfway to the store, his phone rang. Expecting that it was Marie, likely telling him to forget the food and just come back already, he grinned as he answered with, "Seriously, you're wearing me out. Can I at least get a little something for us to eat before you expect me to get right back in bed with you?"

Nothing but silence for a moment. Then, Drew's voice. "Well, hello to you, too, man."

Scott laughed out loud. "I thought you were someone else!"

Another pause. "Well, I'm glad that you're not talking like that to me, obviously, but I've got to say that I'm concerned, as your pastor and your friend, that you've got some woman –"

"Not some woman," Scott said. "I thought I was talking to Marie."

Again, a pause. "Okay, well, that's even worse, Scott," he said. "Marie is –"

"My wife," Scott laughed. "She's my wife, Drew. I married her last week. That's why she didn't come in on Sunday. She was... well, otherwise occupied on Sunday morning."

"You what?!"

Scott was prepared for some disbelief from some of the people in his life. But in his mind's eye, even now, he saw Marie, smiling at him as she'd murmured her vows, then wiping away tears as he'd whispered his to her, so certain and so sure. He saw how she had looked at him that night, adoration in her eyes as he'd given her every part of himself, and how he'd very nearly been speechless over how God had redeemed even this part of his heart, allowing him to hold and love a woman in a way he never had before, honestly treasuring her and counting her above himself.

Finally. Marie. It was all the grace of God, finding her and feeling this way, even with his past.

"I made the best decision of my life, after following Christ, of course," Scott said to Drew, beaming at the thought of it all. "Order her some new business cards, Drew. She's changed her last name. Or will once we get all the documents sorted out. It all happened kind of fast."

Drew was silent for a moment. "Scott, she needs to come into the office and speak with me. Can you give her that message?"

"Well, sure," he said. "Is everything okay?"

"Yeah," Drew said shortly.

"Hey, man, why were you calling me anyway?," Scott asked.

"Just wanted to see how you were doing," he said, a great sigh in his voice. "Hadn't seen you at church. Just wanted to make sure you were doing okay."

"Better than okay," Scott said, hanging up the phone and smiling at how amazing everything was turning out for him.

Marie

Her parents called while he was out.

She'd gotten the text as she'd laid in his bed, grinning at the screen, expecting that it would be him... then, panicking when she saw who it was.

Now was as good a time as any to tell them what had happened.

So, she slipped on one of Scott's shirts, tried to smooth down her hair, and sat down in front of her laptop.

"Marie," her father said, smiling when their faces both appeared on her screen.

"Hey, Dad," she said softly.

"Marie," her mother began brightly, "we've been…" Then, confusion. "Where are you, Marie?"

Marie turned and looked behind her. Scott's bookshelves, his giant big screen television, the picture window framing the acreage behind his house, his living room furniture… all of it familiar enough to her all these months later but totally foreign to her parents.

"Home," she said softly.

"Did they give you a really big raise at the church?," her father asked, squinting as he checked it out as well.

"I need to tell you something," Marie managed.

"Okay," her mother said, and Marie could see her put her hand to her father's. She could tell the news was big.

Oh, boy.

"I've gotten married," Marie practically whispered. Then she smiled, as if that would make this the best news ever –

"What?," her father asked as they both stared at her.

"I'm married now," she said.

"But… how?," her mother asked weakly.

"How?," her father spat out. "I think the better question is who?! Who did you marry?! Who will I have to kill now?!"

"Chad," her mother said, sighing. "Oh, Marie, is it the missions student?"

That probably would've made better sense, of course. How to best explain –

"How did… when did… married?!" Her mother wasn't going to take any of this well. The reality seemed to be hitting her slowly.

Marie held up her left hand weakly.

Her mother gasped again. "How did a seminary student afford that?!"

"Seminary student?!," her father bellowed. "Who are we even talking about?! Who?!"

"Chad," her mother gasped. "I don't even know his last name!"

"Harper," Marie offered, "but –"

"Marie Harper," her father said severely. "We've got to have a serious talk with you –"

"Oh, no," Marie held her head in her hands and tried breathing evenly. "I'm not Marie Harper. Huntington. Marie Huntington. I'm married to Scott. Scott Huntington."

Her parents continued staring at her.

"Who is Scott Huntington?!," her father yelled.

"Wait," her mother gasped again. "Huntington… Marie, is he Thomas Fisher's grandson?"

Marie nodded, tears lodged in her throat.

"I know him, Daniel," she said. "Well, I *knew* him. Back when he was three, Marie!"

"He's three?! You married a three year old?! What kind of sick church are you at?!"

Was it possible that her father had lost his connection to reality in his rage?

"Daniel," her mother said severely, "he's not three now. He's… oh, he was one of the older brothers, so he must be –"

"Thirty-one," Marie said quietly.

"What?!," her dad yelled.

"Marie," her mother gasped. "How did this happen?!"

"It's a long story," she said, just as the screen began to disconnect. "No! NO! Mom, Dad –"

But she could only see her father continuing to yell and her mother starting to cry as they disappeared.

Marie was still crying when he got home.

"They know," she said. "My parents know."

"Hey," he said softly, putting the food on the counter and pulling her into his arms. "They didn't take it well?"

Understatement of the year.

"Not at all," she managed, laying her head on his chest. "I made my mother cry. And my dad…"

He said nothing as he rubbed her back and held her close.

"I hate being so far away," she whispered

"What can I do to make it better?," he asked. "I'll do anything for you."

And she knew he was telling the truth. What had she ever done to deserve him?

"Nothing," she said. "I've tried calling them back, but they're not answering. And… maybe that's good. Maybe they need to process it all, take the news in over a while since I can't be there to explain it, to make things right."

"But you can," he said, tilting her face up to his. "We can go there. Take a couple of weeks, travel out there –"

"I can't afford it," she said, crying harder. "Why do you think I haven't been back since I was seventeen?"

"You can afford it," he said, smiling. "We've got the money. Whatever it takes to get us both there. You can book it now."

"Really?," she asked, hope in her eyes, shock in her voice. "You would do that for me?"

"Sure would," he said. "Text them now. Tell them that we'll be there to explain it. That we'll explain everything when we get there. Give them time to cool off."

And she thanked God for Scott, who went right to work at fixing this, at finding the flight that would take her back home.

Scott

Giving her parents time to cool off was a great idea.

With the news told and a date on the calendar when she could explain it all, Marie seemed to finally feel free to settle into his home. Her home. Their home.

The weird stuff she'd always cooked and brought to share with him at the church was now being made in his kitchen. He hadn't told her yet that Drew wanted to speak with her. He figured another week of peace, of Marie cooking and dancing around the kitchen wearing some very tiny pajamas was worth the omission.

And how.

He'd caught her in his arms on one particular evening and was working on getting her out of the tiny pajamas she was wearing as dinner cooked on the stove, when they heard a knock on the door.

"Visitors," she said underneath his lips, grinning. "Let me get that, as the lady of the house."

He'd smiled to watch her saunter away with a lift in her step and smiled even further when she opened the door with a very happy, "Hi. Who are you?"

"Uh... is Scott here?"

And Scott laughed out loud at the sound of the voice as Marie turned to him with a questioning look.

Sure enough, he ran to her side just in time to see his brother give his wife a strange once-over.

Sam. Back home.

"What are you doing here?," Scott shouted, reaching out to hug him.

"Uh... extended leave," he said, patting him on the back. He looked at Marie, then back at his brother pointedly.

"Marie, this is Sam," Scott said.

She grinned up at him and put her arms around his neck without any hesitation. "Sam! The Marine who kept him sober!"

Sam returned the hug awkwardly. "Uh... yeah."

"Oh, I'm so glad to meet you! I feel like I know you already from all that Scott's said," she said, kissing him on the cheek.

"And you're... Marie? The church girl?"

Marie grinned over at Scott. "The church girl?"

Scott shrugged, his grin spreading wider. "Well, that's what I usually called you."

"Fitting," she said, smiling back at Sam. "Yes, I'm the church girl."

"And my wife," Scott said, beaming at her.

Sam opened his mouth to say something, then snapped it shut again. Then, opened it and managed, "Well, congratulations. My invite must have gotten lost in the mail."

"It was a quick thing, and –" Marie stopped talking and suddenly realized what she was wearing. "I should probably go change. I'll come back and finish dinner for both of you, though." She left the room, stopping only to kiss Scott.

Scott followed her with his eyes, then turned to Sam with a smug smile.

"What in the world, man?," Sam managed.

"I could say the same," Scott said. "Extended leave? Come in."

"You married her?," Sam said, coming into the house with all of his gear on his back. "When? How?"

"Almost two weeks ago," he grinned. "When you know, you know. Didn't figure there was any reason to wait around. Flew out to Vegas, said our vows, and brought her home. It's been the best two weeks of my life."

Sam's eyes went over to where Marie had just walked. "Well, probably so," he said, dropping all of his stuff by the couch. "But I didn't think you would ever settle down."

"Me neither," Scott sighed. "But big changes. You know that."

"And now one woman for the rest of your life," he said, studying his brother carefully.

Scott grinned. "I know. I really got lucky, Sam."

Sam laughed out loud at this. "You are different. It's good to see you. Though I wonder now if I should stay…"

"Extended leave," Scott said. "What's that? A month? You're welcome. As long as you need."

Sam frowned a little. "It's… not really leave."

"Oh?"

"I didn't re-enlist."

"What?" Scott blinked at him. Nearly half of his brother's life had been spent as a Marine. Scott had assumed, like everyone else probably had as well, that he'd stay in until retirement. "Why?"

"It was time," Sam said simply.

"That makes no sense," Scott said. "And why didn't you tell anyone?"

"Because of your reaction right now," he said. "I can't explain it. I need to figure out what's next before I tell the rest of the family. But I couldn't do it anymore. Just… too much. I have to get my head on straight again. And can I tell you how much freer I'm feeling just knowing that I'm done?"

Scott watched, concerned, wondering over how Sam was really doing.

"Well, you look awful," he noted.

"Thanks," Sam nodded. "I haven't shaved since the discharge. Didn't even know I could grow a beard since I haven't been free to try since I was seventeen."

"Yeah, you couldn't even grow a five o'clock shadow back then."

"I know," Sam nodded. "And now, I probably won't ever shave again."

"Mom will have something to say about that," Scott muttered.

"Yeah, and a few other things, particularly what's going on with you," Sam said. And they stared at one another for a second. Then, they flung their fingers at one another and yelled, at the same time, *"You first!"*

"Oh, no, you don't," Scott said. "I'm not calling her until you do."

"You've got the bigger news," Sam argued. "Seems like you should go first."

"Seems like you should go first to buffer my own news," Scott said, "especially since I'm letting you live with us while you figure out the next step."

Sam sighed. "I can't live here. You have a wife now."

"And she'd say the same," he said. "And we're going to visit her parents in another week. You'll have the house to yourself."

Sam nodded hesitantly. "Okay, then. I appreciate it."

"I appreciate you," Scott said sincerely.

"You're still talking to Mom first."

"No, I'm not."

"We'll see."

Marie

She sat on their bed with him as he talked on the phone.

He told her he'd lost to Sam in some arm wrestling contest, which meant that he had to tell their parents the marriage news before Sam broke the news about his honorable discharge to them.

It made no sense, connecting arm wrestling to big news revelations like this. But Marie figured she didn't know much about siblings anyway since she was an only child. *Was* being the operative word since she now, a week into marriage, had gained Sam as a real, live, live-in brother.

She smiled at this, even as Scott made a face at her as his mother continued screeching on the phone.

"Yeah," he said, "I totally knew that was what you were going to say. Thanks, Dad."

Oh, wow. His mother was so hysterical that she could be heard even when she wasn't on the phone.

"Okay, okay," Scott said, "if she must." He handed Marie the phone. "My mother needs to talk with you."

Uh-oh. Marie swallowed and held the phone up to her ear. "Hi… Jessica." She prayed that there would be some goodwill left between them, remembering how kind Scott's mother had been to her when he was sick, how she'd insisted on being called by her first name, and how she'd told Marie how thankful she was for her.

"Oh, praise God!," she yelled over the phone. "Marie, I am praising God for you right now!"

Goodwill? Most definitely.

"Are you?," Marie asked with some disbelief.

"Oh, you have no idea the grief that Scott has put us through over the years," she said. Scott rolled his eyes at this. "I mean, he didn't have it together. Not even close. And I hoped, when he came to Christ, that it was just the beginning of a total life overhaul and all. Sure enough, we heard about you not too long afterwards, and I told everyone that I had high, high hopes that you were going to be the girl I've been praying for his entire life."

"Really?," Marie asked, touched by this.

"Every day," Jessica continued on. "I prayed every day for the girls that each of my boys would end up with, and I'm telling you, on the day that I met you, I knew you were the one for him."

Scott leaned up next to her, one hand on her neck, the other on her waist. "Hang up on her," he whispered in her free ear, before laying her on her back.

"And you know," Jessica went right on, thankfully oblivious to the way her son was now placing slow, deep kisses down Marie's neck as his hands began to wander, "I figured we'd hear an engagement announcement soon from the two of you, but this? Is just better, right? And I'm sure all of the other daughters-in-law will want to help me throw a wedding shower. Have you got a calendar handy? Let's talk dates!"

"Marie," Scott groaned, his lips and hands still traveling. "Hang. Up."

"And, of course, you'll have to come and plan to spend the whole weekend so I can introduce you around the church, and —"

"Well, that sounds wonderful," Marie said, before Scott took the phone from her hands.

"Mom!," he bellowed into the phone. "We'll call you later. Goodbye."

And with that, he hung up.

"Wow," Marie said, as he went right back to where he left off. "She wasn't upset at all."

"Nope," he managed, pulling his shirt off. "Now, where were we —"

"Maybe it won't be such a big deal after all," she interrupted, sliding her arms around him. "Maybe it was just my parents. Maybe the church here won't think twice about it, huh?"

And Scott stopped what he was doing. "I actually... already mentioned it to Drew."

"When?," Marie breathed, just a tiny bit horrified.

"About a week ago," he said. "He told me he wanted to meet with you."

"Why didn't you tell me?"

"Because you don't need to go back to the church until after we've taken some time. You're on vacation. You don't need to worry about work." And he began kissing her neck again.

"I wonder," she sighed, even as she put her arms back around him, "why I haven't heard from Tracy, then."

The silence, likely very intentional, rubbed her the wrong way. She'd already wondered why Tracy hadn't called in so long, but since their contact had been sporadic the more Scott had gotten involved in her life, she just counted it as more of the same.

Now she wasn't so sure.

"I don't know," Scott murmured. "It's not like you've called her either."

And she hadn't. Because she didn't want to hear what Tracy would likely say.

She'd call them eventually. She tucked away the worry, put it right alongside the anxiety she felt about going back to Namibia, and resolved that it could wait another day.

And she pulled Scott closer and forgot about everything else.

Scott

He woke up a few hours later to find that Marie had left the bed, and when he got up to see where she had gone, he found her kneeling in front of the toilet. She had pulled on one of his shirts and was resting her head on the seat, looking... awful.

"You look so hot in my shirt," he said, wisely declining to state the obvious.

"I don't feel so hot," she said, closing her eyes.

"Hey," he said softly, "are you okay?"

"No," she shook her head at him, wiping her mouth with the back of her hand. "I feel like death."

"You finally caught the flu, didn't you?"

"If I didn't catch it taking care of you, I'm completely immune."

"Maybe it's just nerves," he said, feeling a little like death himself at the prospect of facing Marie's parents in another week.

"Scott," she said softly, closing her eyes again and cradling the toilet closer. "I'm just so..."

And then, she sat straight up and gasped. She looked at him with rounded eyes and shook her head.

"Oh, no. No, no, no..."

"What?," he asked, even as she stood up and rushed past him into their bedroom, searching for her purse, then pulling it open and rustling through its contents, biting her lip all the while. "What's going on?"

"I need my calendar," she said. With a slim pink book in her hands she sat on the bed and opened it up, looking at it intently, flipping a page, counting again, and letting out a tiny whimper. "Oh. Oh, no…"

"What?," he asked again.

"Scott," she said softly, still staring at the calendar. "I think I might be pregnant."

Well, that sure wouldn't make meeting her parents any easier. He didn't say anything for a moment. Then, "How is that possible?"

She leaned her head in her hands. "Oh, I think you know how that's possible."

"Was it last night?," he asked. "I mean, that seems kind of quick and all, but –"

She made a face at him. It was the first truly mean face she'd ever made at him. He was a little shocked by it.

"Are you being serious?"

He nodded. "I mean, it was really great and all, but –"

"Oh, good grief," she said, rolling her eyes at him. "I'm going to need to buy you a book about how this all works, aren't I?"

Scott couldn't imagine what kind of book she meant with the conversation they were having and opened his mouth to offer his opinion when she cut him off.

"Not tonight, buddy," she said. "It wasn't tonight. Although tonight wasn't smart –"

"But… we've… there's… I've been –"

"But we didn't last night, which matters very little now since we didn't that *first* night, Scott," she said. "Which is when we *really* should have."

"Only two times!," he exclaimed. "We've been so careful –"

She threw the calendar down and shrieked at him, "It's only takes *one* time, Scott! The *right* time!"

Whoa. He'd never seen this side of Marie before. He was a little scared.

She couldn't tell, though, as her preoccupation with days and their cavalier approach to birth control continued to infuriate her. Or maybe it was him who was infuriating her, he noted, as she glared at him with her intense eyes. "We should've been more careful. Because I've gone back and looked at my calendar and counted. We got married on day fourteen. We didn't use anything on day fourteen. Fourteen, Scott!"

He frowned at this. "Fourteen... what?"

She sighed and groaned just a little. "Really, Scott?"

"*Oh!*," he exclaimed, finally getting what she was saying. "You keep track of that?"

"Been keeping track of it ever since I was a teenager," she said. "Because it –" Then she stopped and blushed a little at this. And he wondered at why she would have been concerned about it as a teenager, but before he could ask, she spoke over the question in his eyes. "I think I'm pregnant."

"But two weeks?! How is it –"

"I don't know," she groaned. "It's a very slim possibility. But I need to take a test now, or neither one of us will get any rest."

Scott praised God for twenty-four hour pharmacies. Of course, he felt like a total moron trying to pick out a test from the numerous options on the shelves. And how ironic, that pregnancy tests were kept right next to various birth control options. Almost as if to say, "Should've come by here a lot earlier, you idiot."

As he stood in line with the little pink box in his hands, biting his lip and considering all the thousand and one reasons why he wasn't ready to be a father, he didn't notice the nosy lady behind him staring his direction, then grinning when she saw what he held.

"Good luck to you and your wife," she said with a smile.

Scott looked at her dubiously. "My what?"

"Your wife," she said, pointing at the test. "You must be so excited."

He sighed. "No way, ma'am."

But he pretended he was when Marie placed the completed test on the sink, wrapped her arms around him, and held him as they stood and waited for the news that would change their lives.

Positive.

Oh, wow.

CHAPTER SEVEN

Marie

A mother. She was someone's mother.

Not *going to be* someone's mother, she noted, as she pictured a tiny heart, hidden away, already beating, already claimed and called out by God Himself.

Already someone's mother.

Scott put his hand high up on her stomach, shock still apparent in his eyes. This was a little more than surprising for him, obviously. And though he had seemed to know his way around her body without needing to ask for directions or clarification these past two weeks, he regarded the place where his hand rested with newfound wonder.

"Actually, Daddy," she said, "it's a bit lower than that." She moved his hand to the place where life had already taken up residence.

"Wow," he breathed, staring intently. "And how long does this whole thing take?"

She sighed a little. "Pregnancy?"

"Yeah."

"Forty weeks," she said. "Nine months."

He nodded. "We don't have much time," he noted. "Is it even safe for you to travel?"

She blinked at this. Was it? Was it safe to travel? Was it safe to drink coffee? Safe to go out and run a mile? Safe to go back to the smoky bar where she'd been teaching Ephesians? Safe to play the rough games at rec on Sunday mornings? Safe to sleep on her stomach? Safe to take a hot bath?

She had no idea. She hadn't been prepared to be a wife, to transition to his house and his life while continuing on with her own as normal... but she was even less prepared for this.

She shrugged fractionally, feeling deflated at the thought. "I don't know." And she blinked back tears as she looked at him. "I don't know anything about it."

He swallowed and managed an uncertain smile. "Maybe we both need a book, huh?"

And as he held her in his arms, she tried to believe the whispered assurances that he gave to her.

Scott

With Marie finally asleep, he left the bedroom.

He needed a drink. Oh, wow. He *needed* a drink.

It wasn't that he didn't like children. He loved his nephews and nieces. But they went home with someone else at night, and he, praise God, had never had to share a bed with one of his pregnant sisters-in-law. He tried to imagine what Marie would look like all round and full with a baby. He'd hardly gotten acquainted with her body in its normal, beautiful, slim state. That wouldn't last much longer now, and who knew what it would be like, being with a woman whose shape changed week by week?

There was that, of course. But he was even more freaked out by the thought of a baby. A tiny little baby, depending on him to stay sober, to keep working, to be a success, to make something of himself, to be the man God was just now showing him he needed to be.

He was so *not* ready for this.

His keys were on the counter. He could take his truck, go out, get a drink, and calm the panic he was feeling. It would be a comfort, like an old friend, understanding and warm, familiar and close.

Just one drink. It would be enough.

He took a step towards the counter. And another. He kept on walking until he had walked right past the counter and the keys both, and then he hit the stairs running. He forced himself into the spare room where Sam slept and forced himself to kick his brother right out of the bed before he could talk himself out of it.

Sam hit the ground with a thud and came to quickly enough. He grabbed Scott's ankle reflexively and pulled him to the ground, jumping on top of him once he was down and putting a hand to his throat in an instant.

"Hey!," Scott shouted, taken aback by this. "What are you doing?!"

Sam stared at him, coming back to himself. "Where am I?," he asked calmly, curtly.

"In my house, Sam," he moaned.

"Where?," Sam hissed, gripping his throat tighter.

"Houston, you idiot!," he yelled. "Stop trying to kill me!"

Sam took a deep breath, then let go with great hesitation.

Scott took the opportunity and scurried away from his brother quickly.

"What was that?!"

Sam sighed deeply, closing his eyes as he continued to sit on the floor. "Bad dream."

"Bad reality, man," Scott yelled. "You almost killed me!"

"If I'd been trying to kill you," Sam said, very calmly, "you'd be dead."

"Duly noted," Scott groaned.

"Was I yelling in my sleep?," he asked.

"No," Scott said.

"How'd I end up on the floor?," he murmured.

"I kicked you out of bed so you'd keep me from going to get a drink," Scott said.

Sam looked at him. "Then I should have killed you."

"Thanks."

"Would have kept you from drinking, though."

"Well, I got you up," he said. "And now that you're up and I'm still alive, you won't let me get a drink, right?"

"Why do you need a drink?," Sam muttered, leaning back against the bed.

"Because I'm having a baby," Scott moaned, his head in his hands.

A long pause as Sam watched him. "I'm sorry... what?"

"I'm pregnant!"

Sam frowned. "Then, you really don't need a drink."

"What?"

"Fetal alcohol syndrome. Horrible stuff," Sam noted. "Though you're probably more upset about losing your girlish figure."

Scott shot him a look. "Could you be serious for a minute?"

"I think I was plenty serious when I attacked you," he said.

"Serious about this conversation, Sam. Now, Sam."

"Okay, okay," Sam said. "You say you're pregnant –"

"Marie," Scott hissed. "Marie is pregnant."

Sam let out a breath. "Well, the quick wedding makes sense now."

"Oh, no," Scott said. "This is a wedding night baby! First time. Pregnant. What are the odds, right?!"

Sam watched him for a moment, then shook his head. "Only you, Scott. This would only happen to you."

"Ugggghhhhh..."

"You should have figured," Sam noted. "I mean, you come from a family of six children. Sean has twins, Stu had a baby on the way before he'd even been married a year, and Seth just has to look at Chelsea to get her pregnant. You could probably just wave your boxers in Marie's direction, and that would do it. Fertile Myrtles, the whole lot of you."

"I'm so glad that you're taking on my role as the funny guy of this family," Scott said sarcastically. "Because I have no humor at the moment."

Sam smiled. "Hey. A baby. Congratulations. How can that be a bad thing?"

"I don't know anything about babies," he said. "I don't even know that I want children."

"Well, you've got one now," Sam noted. "Seems like the decision has already been made."

"Yeah," Scott said. "What am I going to do?"

"It's probably a stretch at this point to wrap your mind around how to be a good father," Sam said. "Maybe that's why God is giving you nine months to work it out."

"That's not a lot of time," Scott said, thinking about how the clock was already ticking.

"It isn't," he said. "But the way you can get there is by doing your best to love Marie."

"Done a great job of that, Sam," he said sarcastically. "Two weeks married, and she's already pregnant!"

"I didn't mean that, you dolt," Sam said, reaching out and whacking the back of his head.

"Oww!"

"And be quiet," he said. "The mother of your child is asleep downstairs. Let her get her rest."

"Fine," Scott hissed.

"You need to do your best to love her, to take care of her, to treat her better than you treat yourself."

And Scott had an epiphany. Hadn't he just been studying this?

"Ephesians 5!," he shouted. Then, in a whisper, thinking of Marie and how he was doing a poor job of this already, "Ephesians 5!"

Sam wrinkled his nose at this. "What?"

"It makes sense," Scott said. "And I... I can do this, Sam. I can do it." He swallowed. "I think... right?"

"You can," Sam said. "You can be exactly who God is calling you to be here."

"Just another new tune," Scott murmured, praying that he was right.

Marie

They got a call a few days later. Scott's parents, in town for a surprise visit so his dad could meet his new daughter-in-law. Scott had been fixing breakfast for Sam and Marie when they called, and he wisely suggested that his parents meet them somewhere away from the house, given Sam's panic and the green way Marie was looking as she stared down at her toast.

A trip out would be good for her.

And it was, as Marie felt great comfort at the embrace her new father-in-law gave her, acceptance and warmth in his eyes as he'd told her how glad they were that she was one of them now.

"One of you," she had said, looking to Scott for another nod that this was the right time to tell them. "Well, it's actually me and... another little Huntington on the way."

His parents questioned nothing. Which was a relief to Scott. And a pleasant surprise to Marie.

"Another grandbaby!," his mother squealed, hugging Marie close. "Oh, I can't wait! Are you feeling well? Any morning sickness?"

"Um," Marie smiled, "just in the mornings... and the afternoons... and the evenings, actually."

"Isn't that the worst?," his mother said. Then, smiling, "I was sick with all six of mine. Boy, girl, no difference. Puking all the time." She clasped her hands together. "What do you think it is? A boy or a girl? Mothers have intuition about these things, you know."

Marie shrugged, thinking of how she'd imagined the baby. "I see a... boy. But it could be a girl."

"Loved my boys," his mother said. "Was always so thrilled to hear that we were having another boy, you know. Just couldn't wait to hear the doctor confirm it –"

"Yeah, which is why you stopped having babies just as soon as you got a girl," Scott noted wryly.

His mother frowned at him. "No, that was because we only have eight seats at the dinner table. Couldn't fit anymore of you in." She smiled at Marie. "Then, they went and got married and brought home spouses, so we had to buy a new table anyway. Should've kept having babies!"

Marie smiled at this.

"Well, it sure is fast," Jess continued on. "A baby this soon. But I myself was a honeymoon baby, you know." She smiled.

"Really?," Scott asked. "I didn't know that."

"Oh, yeah," Jess nodded. "Scandal at the church, I'm quite sure. But Mom was so young and Dad was... well, not, so there was plenty of scandal already."

Marie thought on this, wondering what this newest development in the Marie/Scott drama might do to her ministry, to her livelihood, to her only dream –

"But enough about that," Jess said, smiling. "Let's talk baby names!"

She couldn't think of anything for days without a headache coming on.

The baby. She had very nearly wrapped her mind around what was to come. Her in-laws' reaction had been so unexpected, and she'd found herself, at the end of their time together, actually anticipating all that was up ahead.

She loved children, obviously. She'd always wanted her own family one day. She could imagine a little boy even now, with Scott's smile, his mother's laugh, her own musical ability, her father's eyes...

... oh, her father.

Her parents. They would be shocked. And disappointed. Not just because of the marriage and the baby but because of all the dreams ruined. They'd sent her to the US all those years ago to prepare her for a future. And in one twenty-four hour stretch, Marie had made the biggest decisions of her life, putting it all in jeopardy.

Her seminary program would probably have to be put on hold for... eighteen years? And her job. What would the church say?

Headaches. So many headaches.

She laid down on the bed that night, closing her eyes and willing away the headaches for just a moment.

"So," Scott said, with no clue as to what she was feeling, "it says here that you're likely going to poop right there in front of everyone in the delivery room when you push out our baby."

She sighed, opening her eyes to look at what he was reading.

"Great," she murmured. "You got a book."

"You're the one who suggested it," he smiled. "And it says that the hard part of labor can take hours. Literal hours of pain. Unless you opt for this thing called an epidural. Which involves a giant needle stuck right into your spine."

"That sounds fun," she said.

"Yeah, and it says here that you might tear. But that the contractions at the end will be so bad that you'd rather tear right in half than keep having the contractions."

"That's a scary, scary book you're reading, Scott," she said irritably.

"I wonder if it heals up okay," he said, concern in his voice. "Tearing like that. Or are you off sex forever if that happens?" He released a breath. "I really hope not."

"I hardly think your parents would have been able to have six children if childbirth put you, and I quote 'off sex forever,'" she said, looking up at him.

"The stork brought all six of us," he said.

"Please," she murmured. "I saw your parents together this morning. They're still, even at their age, getting –"

"And you've taken this conversation to a place where I just can't go, Marie," he said. "Whoa! Look at this picture of what breastfeeding is going to do to your –"

"Scott," she said simply, reaching over and grabbing the book from his hands. "No more. Come here."

He laid down so that she could rest her head on his chest as he put his fingers through her hair.

"I started packing our bags for Namibia," she said softly.

"Gonna be my first time overseas," he grinned. "I'm looking forward to it."

He obviously thought this was going to be like a tropical vacation... not a trial, complete with a judge and jury. She was dreading it so much. Dreading it and yet longing for it all at the same time. The smell of the air, the taste of the food, the comfort of her family and friends, all these years later...

... all the explanations.

"I don't feel so well," she murmured, thinking of all the unknowns.

"You need to see a doctor," he said, looking down at her and kissing her on the forehead. "We need to get you to a doctor. Need to make sure everything's okay. Get some blood work done. Screening. A complete workup. That book is full of everything you need to do –"

"I need to go home," she said, tears in her throat. "I need to go home."

And he said nothing as he gathered her close and let her think over all that would happen as soon as she went back to Namibia.

In the morning, she felt better.

Well, not physically. No, all the nausea she'd been feeling finally gave way to real action, and she threw up everything she'd ever eaten. In her entire life. Or so it seemed.

"You okay?," Scott asked from behind the bathroom door.

"Nooooo," Marie groaned.

"My book says you should try eating a cracker before you get out of bed," he said.

"So I can vomit that up two minutes later?," she asked, hearing the rudeness in her voice.

A pause. "Just trying to help, Marie," he murmured. "Not much I can do for you, you know? Just trying my best."

She closed her eyes at the discouragement in his voice. He was just trying. "You can help," she said softly. "Fix me some tea. The Rooibos."

"The what?"

"The red tea," she said. "Just a cup of it."

"I can do that," he said eagerly.

"And Scott?"

"Yeah?"

She took a breath. "Can you call Drew? Set up a meeting today?"

Another pause. "Are you sure you want to meet him today?"

"I want to get it all sorted out before we leave," she said. "I feel better about things today. It's a good time to see him."

"You want me to come with you?"

She thought about the security of going in with him, of having him there to take whatever it was that she had coming alongside her. But she'd done this herself, made these choices on her own, and she felt obligated to explain it all alone.

"No," she said, finally getting to her feet, walking to the sink to rinse out her mouth. "I can handle it."

And she got herself ready, growing more and more confident as she did so, convincing herself that this wouldn't be such a huge issue at the church. Drew and Tracy had always been friends, the elders had always appreciated her work, and the church loved her. She knew that they'd need the whole truth from her, all of it, and that with it, they'd be able to advise her how to best share her news with those connected to the children's ministry, how to move forward in this, and how to do what work she could from Namibia.

They'd figure it out together.

She could even smile about this as she made her way to the kitchen, where Sam and Scott were both pulling on their boots.

"You look great," Scott said, smiling up at her appreciatively. "Your tea is on the counter. Put it in a travel mug for you."

"Thanks," she said. "Where are you guys headed?"

"Work site," Scott sighed. "Thought I'd show Sam some things he can keep an eye on while we're gone."

"Yeah, I'm his newest employee," Sam muttered.

"And you sound so enthusiastic about it," Scott slapped him on the back before standing and going to Marie. "Hey," he said, slipping his arms around her, "we'll drive you over there."

"I'd rather take my car," she said. "I don't know how long I'll be there. What time did Drew say he could meet me?"

"Said he'd be there in about thirty minutes."

"Then, I better get going," she said, kissing him.

"Let me take you," he said. "I don't want you getting sick."

"I'll be okay," she said. "Really, Scott... everything is going to be fine."

And as he smiled at her and squeezed her hand, reaching out to touch her stomach with his other hand... she actually believed it.

It would be fine. Everything would be fine.

Everything was *not* fine.

Drew and Tracy had both been waiting for her in the office. There had been no congratulations, of course, and there had been very little kindness. Marie had been honest, and the news of the baby had only made things worse.

"What were you thinking, Marie?," Tracy asked, real sadness in her eyes. "You told me that you weren't going down this road. You promised me."

She had. But she hadn't known him. And she hadn't known herself, that she would give herself the freedom to feel what she felt, to do what she did, and to make a home with him.

"He's different than he was," Marie said simply. "And it happened quickly... but I don't regret it."

And she didn't. She sincerely didn't regret any of it. This, sitting here and explaining it all, was the hard part of living with those choices, but she would make them again if given the opportunity. She thought of Scott's face even as she kept her hand on her midsection, confident in what was already done.

"Marie," Drew sighed, "I know Scott. And I knew him long before he even came here. And I should've done my part in protecting you from him and the kind of guy he is —"

"First of all," Marie cut in, more than a little irritated by this, "I don't need you to protect me. And second of all, this really has no bearing on my job."

"Actually," Drew said, "I had to talk to the elders."

Marie's heart faltered a little at this. "Oh." Perhaps it all *did* have a bearing on her job now. When ministry was your life as much as it was your occupation, you had no personal life to speak of as it was all on display for everyone.

"Of course, it was only about the elopement," Tracy noted, obviously having discussed the implications of what Marie had done. Discussed it with Drew, of course. And maybe with other people in the church as well. "And now... this."

This. A child. A pregnancy. A very badly-timed pregnancy. Still, Marie bristled at Tracy's use of the word "this."

"So, we'll tell them what happened," Marie said, knowing that her friendship with these two, who had felt like family, would never be the same. But her job could be salvaged, surely. She wouldn't lose that today, too. "They can know the whole story. The elders. The volunteers. The whole church."

"The elders already have some reservations now, about your integrity as far as what's happened with... well, with you running off and marrying the contractor for the building. Especially since he just so recently became a believer. They've expressed some concern over all the hours you spent alone with him here, right in the church building."

Marie felt her face grow hot at this. She could understand how they felt they had the right to question her as an employee of the church. But that they would feel free to question Scott, to label him by what he did, to assume that he was beneath her somehow and that they had done what they hadn't done—

"I'd love to speak with the elders," she said, trying to keep the edge out of her voice. "To get a chance to tell them the truth."

"Marie," Drew managed, softening his voice as much as possible, "it doesn't matter what the truth is... just what people will think. And they're going to think —"

"I know what they'll think," Marie managed, swallowing with great difficulty, feeling sick all over again. She looked to Tracy, expecting something, anything, from her old friend, who'd been like a sister all this time. Support, understanding, even just sympathy for her obvious downfall…

Tracy wouldn't look at her.

Well. That was it, then. "Okay, Drew."

"Do you know what I'm saying?," he asked.

"I do. And I understand."

"You're wonderful at what you do," he said. "But I don't know that we'll be able to…"

"To let me continue on here," she swallowed past the lump in her throat. "I understand. I'll announce my resignation when I get back from Namibia then."

And she walked out of his office feeling, for the first time ever, ashamed of what she hadn't even done.

Scott

Scott was mad. So mad.

She'd come home with her office loaded into her car. He'd come out to the driveway, saw what she had, and exploded.

Not at her. But on her behalf.

Half an hour full of explanations later, he was still upset.

"You didn't do anything wrong!," he bellowed.

"Oh, Scott, surely you can understand how things sometimes work in ministry," Marie said softly. "I mean, your grandfather was a pastor for how many years, and —"

"You didn't do anything wrong."

She sighed. "I know. But Drew can't put what's going on at the church, with all the success he's having... well, he can't put it at risk by having me there, with people talking and assuming things."

He fumed even more at this. He knew Drew, knew what a sycophant he could be. And that horribly prissy, judgmental wife of his. Half the success they were seeing at their church had more to do with the other staff members than it did with anything they were doing. Wasn't the church growing so much because of what Marie was doing in the children's ministry? Hadn't that been why they brought him in to build more space for her growing group of kids? Wasn't she one of the reasons that his leadership looked like it was working so well?

He'd love to have a long talk with Drew about who Marie really was.

"Drew should be a man."

"Scott..."

"Seriously, if it's right for you to stay there, he should stand by the truth. He's never been able to stand for anything, Marie. This is just like when we got arrested for the DWI and how he fell apart over it all. Couldn't even get the idiot to stop carrying on in the cell, and —"

He stopped short at the horror in Marie's eyes.

"What?"

"DWI?," she asked softly.

"You know that about me," he said, holding her hands. "I told you I was an alcoholic. That was the turning point. That was when it all changed."

"I'm pregnant with a felon's child," she whispered, beginning to cry.

"A DWI is not a felony in the state of Texas," he said. "It's a misdemeanor."

"That's not any better, Scott!"

"It was the past," he said, just a little hurt by this. "Not who I am, but who I was."

She watched him with disbelief for a moment... then nodded. "You're right. You're right."

"And I'm right about Drew. He needs to tell people that –"

"He shouldn't," Marie said firmly. "If we had married in the church, actually *planned* a wedding, had a real engagement, and then a baby? People still would have talked. But what we did? What would you think, if it was anyone else?"

Scott considered this. "Well, obviously, I would think the worst. But is that really so bad? Even if that's how things really went down with us? Shouldn't the church show some grace?"

"They should, Scott, but I'm a leader in the church," she sighed. "And people have expectations. Would you want your pastor continuing to preach if he was involved in something shady?"

"Probably not."

"And it's worse because I work with children. Impressionable, young children. And I'm a woman."

"Why does that complicate things?," Scott asked, totally baffled.

"It just does, Scott," she smiled grimly. "But we're not out of options. I... I still have a degree. I can teach. I can... can find another ministry job maybe. One day."

"Hey," Scott caught her hands in his. "You can do whatever you want, but you don't have to do any of it, Marie. You can stay here at home, let me take care of you. You don't have to work."

She swallowed, her eyes brimming with tears. "I appreciate that, Scott," she managed. "But it wasn't so much about the financial part of it. It was more about... well... who am I now, if I'm not in ministry?"

"You're *my* wife. The mother of *our* child."

A few tears made their way down her cheeks.

"I mean," she explained, "is that all I am now? *Just* someone's mother? Someone's wife?"

"Not someone's. Mine. And his. Or hers. And *just* a mother and a wife?," Scott asked. "There's no bigger job in the world, Marie. Do you think my father could have been half the man he is today without my mother doing what she did at home?"

She smiled and shook her head. "It's putting an awful lot of faith in you," she said, "to just give it all up and trust that you can really…. take care of us, you know? And that you're not just going to run out on us if things get tough."

"And it's not taking faith on my part, to trust you? If you left me, especially with our child, you'd get everything, you know. My house, half my business, everything I have. It takes faith both ways."

He thought on the truth of this, how they both had a lot to lose now. How something as simple and right and amazing as choosing one another had forever linked them together like this.

There was nothing simple about marriage after all. Especially with a baby on the way. He was thankful that he was in this with her.

She put her arms around him. "I won't ever leave you."

"And I won't ever let you down. We've got to trust each other."

He did his best to keep her trust. On both continents and in between.

From one flight to the next, he took care of her, made sure she had what she needed when she felt sick, made sure she could count on him, and made sure to not let her down.

They reached their destination after what felt like thousands of hours. Walvis Bay. No more plane rides ahead, just a car ride up along the coast to Swakopmund, where Marie had spent her childhood.

Scott held her hand as they left the plane, noting that her color had gone from bad to worse on the last flight. But that was the least of his concerns as he raised his eyes up past the counter at immigration and found his gaze matched with a man who stood just beyond the glass in the lobby.

He looked just exactly like Marie... except with a murderous, chilling glare in his eyes.

Ahh, his father-in-law. Wonderful.

Scott took his passport and Marie's in his right hand and reached out for her with his left, exiting to the lobby with the rest of the passengers. He kissed her fingers one last time, looking back at her for just a moment, then steeling himself to meet the man who waited for them.

Before he could reach out to shake her father's hand, though, Marie fell right to the floor in a dead faint.

Scott was doing a great job of taking care of her.

Obviously.

Marie

"Marie?"

She could smell the sand. And it was likely her brain playing tricks on her, but she swore that she smelled the sea as well. Could almost hear the soothing sounds of the waves against the dunes…

"Well, you've killed her. I managed to keep her alive for twenty-two years, and you've killed her after only three weeks of marriage. Well done."

Oh, no.

"Marie, I really need you to wake up and help me out here, sweetheart."

She felt the arms around her tighten, felt a hand on her face.

"Scott?," she said, weakly.

"I'm right here," he said.

She opened her eyes, expecting to see him, her eyes filling with tears when she saw that the face that stared into hers was her father's. How was it possible that he'd aged so much in just these few weeks?

"Dad," she sighed weakly.

"Welcome home, Marietjie," he smiled. Then, shooting a glare Scott's direction, "This is him, then?"

Ahh. It was going so well already.

"Yeah. Dad, this is Scott. Scott, this is my dad, Daniel." She tried sitting up.

"Whoa," Scott said. "Take it easy. I'll carry you over to those chairs."

"Your mother's coming with something to drink," her father said. "What did he do to you, Marie?"

Scott hoisted her up in his arms, whispering "wow, so many issues" close to her ear as he did so. She suppressed a smile at this, touching his face softly, her heart warmed as he smiled back at her.

"He brought me back home, Dad," she said, her eyes never leaving Scott's.

CHAPTER EIGHT

Scott

Thirty minutes later, they were loaded up in the car with all of their bags and Marie's parents. They were concerned, obviously, as was Scott, but her mother had managed a few pleasantries with her new son-in-law even in her anxiety over Marie's health.

Marie's father, however, hadn't managed any pleasantries. Just glares, even as they drove, glancing up at Scott in the rearview mirror every few seconds.

"Your dad called Piet," Sara said to Marie. "Just to let him know that you were ill. He said he'd meet us at the house, just to check you out and make sure you're okay."

Marie sighed at this.

"Who's Piet?," Scott asked. The question brought some surprise to Sara's face and a deeper glare to Daniel's, but Marie simply smiled at him. "Just an old friend. A childhood friend who's now a paramedic."

"Who she'll need since you've made her sick," Daniel muttered.

Scott opened his mouth to respond to this, then snapped it shut again. There was a long list of things that Marie didn't need right now, and a rousing good fight between her father and her husband was at the top of that list.

Marie squeezed his hand tighter as he sat in silence. He squeezed back and managed a small smile over at her.

Who cared what Daniel thought anyway? Who cared what anyone thought? Marie with him, right now... nothing else mattered. Nothing could ruin this.

Not even Piet, who was, as promised, waiting on them as soon as they arrived at the mission house.

"We built the house when Marie was nine," Sara murmured as they all climbed out of the car. "Moved out here from Windhoek to be closer to friends who were part of our team. Are still part of our team. Like Piet here."

Scott watched with a growing amount of discomfort as Piet stood to his feet and stared at Marie. His gaze swept her from head to foot as he seemed to wordlessly communicate something with her, adoration in his eyes... adoration that seemed to make Marie wilt at first, then blush, then finally stand tall.

"Goeie middag, Piet," she said very simply. "Hoe gaan dit?"

"Baie goed, Marie," he smiled back at her, reaching out and pulling her into a close embrace.

Marie stood woodenly as he held her, then pushed away a moment later.

Scott was wishing she'd pushed him just a little harder.

"Piet," she said, her voice strong and confident, "I want you to meet Scott." She turned to her husband with an uneasy look.

Scott held out his hand, giving Piet a good once-over… which Piet returned with a friendly enough smile that failed to mask the open hostility in his eyes.

"Ja… Scott," Piet said evenly.

Scott eyed him and took stock of the situation.

Piet? Was a big dude. A big, freakin' sexy dude. Not that Scott cared either way, but he knew women. And Piet? Was just what women tended to like. Scott was a foot shorter, even standing as straight as he could, and all the muscles in both of his arms couldn't compare to just one of Piet's biceps, which were nicely on display for the entire world in the tight shirt he wore. And he was, even still, even as he shook hands with Scott, looking at Marie as though she was the only woman in the world.

Ugh. *This* was Piet. Of course it was.

"Pieter Botha," he said, squeezing Scott's hand with more force than necessary. "Marie's best friend."

"Scott Huntington," he said back, giving as good as he got. "Marie's husband."

"Ja," Piet said softly. "Daniel told me all about how you swept our Marietjie off and married her in some casino without even letting her call her parents. Sounds sooo charming."

"Well, it wasn't like that," Scott said, wondering why he felt the need to defend himself to this twit.

"Shame, man, I'm sure it was just lovely." His cold eyes swept over to

Marie and filled with warmth, joy, and clear affection. "But not as lovely as Marie would have been had she been allowed to be the most beautiful bride in all the world –"

"Piet," Marie said, stopping Scott from saying many, *many* things, "eloping was my idea as much as it was Scott's. Maybe more, actually." She smiled while pulling Scott close to her, a move that Piet couldn't miss, which was likely her intent, given the way it seemed to deflate him. Scott gave him a condescending smile.

"Marie," her father barked out as he came up the walk with the luggage, causing Marie to pull her hands from her husband. "Go inside and lie down." He looked to Piet and began speaking a language Scott certainly didn't understand. Marie joined their discussion – his wife spoke another language?! – and after much protesting on her part, she finally sighed.

"Fine, whatever," she said in English. "Scott," she said, by way of explanation, as they moved into the house, "My father is under the impression that I need medical assistance. And Piet here," she said, with a hint of sarcasm in her tone, "has so graciously volunteered to help out with that."

"Pleasure, Marie," Piet murmured.

And, wow, Scott sure didn't like the way *that* sounded coming from such a big, freakin' sexy dude, but he simply shrugged. "By all means, then, right?"

She turned to Piet and explained the situation in the mystery language as her father loomed over them. Scott wondered if there were details she was omitting concerning her most recent condition. Judging by the way he was still breathing, even as her father shot him glares, he assumed she hadn't divulged the obvious.

After checking vital signs and asking more questions Scott couldn't understand, Piet spoke to them all in English.

"She's dehydrated," he said, shooting Scott a sideways glance. "And hasn't been eating enough, I imagine. Been feeling a little under the weather, Marietjie?"

"Ja," she breathed.

"And... based on my best guess, I think there's probably a very good reason."

"Dankie, Piet," Marie said softly. "There is."

Piet smiled at her. "Ja, congratulations. Women in your condition need to take better care of themselves, ne?"

"Ja," Marie managed a small smile back at him, then glanced over at Scott. "We should probably tell them."

"Tell us what?," Sara asked, brushing the hair back from Marie's face.

"We're having a baby."

Scott was overwhelmed by the silence that followed her declaration. He was beginning to think that he'd lost his hearing temporarily (perhaps an effect of all those hours on a plane?) and thought that something more needed to be said.

"Surprise!," he offered with a little laugh.

Which wasn't the smartest thing to say, he realized a moment too late. Before he could think of the best way to explain it all to them, Daniel's hand was on his shoulder, squeezing past the point of comfort.

"Think I'm going to take my new *son* out for a congratulatory drink."

And as his eyes met Marie's rounded ones, Scott knew this wouldn't end well.

It didn't begin well either.

He took Scott to a bar. Like father, like daughter. Except Daniel didn't ask about the drinking. Just ordered for them both and put the beer in front of Scott.

He had two choices... drink the beer and have this talk. Or stay sober and possibly have the man kill him for wasting a perfectly good beer. Which sounded illogical, but wow, the scary missionary was already probably on the edge and even the slightest slight would send him over the cliff and into a psychopathic rage.

Scott decided to drink the beer.

"So," Daniel began, staring at him. "You're the man who knocked up my little girl."

Scott couldn't stop himself from choking. His first beer in five years, and there would be no joy in it.

"Well?"

"Yes, sir," he managed. "I mean, it wasn't like that."

"How was it like, then? Do tell."

Scott watched him warily. "There's no right answer to that question, sir."

"You're right," Daniel took a drink of his own beer. "There's not. But I'm telling you, I need *some* answers because I hear that my daughter ran off and married someone I hadn't even heard of, denying me the pleasure of giving her away and throwing her the wedding of her dreams, and I can't imagine *why* she'd do such a quick wedding. And, then, she comes home and announces that she's expecting. Doesn't take a genius to figure out what happened."

"But, see, that's where you're wrong... sir. I swear to you, I didn't touch

Marie until we were married."

Daniel gave him a dubious look.

"I swear it. I've not always done the right thing, granted, but I did right by Marie. I give you my word on that. She's a treasure in Christ, and I would've never... well, never in good conscience. Which is one of the reasons why I married her so quickly, sir, because I know just how much I can handle, and, honestly, being around Marie was making me –"

"Okay. You've said *more* than enough now."

Scott blew out a relieved breath.

Daniel regarded him coolly over his bottle. "You know, Marie isn't without options."

Scott matched his gaze. "And that means...?"

"That we sent her to the US so that she'd go to college and get her education," he said. "She would have stayed here, married Piet likely, and started having his babies. And been perfectly happy."

"Well, that's nice," Scott managed.

"But we wanted her to have options. To be able to support herself here or stateside, to not have to depend on a man or even be bound to one culture. Because a woman who has no options? Has a hard road ahead of her."

"Clearly," Scott said, "this won't be Marie's problem. And besides, sir, she's married to me now, and I have no intention of –"

"Does she even have a doctor yet?," Daniel interrupted him. "Have you even thought through how you're going to pay the medical bills?"

Scott hadn't thought about this. The wedding, as it was, had come and gone so quickly, and the baby even more quickly and –

"And there are other costs that you haven't thought of probably," Daniel continued on. "Furniture, clothes, formula, diapers, doctor's visits, car seats... and a car, while we're at it, since Marie is still driving around that piece of junk that should have died two years ago."

Scott could feel the beginnings of a headache. "Well, I own my own business. And honestly? Things are good, financially speaking."

"Do you intend for Marie to continue on with her work?"

"I intend to support her in whatever she wants to do. Sure, I'd love it if she'd let me support her entirely, but if she wants to work, I'm going to let her do what she needs to do. I'm not her boss."

"I don't suppose she's been able to keep her job, thanks to you," Daniel said.

Scott bristled at this. "Thanks to me? Marie married me, too, you know, so it's not entirely my fault, and —"

"So," Daniel raised his eyebrows. "She's lost her job? Lost probably her entire future in ministry?"

Scott sighed. "Well, if her pastor wasn't such a wimp, he would have explained to people that... well, she wouldn't have to..."

"Let me tell you something, Scott," he said. "They'd likely forgive a man in her position."

"She didn't do anything wrong!," he insisted heatedly.

"You and I know that," Daniel said. "But they don't. And while they'd forgive a man in that position, they're not going to extend the same grace to a pregnant woman who honestly? They probably think should be at home with the baby anyway."

"Nothing wrong with a woman staying at home and raising a child," Scott managed.

"Nothing at all," Daniel said, "if it's her choice. But you've left her no choice, have you, Scott?"

"It just happened," he said. "And Marie's happy. Really." She was... wasn't she? There had been a lot of crying, and she'd been quiet... but pregnancy did that to women, right?

"Hard for her, though," Daniel said. "Losing her job, having a baby, trying to figure out who she even is now."

"No one forced her into life with me," Scott said. "And besides, she trusts me. She can trust me forever."

"Hmm," Daniel said. "A woman can trust like that if she's married to a man who will lead, support, and protect her. Not some guy who's just going to take things as they come without any sort of plan. Hard for a woman to trust a man who has no idea what he's gotten himself into."

"Oh, I know what I've gotten myself into," Scott said, doubting very much that he really knew.

"What if she has trouble with the pregnancy? What if the baby has problems? What if her health starts to affect *your* work?"

"Well, we'll figure it out," Scott spat out, exasperated. "This is all new to me, too, you know. Neither one of us thought through it all, sure, but –"

"But she has options. I just want to make sure that *you* know that." Daniel gave him an icy glare. "She can come back here, to us. I can take care of my daughter. And my grandchild. She's not stuck or trapped or in any great need of you. Just remember that."

"Are you saying she should leave me?," Scott practically whispered.

"I'm not saying that," Daniel said, calmly. "But I'm saying if you think you can't handle what you've gotten yourself into, you need to man up now and step away. Because Marie can take care of herself."

"I'm aware," Scott said. "But she won't have to."

"You know," Daniel said, with a smile, "this is a crazy place. The other night, I saw two guys driving by, right near the mission house, out in the open veld and all, on these ATVs, right?"

"Yeah?," Scott asked, with absolutely no idea where he was going with this.

"And they had guns. I mean, like, semi-automatic weapons. And they were firing them right into the air. And did they get arrested? Or even stopped by the police? Not at all. It's like the Wild West out here, Scott." He gave him a pointed look. "I mean, a man could end up dead, and there would be no way to know how it happened. And the law wouldn't even care, likely."

Scott said nothing.

"Not to scare you or anything, but... well, I wouldn't... yeah," Daniel looked at him meaningfully. "But just so you know."

"You're scaring me, sir."

"Well, good," Daniel said, clinking his bottle on Scott's. "Cheers."

There were many, many beers that night. More than Scott certainly would have had himself even before sobriety, but Daniel kept having more brought to their table, and Scott? Well, Scott saw no reason to hack the man off any further by refusing to drink with him.

So, he kept on. Until he was drunk enough to probably say some things he shouldn't have said.

Like, "Sir, you're freakin' evil, you know? I mean, like, if Satan himself had a kid brother, it'd be you" and "Kudos to you, sir, for raising a daughter who is? Very frankly? The best I've ever had. I'm talking *wild* and crazy, sir."

And best of all? "When she told me she was pregnant, I actually considered throwing myself in front of a bus, sir. Because I'm not even sure I *want* a baby."

If Scott had been sober, he would have noted that Daniel, who was still somehow not even tipsy at all (confounding tolerance, actually), kept careful track of every word.

But as it was? Scott missed it all.

Marie

Marie waited up later than she felt like, certainly, talking with her mother and waiting for Scott.

She'd known it was a bad idea the moment she'd mentioned the baby. The reaction had been playing through her head all night. Her mother gasping in surprise, her father narrowing his eyes at Scott, Piet giving her a sympathetic smile, and... poor Scott. Grinning like he honestly expected someone to congratulate him. She thought of him with his pregnancy book, becoming a self-assured expert on the subject, and how nothing that was unfolding tonight had likely been in that book.

Chapter One. Protecting yourself once your insane father-in-law has had it confirmed, beyond a shadow of a doubt, that you've had sex with his daughter.

That probably would have been more helpful than the graphic descriptions of childbirth.

"Do you think Dad's being...," she asked her mother, not knowing how to finish the question.

Sara thought about this for a moment. "Do I think he's being... him?"

Marie sighed and bit her lip. "Shame, man."

"It *is* a shame, Marie," Sara sighed herself, turning to look at her daughter. "It's a shame that you gave us no indication at all that this was about to happen. *Any* of this. We would've understood. Or at least, *I* would have understood."

"I know, I know," Marie said, looking at her hands.

"You've always been so honest with me, ever since you went back to the States," Sara said quietly. "And I'm your mother, of course, but I've always thought that you could confide in me as your friend as well. You always have."

"I have," Marie said, thinking through the reasons she hadn't confided this, even early on when there was no marriage and no baby. She thought of Tracy's silence in Drew's office, how she'd known a relationship with Scott would lead there with her, how she'd assumed it would lead there with everyone else. She hadn't given anyone a chance to prove her wrong. And so, she'd rushed into it all without telling anyone. She'd fallen in love with him, so when he'd promised her forever, she'd done what she wanted to do.

"It just all happened so quickly," she managed.

"How long have you known him?," her mother asked.

"A while."

"And how did you meet him?"

Marie sighed. "The elder board at church told me that I was in charge of overseeing the children's ministry wing construction. And I, of course, was in way over my head with all of that, but Drew knew Scott."

Her mother frowned at this, confused. "And..?"

They didn't even know what he did for a living. There was so much she hadn't even bothered to mention.

She swallowed, regretting that she'd failed them all so much.

"He owns his own construction company. Custom homes, small business expansions, remodels. That kind of thing."

"Really?," her mother asked appreciatively.

"Yeah," Marie nodded, thinking of how hard Scott worked, thinking of how good his work at the church had been. "I set up a meeting with his foreman, and my plans were... well, awful. Scott said I was trying to build Whoville."

Sara smiled at this.

"Anyway," Marie continued on, "he came up and took a look at the building. And I remembered his name, recognized him because... he looks just like his grandfather."

Sara nodded. "I thought the same thing. Dr. Fisher was my pastor, remember?"

"I do."

"I'm guessing Scott had no idea that there was a connection there, that we know his family?"

Marie shook her head. "No. And I didn't know them. And he didn't know me, of course."

"He does now, obviously," her mother said.

"Yeah," Marie nodded, feeling remorse again for keeping this all from her.

"Marie," Sara sighed, looking at her sincerely. "We're working through this, too, you know. You'll have to forgive us if it's hard." She said nothing for a long, thoughtful moment. "But I'm trying. Really. I am."

Marie blinked back tears, understanding this. Or, at least, trying to.

"So," her mother sighed. "Love at first sight? He walks in, takes a look at the building, and he's so in love with Jesus that you fell in love with him?"

Oh, boy.

"Um...no," Marie managed. "His crew started working on the project, and he was there all the time, too, and... well over time, we talked about Christ, about what it means to live for Him, and... well, we were just friends. And Scott? Became a believer."

"Wait... he just now became a believer?," Sara asked.

"A while ago," she affirmed quietly.

"Marie, you keep speaking in generalities," her mother answered. "I... I don't want to know specifics, do I?"

Marie shook her head, thinking again about how quickly it had all happened.

"Okay," Sara nodded, trying to process and accept this. "He becomes a believer. And you marry him. Just like that. Without any pause or thought as to how that might not be the best idea you've ever had. I mean, regardless of his maturity in Christ, of whether or not you're in the same place spiritually, or –"

"It wasn't like that," she said. "I hadn't really thought much about him, apart from how fun he was and how cute he was, until all of a sudden, he actually started caring about what I was doing in the ministry there, about what God was doing, about what Christ had done in his life. And then, suddenly? Well, I started thinking differently. He was so genuine, so real in Christ, so appealing. Even though he still thought I was just a cool guy to hang out with, watch the game, eat some wings, you know."

"Well, you are a cool guy, Marie. Always have been."

"Yes," she sighed. "But you know how it is, when you feel... well, more."

"Yeah," her mother nodded.

"Anyway, I'm not sure when it hit him that there was more, but he totally wrecked a date I was on, then took me out himself, and spent the whole morning looking like a springbok in the headlights, you know?"

"Shame," Sara breathed.

"And just as I was telling him that it was okay, that we could go back to hanging out like the two guys that we are, right? Well, he leaned over and kissed me. And I... married him a week later. And got pregnant that same night." She exhaled heavily. "And when I say it all out loud like that, it sounds even worse."

"Well, yeah," her mother agreed.

"I decided it, you know," she said. "Right before I told him I'd marry him, I decided that he was going to be it. There wasn't any going back after that. We were going to be home to one another."

Her mother frowned sadly at this. "So eager to find a home."

Marie nodded. "He's a good man. He makes me happy. And I know I can build a future with him."

"Already are building a future," Sara sighed. "And it's not like I can judge you when I did the very same thing. Deciding on a man so quickly, even though it didn't look smart to anyone else."

Marie wondered at this for a moment. "But you picked Dad."

"Marie, have you met your father?," Sara said incredulously.

Marie thought on this. "Well... okay, I can see how loving him didn't look smart."

"Not at all," her mother confirmed. "He was in Christ, sure, but he had his own struggles. And it didn't look smart at the time, buying into that, yoking myself to those issues... but it turned out better than okay, didn't it?"

"I don't know," Marie sighed. "He's still crazy."

Sara laughed out loud at this. "But we've been heading in the same direction all these years now. And you and Scott... just may be the same. Or even better. Just because Scott is young in his faith and just because you've rushed into this... doesn't mean it isn't something God is going to bless."

"He will," Marie said, affirming it to herself.

"And," her mother smiled, "there are already blessings from it all. A baby. Wow." She shook her head. "I'm going to be a grandmother."

"Yeah," Marie managed, her eyes filling with tears again. "You are."

"Wow," Sara leaned back on the couch and shook her head. "I like Scott, though. I think you picked well, even if you did it quickly."

"I know," Marie said. "And I know that he's a good man, that he's new in Christ, that he's going to live the rest of his life to honor Him. Isn't that enough to build a future on?"

Her mother patted her hand. "I think so, Marie."

And Marie resolved that it would be. And she looked at the door even more expectantly, eager for Scott to be back with her.

Scott

When they finally arrived back at the mission house, Marie was looking much better.

She looked amazing, actually, as she smiled up at him from where she sat on the couch. She'd probably had a good conversation with her mother.

"Hey," Daniel said as he came in, "how are my girls?"

"Much better," Sara said, eyeing him with concern. "Marie was telling me about the wedding. She even has some pictures, Daniel. Beautiful bride and handsome groom…"

"You feeling better, Marie?," Daniel asked.

She nodded. "Yeah, Dad. Just… normal pregnancy stuff, I guess. I don't really even know." She looked over to Scott, who leaned in the doorway with a silly grin on his face. "Scott, are you okay?"

"Oh, me? Just great."

"Yeah, lucky him," Daniel said. "Though I can probably get him to throw up, too, if that would make you feel better."

"No." Marie looked horrified by her father's words and the chilly glare he shot in Scott's direction.

"Daniel," Sara intervened, "why don't you sit with Marie for a while? I want to get reacquainted with Scott." She smiled at him. "Maybe something to eat?"

"Sounds great," he said.

And he followed her to the kitchen, after waving to Marie and smiling at her, trying to put her mind at ease, even though his most certainly wasn't. Sobriety was coming back to him slowly, and he was worried about all that he had probably said. He wasn't sure he could take much more of this getting acquainted or reacquainted.

"Mrs. Boyd, I'm not sure we've ever actually met before today," he said as he sat across the table from her, where she put out a plate full of cookies.

"It's Sara," she smiled at him. "And we have. I taught the three year old Sunday school class for years at Grace. Had Sean, Sam, and you before I left for the mission field."

"Well, that would explain why I don't remember it," he said, biting into a sugar cookie. "Being three and all."

"Oh, but I remember you," she said. "Sean was very vocal, very precocious, typical oldest child stuff, you know. And Sam was so sensitive and tender-hearted, the quietest in the class, actually. And you? You were the one dancing on the tables if I didn't catch you in time. And kissing the girls. At three."

Scott rubbed the back of his neck. "Well, that sounds about right. We're all pretty much the same now. Except I'm not kissing anyone but Marie. Of course."

She smiled. "Oh, I so admired your mother. Still do, actually. The way she'd line you boys up like little ducklings and parade you around to your different classes and play groups at Grace, acting as though it wasn't at all difficult, having so many little ones. I wanted to be like her. Would've had just as many children, too, probably, had we not had so much trouble with Marie."

Scott imagined late nights in his immediate future with comments like this. "Was she a difficult baby?"

"Oh, no," Sara shook her head. "She was wonderful. It was getting her here that was the problem. I was pregnant, doing work for the mission up north, and I caught malaria. We weren't very smart about it all, and Marie came early. We almost lost her. Daniel almost lost me. And we couldn't have anymore."

"I'm sorry to hear that," Scott offered.

"I only tell you this because you've got to understand where Daniel's coming from. Why Marie... well, why her being married is enough of a shock, but being pregnant? And passing out like that on us? It scares him, reminds him of those days, I'm sure. Plus, he has such a complicated history with his own childhood, a father he never knew, and a mother with real problems... and I don't know what he said to you tonight–"

"Well, I think the conclusions I drew from what he did say and what he didn't say was that he could easily have me killed, make it look like an accident, and have Piet marry Marie and raise our child." He was being really honest. He stuffed another cookie in his mouth to keep himself quiet until he was a little more sober.

"Shame, man," she murmured. "I like Piet just fine, of course, but Marie has never looked at him the way she looks at you." She smiled at him. "And I see how you look at her, even though she comes with a very grouchy father."

"Grouchy?," Scott sighed. "Well, psychotic is probably closer to the truth." Oh, yeah. He was still drunk.

"He'll come around, Scott," she laughed. "I'll tell him to call off the dogs, so to speak. And you just wait until my grandbaby is born. He'll be an entirely different man."

They found Daniel alone, glaring from his seat on the couch, once they went back to the living room.

"Marie went to bed," he said softly. "She's completely exhausted." He shot a look at Scott.

"Well," Sara said lightly, running her hands over her husband's shoulders and looking at him meaningfully, "we should probably head to our room and let Scott get some sleep as well. He's probably just as tired as Marie."

"Hmm," Daniel muttered.

"Thanks for the evening out, sir," Scott said. "It was... well, awful. But I thank you for it all the same." He saluted his father-in-law with a flourish and started walking in the direction of Marie's room.

"Hold up," Daniel said. "You're not sleeping in there."

"Well, just where in the –"

"Daniel," Sara said, warning in her voice. The two exchanged a long look, before Daniel broke the gaze and pointed his finger at Scott. "You just keep your hands to yourself in there. You've done enough damage as it is, and –"

"No worries there, sir," Scott laughed. "I'm so drunk I don't know where my hands or any of my other parts would actually go."

"Drunk?," Sara looked at Daniel, who wouldn't meet her eyes. "Scott," she said, compassionately. "I'm so sorry. Things –" she shot her husband a look "—will be better in the morning."

"Well, they couldn't be worse," Scott said, stumbling back to Marie's room.

She was waiting up for him, wearing one of his shirts and looking up at him from where she was comfortably stretched out across the bed.

The nausea was gone, if the look in her eyes as she climbed up on her knees and motioned him forward with one finger and her seductive smile was any indication.

"Well, hello," Scott said, drinking in this vision of his wife, his pregnant wife, who looked amazing. He began to second guess every thought he'd had about what it would be like to be with a woman who changed from week to week with new life. As she smiled at him and he came closer, he concluded that he'd be okay as long as that woman was Marie.

Praise God.

"Hey, buddy, I'm so jet lagged that I don't know how this is going to go," she said, sliding her arms around his neck, "but I'm willing to give it a try because for the first time this week I don't feel like puking."

"Wow," he said, grinning and breathing in her face. "I'm not sure what was in that weird Namibian beer, but I might need whole cases of it shipped back to Texas if this is the kind of hallucination it produces."

"Beer?," she asked, putting her hand to her nose. "Oh, wow…"

"Can smell it, can't you?," he asked.

"Scott, what happened when you went out with my dad–"

"He's the first real missionary I've ever met, you know," Scott said, sighing. "And he got me drunk. Is making me really, really rethink all that I once thought to be true about vocational ministry."

"Oh, I'll kill him," Marie swore. "I will kill him. Scott, lie down, sweetheart, if you can –"

He knelt next to her on the bed and leaned his forehead against hers. "Wow, you're *hot*," he breathed out.

"Well, yeah," she said, sympathetically. "Probably even more so than normal, thanks to the –"

"Oh, no, it's not the beer talking," he said, putting his hands on her clumsily. "Your dad said not to touch you, but I want to touch you *everywhere*, Marie."

He pulled her close and moved his lips down to her neck… then seemed to forget what he was doing.

He looked at her blankly. "What was I saying?"

"That you wanted to –"

"I remember! Your dad! Your really crazy, psychotic dad! I don't freakin' care what he said. Thinks he's so big and bad and –"

He stopped short and stared at her.

"What, Scott?," she said, putting her hands on his face, concerned. "Are you okay?"

Scott continued staring at her. "No," he breathed out. "I'm *not* okay. What kind of crazy language were you speaking earlier? Was I already drunk?"

She smiled and kissed his lips. "Earlier? When Piet was here?"

"Oh," he said, "and that's another thing. *Piet.*" He didn't finish his statement, just rolled his eyes.

"Shame, man," she said. "We were speaking Afrikaans. It's Piet's first language, though he speaks English as well as I speak Afrikaans and... well, we just switch back and forth without thinking. I'll keep everything in English from now on."

"How many languages do you know?," Scott asked, incredulous, wrapping his arms around her and leaning on her shoulder.

"Four," she said, nearly cradling him now as he drooped lower and lower. "Here, Scott, why don't we just lie down, and –"

"Four?! Why did I not know this about you? Which ones?"

She smiled as she rubbed his back. "Well, I've never had cause to speak them around you, I guess. I know English, of course, and Afrikaans about the same. I actually dream in Afrikaans half the time. I know

German pretty well. And I understand Oshiwambo, though my ability to speak it has probably faltered a bit since I've left home."

"I've never even heard of that one," Scott said. "My wife's a freakin' genius, and I never knew. And you look so freakin' hot, but there's nothing I can freakin' do about it tonight because I'm so freakin' drunk and your father is a –"

"Freakin' jerk, I know," she said. She managed to pull him up towards the pillow, then took his shoes off for him, even as he was starting to doze off.

"You're so beautiful," he murmured, already half unconscious. She kissed his face, kissed the wedding band he wore, and curled up close to him.

Marie

Marie waited until he was peacefully asleep... then she silently crept out of bed and down the hall until she was standing in front of her parents' door. Knocking quietly on it, she clenched her fists and counted to ten, under her breath, willing herself to speak in a civil tone with her father...

... who even now opened the door and gave her a worried frown. "You okay?," he asked softly.

"No, actually," she managed. "I'm not okay. We need to talk."

He saw the challenge in her eyes. She had his eyes. And she had his attention, fully and completely.

"We probably should talk, huh, Marie?," he managed. "Just get this out in the open, now that you're back, now that you can't hide anything else from us anymore. Clearly."

"Then let's," she said. She could see her mother glancing between them from where she sat on their bed, taking a breath, preparing for the worst.

This wasn't the first time they'd had it out like this. Her entire teenage life had been spent like this, hadn't it?

"You got him drunk," she said.

Daniel frowned at this. "I hardly think he drank enough to even get tipsy, honestly."

"Drunk, Dad," she said severely. "Which is bad enough on its own. And something you should repent from –"

"Oh, let's talk repentance, Marie," he hissed back.

She held her hand up to stop him. "He's a recovering alcoholic. Five years sober. Until tonight. Baie dankie, Dad."

"Oh, Daniel," Sara sighed.

"Nice," he said, his eyes narrowing. "An alcoholic. Hear that, Sara? Our daughter's secret husband is a loser."

"He's not a loser," Marie challenged before her mother could speak. "He never has been, and in Christ, he never will be –"

"An alcoholic, Marie," he said. "You know what addicts are like? They don't change. They don't recover. They're addicts for life. For. Life. If you should take any lessons away from your own family history, it's that – addicts don't change. And he won't."

She counted to ten in her mind, willing herself to calm down. Her father had grown up in and out of an addict's home, so he was particularly sensitive to this. She understood that. But he was a man of God, who called men out of sin, who called them to grace, who believed in transformation in Christ.

"You, of all people, should believe better than that," she said. "Christ calls men out of more than addictions, Dad. You believe it. Or you say you do."

He glared at her, unable to offer a rebuttal to this.

"He's a good guy," she said. "Honestly, if you'll give him a chance –"

"He doesn't want the baby," Daniel cut in. "Did he tell you that? Told me he'd rather be run over by a bus than be a father to your baby."

Surely he hadn't said that. Marie was breathless for a moment at even the possibility of this, that Scott didn't want the baby. More than that, though, she began to struggle with the impossibility that he could want her and not want this child that was already so much a part of her.

Impossible. He couldn't want one and not the other.

Maybe he didn't want her either. Hindsight is twenty-twenty and all.

She forced the thought away. Now wasn't the time to deal with that, with what Scott had likely said in his drunkenness and surely hadn't meant. Now was the time to deal with her father, to say what needed to be said, to do what was right.

"Our business is ours," she said. "Mine and Scott's. And not yours."

"Marie!," he practically shouted. "Do you see what you've done?! Do you see what a mess you've walked yourself right into?!"

She took a breath and felt it catch in her throat, even as she said, "I know what I covenanted. What I promised. And I'll not regret it."

"You won't... but do you? Do you regret it right now? Knowing what you do?," he asked.

"Not that it's your business," she said, fighting against the small voice whispering warped reason to her in the back of her mind. "But no. Not for a minute."

"Then you don't know what you've gotten into," he said simply.

"I know," she said, getting to what she'd been heading towards all along, "that the moment I married him, I stopped being under your authority."

His eyes bulged at her. Her eyes looking back at her. "My authority? Oh, were you *ever* under my authority? In all your life? Because if you had been, I don't think we'd be having this conversation right now, because I would have forbid this!"

"Maybe not your authority, as you would define it," she said, blinking back tears, "but I have, from the moment I came to Christ, tried my best to honor you, Dad. Like Christ called me to. But if you refuse to acknowledge and accept this marriage and accept Scott, then I'm done here. Forever."

She could see her mother visibly panic at this. But her father remained focused on his tirade.

"Leave and cleave, huh?," he asked. "Fine adherence to one biblical concept there, Marie, when you've ignored so many others."

She felt her throat grow heavy with unshed tears. He was being awful. She'd counted on this, though. "What do you mean?"

"That you have this habit," he said, "of picking and choosing what to believe. When it comes to how to live, how to conduct yourself. And all the provisions God had made, all the checks He had in place to help you do the right thing – you ignored them all. Your church. How many people at your church even knew that you were seeing Scott? Did any of them? Or did you keep that from them?"

It had been a secret. She'd kept it from Tracy willfully, knowing that hearing admonitions to slow down and give Scott time to grow and mature in his faith were warnings that she didn't want to heed.

"Why did they fire you, Marie? Was that what they said?"

She saw her mother visibly flinch at this. "Marie… your job…"

"I resigned," Marie said. "And I did nothing wrong. Maybe I didn't do everything the right way –"

"You had to be above reproach," he said. "Above the suspicion of reproach in ministry. How often were you alone with him before? Were people already talking? Were they already suspecting any number of things that weren't even true?"

Likely so. Marie nodded, swallowing tears.

"We sent you away," he said, furious, "so that you'd have options! And you've wiped away all of your options over this man! An alcoholic you've known only months. And now, suddenly, he has the authority to speak truth into your life over your own parents, who've cared for you and sacrificed everything for you, and over your church, which was there to protect you?"

"Yeah," she said, her eyes never leaving his, knowing that there was hard truth in this.

But she'd decided. There was no going back. Ever.

But there was truth in something else as well. "Not like the church has gotten it right every time, Dad. Not like I have either. And not like you have, most of all," she said. "And I'm not sorry for what God's going to do through all of this. What He's already doing."

They stared at one another for a long moment, glare to glare. Finally he broke the gaze, threw his hands up in the air, and said, "Well, there it is. I can't do anything. Can't say anything. Can I?"

"You can tell me to leave," she said, "and I'll do it gladly. I'm sorry to have upset you, but I'm not sorry for the choices I've made."

"Well, you can't leave," he said. "An alcoholic and his pregnant wife out on the streets. That can't be safe. What would that do for my image as the good-hearted, kind missionary?," he muttered sarcastically.

"No more damage than your poor example of godliness tonight has done," she said calmly. "And to Scott, who is new enough in his faith that he was likely looking for you to share from the riches of grace you yourself have known so well all these years. Or so I thought, though I'm beginning to doubt it now."

And that was likely pushing him too far. Her mother watched him from the bed. Marie watched him as well, her breath held.

"Hmm." This was all he managed. Then, with lowered voice, laced with irritation, "Well, you've just put me in my place, haven't you?"

"I probably shouldn't have," she said, apologetically.

"No, but good for you," he said, glaring. "This is hard for us, Marie."

She nodded. "I know."

"I'm not sure you do," he said. Then, pointing at her stomach, "But you'll know it soon enough."

Marie thought on this, about the child already with them, here in this room.

"And you'll know," he said, "that you're never more sinful, never more full of self, than when the best part of you is out there in the world, making her own choices, going somewhere beyond your protection... and you can't do anything."

"I'll know it, then," she confirmed.

"So, you'll forgive me if I'm a jerk," he said. "Or the devil's kid brother, as your husband described me tonight."

"Well, he was drunk," she said, sighing at this horrible tidbit from Scott's evening with her dad.

"Which again, is on me," he said. "I've got it."

They watched one another for a long moment.

"I'm hard on you, have always been hard on you," he said softly, "because I've spent the last twenty-two years praying God's calling into your life. And it comes naturally to you, being Christ to the world, as easy as it is for you to sit at a piano and pick up a new tune like you've known it all your life. And I can't stand to see you rob God of the glory He can get through your life... and I can't stand to see you rob yourself of the joy that would come with it."

She nodded at this, feeling her heart ache. "Maybe God's teaching me a new tune right now."

"Maybe," he said. A pause. "I'll be better, Marie. A better father. A better follower of Christ."

She nodded, tears now making their way down her cheeks. "Thank you, Dad," she barely got out.

And he put his arms around her, as she saw her mother visibly exhale.

Scott

Scott woke up with the worst headache of his life. Marie was still sleeping peacefully, so he leaned over to kiss her, then got up and made his way to the kitchen, hoping he could find a couple of pills to help.

"Good morning, Scott," Sara said softly when he entered, smiling at him from where she stood at the stove making breakfast. "Sleep well?"

"No." Oh, the very effort of saying that was excruciating.

Sara frowned. "Daniel," she said, glancing over to the table, where his father-in-law was already glaring at him, "don't you have something to say to Scott?"

Daniel regarded him coolly, with a faint trace of repentance on his face. "Yeah, I'm sorry... about last night. And I was wondering," he said, as Sara shot him a look, "if you'd be willing to come with me today on a little trip up north to look at some repairs on one of the mission houses."

Scott's head was fuzzy enough that he wasn't sure he was hearing things correctly.

"Mission house?"

"Marie told me last night about how you own your own business," Sara said to him. "I was telling Daniel that you build houses and how you know all the ins and outs of wiring, plumbing, and... well, all of that."

Scott nodded, shrieking inwardly at the immense pain this caused. "Yeah, I do."

"You would actually be a big help to me today," Daniel offered, clearly struggling to do even this, "if you can lend some of your expertise."

"Sure," Scott said, hoping to turn over a new leaf with this scary man. "I'll be happy to."

"Goeie middag!" The door slammed open, and Scott winced. It didn't escape Daniel's notice, as he smirked and leaned around the doorway to nod at the big, burly man who had just come in with Piet. "Hoe gaan dit?," the stranger continued practically shouting, even as he noticed Scott in the room.

"Baie goed," Daniel said.

"Ag, shame, man," the stranger said, holding out his hand to Scott. "Are you Marie's lovey?"

Piet gave Scott a rather cynical look. "Ja, Willem, this is Scott," he responded, before turning to Sara and kissing her on both cheeks, then plopping himself in the seat next to Daniel as though he belonged right here in the big middle of their family.

"Willem Kotze," the large man bellowed at Scott, who took his hand even as his head pounded.

"Scott Huntington, Marie's... lovey, I guess."

"You look a little green this morning, Scott," Piet observed wryly. "Drinks with Daniel last night?"

Sara pursed her lips together, irritated, while Daniel struggled to look repentant and Piet gave him an appreciative glance.

"Shame, Daniel," Willem barked. Then, lowering his voice towards Scott. "Pretty bad this morning, ne?"

"Not great, sir."

"I have just the thing," he said, moving into the kitchen and squeezing past Sara, opening up cabinets as he went. "Something I used back in my younger days when I... well, I was in your condition half the time, honestly."

A few moments later, Willem handed the cloudy drink he'd just concocted to Scott. "Go on," he coaxed.

Well, what could it hurt? Scott drank it all in one gulp, then handed the glass back to Willem.

"Daniel told me on that phone that you might be heading up to Tsumeb with us," he said to Scott, rinsing out the glass and hugging Sara to his side as he passed her at the stove.

"Um... well, is that the north?"

Piet shook his head at Scott's ignorance, while Daniel said, "It is. Willem

230

will fly us up there and save us more than a few hours of driving this morning. Should make the whole trip just a day venture."

"Ja," Willem said, taking a seat at the table. "Going to be a lot of work, based on what I saw last time we were there. You scared of big snakes, Scott?"

Scott shook his head gently. "Not really. I'm from Texas."

"Texas!," Willem shouted appreciatively. "Cowboys and Indians and… well, not really, huh?"

"Not really. But we do have snakes." He rubbed his head absently, wondering at the way that already, he was feeling so much less tension.

"How's it, friend?," Willem smiled at him. "Feeling better now?"

Scott considered this for a moment and chanced a smile. "I don't want to speak too soon, but… yeah, I think that did it. Thanks."

"Pleasure," he said with a genuine smile.

"Piet, will you be joining us?," Daniel asked.

Scott crossed his fingers under the table that Piet would say no and inwardly rejoiced when he shook his head.

"Wish I could, but I have work today," he said. "Just brought Willem by for you. Was hoping I'd see Marie this morning –"

"She's still in bed," Scott said. "Long night last night, you know."

Piet didn't know, of course. But Scott could see the wrong conclusions he was drawing. And he rejoiced to see the disappointment there.

"Ag, well," Piet managed. "Better be getting on my way, then."

And the front door closed behind Piet just as they all heard Marie's door open.

The pale, sickly look on her face couldn't mask her delight as she saw Willem, who stood to greet her. "Oom Willem!," she shouted, running towards him.

He caught her in his arms and swung her around, even as Daniel stepped up and stopped him, muttering a few words in Afrikaans to him, making a grin break out on Marie's face.

"Shame, man," Willem said, putting her on her feet and smiling at her. Then, looking over at Scott, "Congratulations, friend. A papa so soon, ne?"

Scott shrugged. This must be a really, *really* close family friend if they were already sharing all of this.

"Where's Auntie Sophie?," Marie asked in English, for Scott's benefit.

"Back home," he said. "She'll be by later to see you."

"Auntie?," Scott asked. "Are you... well, judging by your accent, you're not Daniel or Sara's brother."

"Shame, man," Marie said. "Did they not introduce you?"

"Not really," Willem said, smiling, "because I was too busy trying to help Scott with his hangover. All better now, right?"

"Better and better by the minute, sir," Scott affirmed.

"Baie goed," Willem sighed, leaning against the counter.

"Scott, this is Willem, who is not technically my uncle," Marie said, moving to sit on her husband's lap, eliciting a look from her father that a look from her mother quickly dissuaded. "But for all intents and purposes, is as close to an uncle as I have or should ever want." She smiled up at Willem.

"I've known Marietjie since she was a tiny baby," Willem said, smiling back at her. "And now, here she is, all grown up and married, and looking very much like her father did back when I beat the crap out of him so many years ago." A devilish look came to his eyes as he smiled over at Daniel.

"Oh, this story never gets old," Marie told Scott, even as Daniel rolled his eyes.

"Yes," Sara said, smiling, "all my fault for coming onto him at the Strand."

"Coming onto... you?," Scott said, looking at Willem.

"I wish," Willem sighed.

"No," Daniel said, "coming onto *me*, which ended up being a convoluted, bloody mess in the end. Literally. When Willem found me later, and we *both* beat the crap out of each other."

"He looked worse than me," Willem affirmed, glancing at Scott. "So, if you need me to hit him again for you, know that I'm willing to do so."

"Noted and remembered," Scott murmured, surprised to see that this brought a smile to Daniel's face.

"I feel better about him now, of course," Willem said, "because his genes have produced Marie, of course. Sophie and I have no children of our own, but we've been content to borrow Daniel and Sara's."

"Ek is lief vir jou, Willem," Marie cooed, smiling.

"I love you, too, Marie," he answered with a matching smile. "Oh, and we've got my nephew, Piet, too."

Scott cringed at the name. "Piet? Oh, please, no..."

"Ja," Marie breathed, when the three friends looked at Scott with some concern. "Piet's mother, Ana Marie, is Willem's sister."

"We actually named Marie after her," Daniel said. "Piet wasn't even a year old himself when Sara got so sick, and Ana Marie saved the day for us, sweeping in with him on her hip, ready to help me figure out what to do with my own baby while Sara got better."

"And Piet and Marie grew up together," Sara said. "Not related but as close as they could be otherwise."

Well, maybe this explained some of the possessiveness Scott had been detecting. Just as he was about to ask more about Piet, Marie pushed her plate away.

"I think I feel worse today than I did yesterday," she said.

"Shame, man," Daniel said. "Are you sure you don't need to go to a doctor here, just to make sure –"

"Daniel," Sara said, placing her hand on his. "Marie, I think if you can eat something, it'll make you feel better."

"Here," Scott said, tearing a bite off of the toast on her plate. "Just try this. For starters."

She allowed him to feed her the bite, then leaned over to hold his face in her hands as she gave him a small kiss. And as bad as this whole trip had been going, he still couldn't be sorry that they were here, because he still had moments like this with Marie.

"Ag, shame," Willem laughed. "Young love, Daniel! Isn't that sweet?"

Daniel rolled his eyes at his friend. Then shifting his attention to Scott, he asked, "Can you be ready to leave in about thirty minutes?"

"Can do," Scott replied.

"Leave? Where are you going?," Marie asked.

"Scott's going up north to help your father get the Tsumeb house back in order," Sara said.

Marie's eyes widened at this. "Oh." She smiled at Scott. "Well, that'll be... fun."

Fun? Was a relative term.

There had been the flight up north. His head was feeling so much better after Willem's remedy, but Willem's haphazard skills at the helm of the tiny plane had him feeling much worse than he had. As he wondered over whether it was the altitude that was affecting him so adversely, Daniel pointed out landmarks from the sky.

And every last one of them was connected to a story about Marie.

Scott could almost see her, a five year old sitting next to her father in his truck, her hand held out the window, catching the wind as they went, chirping away merrily in a language he had been teaching her from birth. He could see her in Daniel's eyes, the little girl he'd never expected and hadn't known he'd even wanted before she'd arrived... the little girl who'd become everything, even as she'd gone so far away.

He could almost empathize, could very nearly feel some connection to this man... until Willem took a hard turn, prompting Scott to grab one of the extra garbage bags they'd brought and vomit his breakfast right into it.

"Sure hope we don't run out of bags now," Daniel had noted wryly, as Willem put his face as close to the plane's small vents as he could, dramatically taking gulping breaths of fresh air.

It had only gotten better once they'd arrived in Tsumeb.

After they had killed two snakes that were, frankly, larger than any snakes Scott had ever seen in all of his life, they moved outside to see what was waiting for them in the yard.

Yes. The snakes had been in the house.

"You sure we can't do anything about the pipes today?," Daniel muttered, looking over at Scott.

The running water in the house was inexplicably brown. Inexplicably for Willem and Daniel, at least, who had turned on the tap and looked to Scott for the answer. He had watched for a moment and declared that it was likely evidence that the pipes had rusted from the inside out, given the age of the house and the poor quality of the pipes that he could see. He'd have to tear out walls to change them out, and because they had no new pipes on hand with them anyway, he'd told them it would have to wait.

It would be no small job and would likely illuminate several other problems with the shoddy house. Scott was tempted to tell them to bulldoze the whole structure and let him build a better one in its place. He couldn't do it now, obviously, but maybe in a year, once the baby was born, when he could take some time from work back home...

He was surprised that his thoughts went this way as they were glaring evidence of his acceptance and his intention of more trips in the future. For the Boyds. For the child that was coming.

For Marie.

They'd done what they could in the house and moved outside to begin the many projects waiting for them there.

They'd cleared out large sections of the brush that was threatening to creep onto the property. They mowed the lawn after Scott fixed the mower. They replaced the gutters after Scott tore down the old ones. The cut back trees that were crowding the driveway.

They did it all... and then some.

Scott was tweaking some wires in the ancient breaker box along the south side of the house and making a list in his head of all that he could bring with him on the next trip to bring the whole system up to

American code (who knew what it was here?) when Willem came to get him.

"Scott, you've done the work of ten men today," he said, wiping sweat off his own brow as he smiled. "Come eat some dinner with us, then we'll head back to Swakop, ne?"

Back to Swakop. Back to Marie. Scott was glad for that as he'd spent a good part of the day wondering how she was feeling.

He followed Willem down the road back to the plane, where Daniel was pulling food out of the cooler they'd packed that morning.

"Baie dankie, Scott," Daniel said simply.

"Buy a donkey?," Scott said, wondering where he could accomplish this new task and exactly *why* he'd want to. "I'm not sure I –"

"Never gets old," Daniel grinned at Willem.

"It got old a long time ago, Daniel," he muttered.

"It means thank you, Scott," Daniel said simply. "For all that you've done."

Scott blinked at the gratitude, surprised by it. "You're welcome," he returned.

"So, how do you find Africa?," Willem said to him, slapping him on the back with a crooked smile.

"I find it to be a lot of hard work," Scott noted, accepting the sandwich that was passed his way. "But my kind of work. I can work on the wiring for the house next time and start changing out the pipes I can see. But, Daniel, the rest of the pipes... it'll have to wait for another trip, when I have more time."

"Another trip!," Willem shouted. "Do you hear that?"

Daniel nodded, sitting down in the dirt with them, beginning to eat his own sandwich.

"Eish, man," Willem sighed. "Marie picked well. Daniel and I do our best with it all, but our skills only go so far."

"Yeah," Scott murmured, looking back at the house. "You guys have plans to change that roof out?"

Daniel groaned. "Not anytime soon. Seems like yesterday that I was re-roofing that thing."

Scott bit his lip, wondering at this. It was in bad condition for a roof that was only a few years old...

"Nee, man!," Willem laughed. "It has been longer than just yesterday!"

Daniel thought about this. "I remember it. Sara came out from the States and drove up here the same day. I was on the roof getting the old shingles off when she showed up."

"She went to the US without you?," Willem asked. "I don't remember that. Was Marie with her?"

"No," Daniel shook his head, smiling at the memory. "She wasn't born yet. Sara and I weren't even married."

"Shame, man, then it's been a while!," Willem exclaimed.

"Doesn't feel like that long ago," Daniel shook his head. "And with Marie back home... it feels like nothing's changed."

But it had, obviously. Scott, the biggest proof of all the changes, sat quietly, eating and watching.

"You're going to be a grandfather, Daniel," Willem laughed, acknowledging the change in this, at least.

"Already am," he said thoughtfully. Then, looking at Scott, he smiled.

"Think it's a boy or a girl?"

Scott was surprised to find that there was no hostility in the question, only curiosity. Maybe even joy and expectation.

"Marie seems to think it's a boy," he offered. "Mother's intuition and all. For what that's worth."

Daniel smiled at this. "A grandson. That'll be fun."

"Daniel was always good with the boys," Willem said. "Hennie, my older nephew, and Piet would follow him all over the beach when we'd go down there on the weekends. Here they had an uncle who is an exceptional –"

"Ooh, big word," Daniel cut in.

"Ja, ex-cep-tion-AL, great English word," Willem grinned. "They had an uncle who was an exceptional surfer, but they wanted to have Daniel teach them."

"And I did," he nodded.

"Which left me with Marie," Willem said to Scott. "And she was just as keen as the boys were. And much more athletic, honestly. Was better than either one of them in no time at all."

"That sounds like Marie," Scott said, smiling. "Where's Hennie now? Marie mentioned him to me before. Told me he was like her big brother."

Willem smiled. "He's in the US. College, then business, and... well, he doesn't come home much."

"She told me how he'd take her out to play rugby," Scott added.

Daniel frowned at this while Willem laughed.

"He did, and it made Daniel plenty irritated," he said.

"Girls shouldn't play such rough sports," Daniel muttered.

"That's what I told her!," Scott said. "And then she, very frankly, wrestled me to the ground and pinned my arms down with her knees –"

And he stopped mid-sentence, wisely discerning that this mental image was one that his father-in-law probably didn't appreciate.

Obviously, Daniel didn't, since the death glare had returned.

"Well, that sounds very interesting, Scott," Willem commented.

"Shut up," Daniel said.

"Ja, well," Willem sighed, "Daniel was always fine with the boys being boys, but he didn't much like Marie running around out there like that."

"I couldn't stop thinking of her like she'd been," he said simply. "So tiny and little, home from the hospital while Sara was so sick. So tiny, Scott, that I swear, I spent all of those nights practically staring at her, making sure her little body was able to breathe on its own. Remember that, Willem?"

"Sure do," Willem smiled. "But she grew up, and you were *still* treating her so gently. Remember that time when you went down to the rugby field and put those players in their place because Marie scraped up her leg and needed stitches?"

"Yeah, and I'd do it again," he said.

"Sho, Scott," Willem laughed. "Those boys were scared. I think some of them may have wet themselves when Daniel came after them. They stayed clear of Marie after that."

"She hated that I did it," Daniel added.

"Yeah," Willem said thoughtfully. "They all stayed clear. Except Piet."

Daniel frowned even further at this. Scott sat up a little straighter, wondering what this could mean, the question on his lips –

"Such a long time ago," Willem sighed. Then, to Daniel, "And I don't know what you and Marie have said to each other about all that's happened," he said, "but I know you were always looking out for her best interests. And she knows that."

"How wonderfully discerning of you, Willem," Daniel said sarcastically, smiling even in this, "knowing that Marie and I have had words."

"Oh, Piet knew they were coming," he said. "Told me that you and Marie both had your crazy eyes on and everything last night. Just a guess that you'd already had it out."

"We had it out."

"Shame, Daniel."

Scott watched silently, wondering at what Marie had said, what Daniel had said, and what he would have said had he known any of it was going on.

"Yes," Daniel said. "And I was a jerk. Which I know you find hard to believe. Both of you."

Scott looked up with what he hoped was innocence. Daniel shook his head at this, smiling even more.

"She put you in your place, then?," Willem grinned. "Sweet, darling Marietjie?"

"And she was really spiritual about it, too," Daniel laughed. "Which made it hard to continue on. So, I didn't."

"You're a good father," Willem affirmed.

"I'm just learning as I go," Daniel said. "Every day, learning how this is supposed to work, relying on grace and the sufficiency of Christ to get me through and to cover my inadequacies when I just don't get it right."

He looked at Scott. "That's a lesson you never stop learning when you're a husband, a father... a follower of Christ. You never get it completely right, but you keep at it."

"Good word, Daniel," Willem murmured.

And Scott nodded at the truth of this, amazed to find that grace was the same on both sides of the world and that the sufficiency of Christ was always there.

They'd arrived home, and Marie had met him at the door with a long, slow kiss. Then, she'd sent him off to shower, telling him that she was feeling nauseous all over again with the way he smelled.

He'd come back to the living room to find Marie and her parents sitting around talking in the front room when the doorbell rang. He offered to get it and immediately regretted that decision when he opened the door and found Piet standing on the porch.

There was something not quite right about Piet and Marie. He'd picked up on it early enough with the way Piet looked at her and the way Marie didn't seem entirely comfortable around him. Then, Willem's comment...

They all stayed clear. Except Piet.

"Yeah?," Scott asked, irritation all over his face, as he shut the door behind him.

Piet looked him over, then smiled. "Ja, man. Thought I'd bring over a little something for Marie. Have you been having a rough night of it?"

"Why do you ask?"

"Because you're a little sunburned," Piet said.

No kidding. Scott had nearly screamed in the shower when the water hit his neck. Marie had even given him a double take when he had emerged from the bathroom.

"Oh, it's fine," he said. "Just a little sun this afternoon in Tsumeb."

"Shame, man," Piet said, all out grinning now. "The Tsumeb house. It's a bloody mess."

"Right now, yeah. But I'm going to fix a lot of those problems."

"Hmm," Piet murmured thoughtfully. "Having a good time getting to know the in-laws, Scott?"

"Just fine." He started trying to think of a way to get Piet to leave so he could go back to Marie, forget about him, and –

"Daniel is... hectic, ja?," Piet grinned.

"I have no idea what that means," Scott said, growing increasingly more irritated with the guy the longer he stood there on the porch. "But, sure, he's hectic all right."

Piet nodded. "Ja, he's never much liked... well, any of the boys who liked Marie. I half suspect he has a collection of their... well, you know, back in a room somewhere, as trophies. Except for me, of course. I'm like the son he never had, actually."

"Well, isn't that special?," Scott spat out, this new comment beginning to nibble away at him like Willem's words had. "So, what did you bring your little Marie-key, or whatever it is you were calling my wife?"

"Ah, well," Piet said, obviously delighted by his ability to irritate him so much, "just a few of her favorite snacks. Some things she might actually be able to keep down." He handed the bag to Scott, who took one whiff and fought back a gag.

"Oh, wow, did something die in here?"

"Shame, man," Piet shot him a look. "That's biltong. Her favorite."

"Bil-what?"

Piet regarded him for a moment. "You don't know her very well, do you?"

Scott crossed his arms over his chest. "I know her better than you do," he said, smiling, remembering the way she looked that first night as she'd pulled his shirt off, the way she'd laughed out loud a few days later as he covered her face in kisses, the way she'd whispered to him, before they left Texas, *only you, Scott, for the rest of my life...*

Piet smiled at him knowingly. "I wouldn't be so sure, friend."

Well, what was *that* supposed to mean?

Before Scott could say another word, Piet sauntered off with a smile. "Lekker slaap." He turned back with a wink. "It means, sleep well. Which I'm sure you will now, thinking about me and Marie, ne?"

Scott numbly walked back in, the sack of biltong under his arm, flinching when Marie met his eyes with a smile. "What's that? Who was at the door?"

He handed her the sack without a word as she smiled at him, confused. She looked in, gasped, and moaned appreciatively. "Oh, Scott, how did you know?"

"I didn't. Piet did."

And he sat beside her as she averted her eyes from his, and for once, he didn't reach out to hold her hand.

"So, what's the deal?," he asked as soon as they were alone in her room again.

"With what?," Marie asked, pulling on his favorite shirt to sleep in.

"And why are you stealing all of my shirts?," he asked. "I swear, I'm going to be forced to walk around naked −"

"Which wouldn't be a bad thing," Marie grinned at him.

"No, it would be," he grumbled. "I just want a few freakin' shirts to call my own."

She regarded him warily. "You told me that I look hot in your shirts."

He ran his hands over his face, frustrated. "I just... I'm just having a rough time." He exhaled sharply and sat on the edge of the bed.

"With what?," she repeated, kneeling behind him, trailing kisses from his neck and across his bare shoulders. He closed his eyes and tried to concentrate on what she was doing while also trying to cast out Piet's knowing look, and without him wanting them to − not at *all* − the two images came together in his mind. And there was Piet, kissing *his* wife, with that stupid expression on his face, calling her that stupid pet name, while she lauded his efforts in a language Scott couldn't understand −

"*Piet*," he practically growled.

"Shame, man," Marie continued kissing him. "What's wrong with Piet?"

Scott turned to face her. "Well, he's in love with you, clearly."

Marie cast her eyes down shyly. "Well... he... we've known each other forever, Scott."

"And?"

"We were babies together," she said. "Grew up together, and... he just... you know." She reached out to hold his hand.

"No, I don't know," Scott said, prompting her to look him in the eyes. "Were you two ever together?"

She looked down and studied their hands together. "Yeah. Back when we were teenagers."

"So…" Scott prodded. "You dated? He was your boyfriend? That was it?"

"Scott," she breathed softly. "It was a long time ago."

"Oh, Marie, this is so not what I need to hear right now. Please tell me that there was nothing more than just a few kisses and –"

"Scott," she said, catching his face in her hands. "There was more, but we were teenagers. And then, there wasn't anyone again. Until you. I stayed true to Christ. And… it was so long ago with Piet. It's been forgiven and forgotten."

He sat back for a moment, studying her. "I'm pretty sure Piet hasn't forgotten *any* of it. In fact, as he was staring me down tonight, I'm pretty sure I caught glimpses of a whole lot of the details still playing themselves out in his mind, and –"

"Well," she sighed. "I can't be culpable for his choice in refusing to move on. I can only move on myself and live for Christ now." She leaned in to kiss his neck again, only to have him move away from her.

And for a moment, he felt intensely angry with her. At this omission. At this *huge* omission. And he couldn't stop from glaring at her.

She gave him a shocked look. "Did you… did you think that there had never been anyone?"

Scott swallowed past the lump in his throat. Had he? Well, of course he had. And had he not stopped and thought it strange that there was no shyness from her that first night, that there had been no hesitation or reservation, that she –

"Oh, man," he moaned, putting his head in his hands.

"Scott…"

"I feel kinda sick just thinking about you and... him."

"Really?," she managed, indignation on her face. "And what about *you*, Scott? How many women have there been before me?"

"Not as many as you'd think," he huffed. "And certainly none like Piet, who is like an ever-present, beloved fungus in this house. *None* of the women I've been with have looked at me like he looks at you!" He shook his head. "And besides, I haven't been with *anyone* since coming to Christ. Only you. And I *waited* for you."

Marie sighed. "Yeah, all of a week, before you convinced me to run off and marry you, just so you could –"

"*I* convinced *you*?," Scott scoffed at her. "Oh, I seem to remember that someone was more than eager to get me in the sack, and that she was just as quick to jump on the plane, and –"

"That's not what I remember –"

"And how *dare* you act as though the only reason for this –" he jabbed his hand towards his wedding band – "and *that*" – he pointed towards her flat tummy – "was a little action. Because I sure could have gotten that without any of this marriage business, Marie. And I could've gotten it from *anyone*."

She didn't say anything for a moment. Then, softly, she murmured, "I can't believe you said that." She turned away from him.

"I was quite the hot commodity, you know," he said, somehow knowing that this wasn't helping things... but keeping on like the idiot he was. "And I certainly didn't need a hypocritical church girl to take care of any of my needs, and –"

"No, you don't need me at all," she said, her back to him. "Because you've got enough hypocrisy going on yourself. Judging me for the very same things *you* yourself are guilty of."

"Yeah, but I never loved any of those other women, but you and *Piet* –"

"Does that make it better, Scott? That you just went through women without feeling anything? Does it make it worse that I actually cared about Piet? Either way, we both messed up, okay? And either way, neither of us is coming out squeaky clean apart from Christ. So, there needs to be no judgment either way."

"Yeah, well..." He didn't know what else to say. "I just don't like it."

"I've got that. And I know you're angry right now, and you're saying a lot of things about me that you probably don't really mean. And I don't care. I don't care that my newlywed husband just told me that he could've gotten laid by anyone less than three weeks ago. None of that is what's upsetting me now."

"Oh, then," he said, continuing on. "Is it Piet? Are you upset about how I treated your precious Piet? Because I'm not treating him as *good* as you sure did back when you were teenagers?!"

Marie looked over her shoulder and shrugged. "Oh, just keep on making things worse, Scott. By all means."

He huffed at her, lying on his back. "Well, I don't know how to make things better. Unless killing him is an option. And even then, I still have this vision in my head of you..."

Marie said nothing.

"I mean, I'm entitled to feel like that, right? And not because of what happened back when you were teenagers... although, wow, I *really* don't like any of that." A pause. "How many times, Marie? How many times did it happen?"

"Scott," she said softly, "how many times were you with other women?"

"I was someone totally different back then!," he yelled. "You *know* that! You've seen the difference!"

"And you need to trust me when I tell you that there's a difference between who I was when I was with Piet and who I am now. Not who I am, but who I was. Do you remember saying that? How you were changed by Christ?"

He did. He did remember. But he wouldn't give her this.

"This double standard, Scott? It doesn't work."

He said nothing for a moment. "I'm not asking about the... ugh. Just asking about the relationship. Okay, Marie? How long were you with him? How long has it been over?"

Marie sighed. "It ended when I left for college. I thought we were going to get married, but he wasn't ready. I left. And in the US, I fell in love with Christ. Everything about my life changed, including who I had been with him. And this is the first time I've been back to Namibia since any of it. The first time I've seen Piet since I was seventeen."

Scott sighed. "Wow. Well, no wonder he's been all over you like mold on –"

"Ag, man, did you not hear *anything* I just said?!"

"And you *talk* like him now that you're back here! It's like I'm in bed with Piet. Which I wouldn't know anything about, but you –"

She turned her back to him again.

He cursed himself silently for not knowing when to shut his mouth. Then, he opened it again. "It's not even that, really."

Again, she remained silent.

"It's more," he continued on, "about how he's here even now. And he still... he still seems to know all these things about you that I don't. And your parents love him, and *you* did love him at least once, and I'm realizing that I don't know you at all. I mean, you speak all these languages, you have the world's biggest Marie Fan Club here, and... I feel like I don't even know you. I'm freakin' married to a total stranger."

He stopped.

"Is that it? Is that what's upset you? Because you really need to tell me *why* you're mad, Marie."

She rolled over to face him.

"No, Scott, it's not about *me*," she said, tears in her eyes. "It's not even about the fact that you say you want to know me but you totally ignore all that I'm saying because you're so hung up on this Piet thing."

"Well, it's a pretty big *thing*, I think—"

"But that's not why I'm angry. I'm angry because you called this child *that*. Like he's just some *thing*." She gave him a steely glare. "I can forgive the things you're saying about me, and the two of us? We can figure one another out. And even though we feel like strangers right now, I know that I like you, that we liked each other, and that once we *do* figure one another out? We're going to be happy together. We're going to honestly *love* one another. But," she snarled at him, raising herself up on one arm, "I will *not* lie here and have you speak about our child like he doesn't even matter."

Scott was surprised by this. "When did I say that?"

"You said it," she said, the tears rolling down her cheeks now. "And you may not want this baby. You may not even want me. But by God's grace, I'm staying with you, Scott, until He changes your heart."

And she turned away from him and sobbed into her hands.

He had never made her cry before. He'd seen her cry, obviously. But he had never been the reason for her tears.

Her sadness left him feeling... well, like a complete loser.

And it hit him that already, not even a month into this marriage, he was already letting Marie down. Just like he had promised he wouldn't.

Marie

Marie sincerely hated him that night.

This is what she got for rushing into things. This, which was worse than losing her job, making her mother cry, and severing ties to her life. Marriage to a man who she could hate as passionately as she loved him.

Marriage. Holy. Cow. She was *married* to this giant tool. And as if that wasn't bad enough, she was carrying his child.

In all of her life, Marie had never felt trapped. There had never been any limit to where she could go, what she could do, and who she could be. But as soon as the pregnancy test turned positive, it was as if countless little threads began to weave themselves into her, anchoring her to one fate, one direction, and one fixed life. She didn't resent the baby at all, didn't wish him away... but she was beginning to panic at the thought that all those threads that connected her to such a blessing had connected her to... well, to Scott. Who was certainly not acting like he ever had before.

As she laid there in bed, furious with him, she thought through the reasons why she had ever liked Scott Huntington. He was cute, he was funny, he was so much fun to be around... but had there been more? Was there more? And where had this irrational, jealous man been back then?

She prayed. And prayed some more. And kept praying until God brought to mind the sincerity on Scott's face when he talked about following Jesus now. And the way his face lit up as he watched her work at the church. And even how he had endured all that her father had put him through since they'd arrived.

But more than that, He brought to mind the vow that she had made, the promise she had sincerely made that she would love and honor this ridiculously jealous, egotistical, and arrogant man tossing and turning in bed next to her.

And that? Was reason enough to wipe her tears away and begin praying, not for deliverance, but for reconciliation. And stronger feelings than the anger she felt now, the naïve sweetness she had felt before... but instead, *real* love and real commitment.

She woke up to what sounded like a house full of people. Again.

Scott was still asleep, blissfully unaware, and blissfully unaffected by the morning sickness that even now was making Marie force back the bile that was rising in her throat.

She thought about giving him a good, swift kick to the butt so that he could really be a part of this pregnancy with her, but she stopped mid-kick, reminding herself of the reconciliation she was praying back into her heart.

She threw on some clothes, left their room, and directed her feet towards the kitchen...

... but was stopped short by Piet, who was sitting in the front room.

"Marie," he said, standing to his feet and going to her side.

"Good morning, Piet," Marie managed past the nausea, using her English to set the tone for the conversation she knew Piet was intent on having. She would be the one to settle this, on her terms.

"Are you feeling well this morning?," he asked, leading her over to the couch and sitting down beside her, even as she regarded him warily.

"Well... no," she said, allowing herself a small smile in his direction.

Piet smiled back at her. "My mother came with us this morning. Brought you something for it."

"Ana Marie is here?," Marie said, her smile spreading even more, as she moved to stand back up.

"Marie, can we speak with one another first?," Piet asked gently.

She sighed. "Piet, I don't think you want to have this conversation."

"Shame," he said, reaching for her hands, only slightly frowning when she pulled them away from him. "I'm not all that bad, am I?"

"I didn't think so," she said, "but you've been tormenting Scott."

He did his best to hide the smile that came to his face. "But he... he makes it very easy."

This was true enough. Scott wore his feelings so much in the open, without meaning to. He was an easy target for jealous ex-boyfriends or, in this case, the *only* jealous ex-boyfriend Marie had –

"You didn't tell him about us, did you?," Piet asked softly.

Marie shook her head. "No. I didn't. Not until last night."

"Why?," he asked. "Was it because I still mean something to you?"

"It was just... I don't know. I didn't figure it would matter either way, honestly."

Piet thought about this for a while. "Does it matter, though?"

Marie thought about how it mattered a whole lot more to Scott than it should have. And because she had kept it from him? Perhaps it meant more to her than it should have as well. "No," she told Piet. "It doesn't."

He took a deep breath, then fixed his eyes on her. "Well, I'm just going to say it, Marietjie. Because if I don't say it now, I'll regret it. I love you. And I don't want you to keep on with... this..."

"With my marriage, you mean?," Marie interjected cynically.

"Yes, with that," Piet said, "because you feel trapped."

And he? Had hit right on what she had been feeling. But she took careful means to make sure the weight of his words didn't show on her face.

"You stay with him, and you can be assured that coming back here? Won't happen. Maybe for a visit or two over the years, but long term? This can never be home again if you stay with him."

Marie knew he spoke the truth. This had been one of those things she hadn't thought of until she was already so deeply in. That home? Would never be the same. Oh, it hadn't been for a while, of course, but now? It would never return to a new normal. And what of her, if that was true? How much of Marie Boyd – actually, Marie Huntington – was connected to here, to this place, to this man who stared at her even now?

"Marie," he said softly, "you could come here, stay with me. I would take care of you. Of the baby. I would marry you. I would marry you right now, right this minute, if you would have me. You know I would. I would live every day to make you happy, like I did before."

She sighed at him. "Big words, Piet. Really, really big words from the man who wanted nothing of this five years ago. You know, back when *I* lived every day to make *you* happy."

He frowned at her. "I wanted it then, you know. I did."

"You certainly didn't," she said. "And you sent me away."

"Sent you away so we could both grow up," he said. "We weren't ready."

And she knew in her heart that this was true. But still, the sting from that rejection, despite all the good that had come because she had gone away – her faith in Christ, her ministry, and, yes, even her marriage to the world's most annoying man – still stung in a fresh way that took her breath away.

"Do you know what I did when you left?," he asked.

"What did you do, Piet? Mourn my departure? Cry into your pillow every night?"

"Nee, man," he shook his head. "I got a job. I started training to be a medic. I saved my money and bought a cottage on the beach, just like you said you wanted. And I waited. I waited for you to come back to me." He paused, struggling for words. "And you never did. You were living your life in the US. Your parents said you were happy. You were like Hennie, just disappearing on us all. I wanted you to make your own choice."

"And I did," she said. "And now you're trying to talk me out of it, when the choice has long since been made."

"No, Marie," he pleaded. "I'm trying to show you that you still have a choice. With me. Stay with me. I can take care of you. I've spent my whole life getting ready to take care of you."

But he hadn't. There had been that time when he wasn't so sure. Even still, though, she felt the uncertainty of her present circumstances pressing on her heart again, thinking back to the anger she had seen in Scott last night, this inexplicable tug towards Piet. One was a stranger, one was everything familiar in her life. But she couldn't think like this anymore. Couldn't let herself think like this –

"Even if I did... come home," Marie began, "I wouldn't *need* you, Piet. I could stand on my own. This isn't about *you*. Because... I don't *need* you."

"Shame, man," Piet said, rather weakly, "because I need you, Marie."

And he leaned over, took her face in his hands, and kissed her softly.

For a brief moment, she ached and yearned for who he was, who he had been, for all that he represented, for the part of her that had existed here in Namibia. It would have been easy to let herself feel what she shouldn't feel and to let him take care of her the way she knew he could. There would have been no arguments about the past, no double standards, no bitterness, only this, and –

And almost as if it was an audible voice, Marie heard the word *no*.

She thought of the childish man back in her bedroom, of the tiny child growing in her womb, and above all else, of the promises she had made and was doing a poor job of honoring even now, by putting herself in this position.

She pushed Piet away, firmly and resolutely.

She could see it there in his startled eyes – all the memories – and felt weak. But again, the word *no* kept repeating itself to her, and she strengthened her resolve.

"Piet, we'll never be who we were," she said.

"Marie, ek is lief vir jou –"

"*No.*"

And then, there were more words.

So many angry, heated words between them. Marie was sure the whole house could hear, that no one save Scott, who was still sleeping, would need a translation for the hateful, awful way she spat out the words that were certain to destroy Piet's heart.

All the years of hurt and anger came out as Marie visibly shook at the thought of what she'd done, who she'd become, sitting here, letting Piet get even this close.

And Scott. Oh, Scott. What had she done?

After there were no words left to say, Piet finally went away, wounded and uncertain, without looking back. And Marie put her head in her hands and cried.

Scott

Scott woke up to... was someone playing the piano? And singing. Someone was singing. And laughing. A whole bunch of people were laughing somewhere in this house.

He looked over to find that Marie was already out of bed. Worried that the singing had woken her up prematurely and that she was sick in the bathroom, he got dressed and made his way out of the room, intending to find her... and stopping short when he saw the scene in the front room.

Marie was at the piano, playing and singing loudly along with Willem, who sat next to her. Another woman sat on her other side, singing and laughing in that same foreign language that Marie seemed to know so well. Sara and Daniel were there as well, Daniel standing behind Marie with his hands on her shoulders, kissing the top of her head, and Sara sitting on the couch.

The woman he hadn't yet met caught his eye from where he stood slumped in the doorway.

"Ag, man," she exclaimed, standing up and rushing to him. "Are you Scott?"

"Um... yes, ma'am," he said, holding out his hand, then nearly falling over when she brought him in close for an exuberant hug.

"Our Marietjie's lovey," she cooed, holding him out in her arms and touching his face.

Daniel smiled over at them, amused by the expression on Scott's face. "Scott, this is Ana Marie. Couldn't stay away when she heard that Marie is expecting."

"*Shame*, man," Ana Marie said, smiling even wider now, hitting Scott playfully on the shoulder. "Didn't waste any time now, did you?" She winked at him.

Before he could think of a polite response to this, she went right into another exclamation. "Shame, man! Piet told me that Marie was feeling a bit unwell, and I have *just* the remedy for it, you see. Should have been a chemist you know, with my remedies."

"That hangover drink?," Willem said. "*All* Ana Marie."

"Well, thank you for that," Scott said. "And I mean that."

"Pleasure," she said. "And sweet Marie, after drinking my mommy's tonic, is back to normal."

Or even better than normal, Scott noted as she launched into yet another song, to the uproarious laughter of Willem, eliciting an eye roll from Daniel, as Ana Marie dashed back to the piano to join along.

Daniel made his way over to Scott. "They're Afrikaans... well, bar songs, for lack of a better phrase. Bawdy, awful words, of course. But Marie plays by ear, and we honestly had no idea she could until she was sitting there at the piano, four years old, belting out those awful songs that Willem still knew from his rowdier days and..." He shrugged. "It wasn't any cuter when she was four."

Marie belted out another line that had Ana Marie and Willem practically rolling, which made Marie laugh out loud as well. She wrapped up the song and looked at her tante and oom.

"Shame, man," she managed. "I shall have to wash my mouth out with soap now."

"Oh, you sing it just like our Papa did!," Ana Marie applauded gleefully, hugging Marie to her side. "You are more Boer than us, Marie."

"If you didn't look so much like Daniel," Willem smiled, "we should have to ask Sara some questions about her fidelity."

"Shame," Sara said, throwing a pillow at his head.

"You're a lucky man, Scott," Willem laughed, catching the pillow in his hands. "No offense to my own wife, of course, but I would have married Marie myself if she had just come along thirty years earlier than she did," Willem said appreciatively. "The voice of an angel, the mouth of a sailor."

"She's the best of Daniel and Sara… and then some," Ana Marie said, pulling her closer.

"And she *dances*!," Willem shouted, standing up. "Sara, play a little something for us," he said, sweeping Marie into his arms.

"Well, I'll do my best," Sara smiled, sitting at the piano, as Marie set herself up across from Willem with a seductive grin, matching the same one he gave her with a hearty laugh. And then, they were dancing… like two ballroom dancing champions.

Scott was dumbfounded. "She's like a freakin' renaissance man, isn't she?," he asked Ana Marie.

"Ja," she nodded. "Did you know that she could dance, Scott?"

Scott thought back to a few very private moments from the past few weeks, back at his house, honeymooning as it was with Marie, and some of the dances she had done for him. Not that this was anything like what she was doing now or like anything anyone here should know about and –

Daniel glared at him from across the room. Could the man read Scott's dirty mind?!

"Well, I didn't know she could do this," he managed.

Ana Marie continued watching her brother and Marie. "She and Riaan could captivate an entire club full of old Afrikaners with their old style dancing like this, back when Marie was a teenager. And Piet… well, he's quite good as well. And the two of them, Marie and Piet, always… shame, man." She wiped away a tear.

"Tante," Marie sighed, twirling away from Willem, embracing Ana Marie hesitantly, tears in her own voice. "I'm sorry."

Scott had no idea what the apology was for or why both women were now crying.

"Sorry?," Ana Marie smiled, even as she wept, brushing Marie's hair from her face. "I'm thankful that you did it. Piet needed to let go and move on and… well, you needed to. It was well past time, love." She smiled over at Scott. "Although you can blame my son for wanting… well, for still wanting her, even though she belongs to you now?"

And Scott? Honestly couldn't.

And for the first time, he felt like he had something over Piet.

He had Marie.

Marie

Her parents convinced her to take a nap after lunch. Marie, still jetlagged, agreed and was only slightly anxious as Scott followed her to her room. She didn't speak to him, too emotional to start their fight all over again, but simply laid down, not facing him, even as he crawled into bed next to her and put his arm around her.

"Hey," he said, "I'm sorry."

She wiped her eyes, cursing the hormones that made the tears come so easily these days.

"And I didn't mean the things I said. Well, okay. Maybe I meant some of them. But I shouldn't have said them, Marie. It's just…" He laid back again, closing his eyes. "There's just a lot we didn't think through, you know?"

"I know," she sighed, crying harder now, "I feel horrible. And I've broken my mother's heart. And my father still probably wants to kill you. And I'm not even sure that you still like me –"

"Oh, I like you," Scott breathed, running his hands down his face. "If I'm certain of nothing else, I'm certain of that. I like you. And the more I'm around you here and back home… the more reasons I find to like you. I think I could spend the rest of our lives together and never figure out everything about you or ever run out of reasons to like you. You're like the world's most interesting woman, Marie. Speaking all these languages, playing nasty bar songs by ear, seducing Afrikaner men of all ages –"

She laughed at this, then began crying even harder.

"What's wrong?," he asked, gently brushing her hair back from her face.

"It's Piet…"

"Hey," he said, softly. "I was wrong about Piet. I'm sorry. You shouldn't feel guilty for what happened all those years ago. I was being a big, mean jerk."

"No, Scott," she continued to sob. "You were right. He kissed me."

Scott didn't say anything for a moment. "What?"

"Just for a moment. And then, I ended it. Oh, Scott, I ended it forever."

Scott

Well, this was really, really bad news. Every bad thought he'd had since meeting Piet had just come to fruition.

Not. Good.

"When did this happen?," he asked.

"This morning," she cried.

He thought on this for a moment, stopping just short of letting himself imagine what they must have looked like. It did no good letting his mind go to these places. He thought of all the potential responses to this confession of hers, the feelings that he was actually justified to have...

Anger. Jealousy. Self-righteousness. All understandable. All allowed. All totally merited and fair and –

But what would be the point? Letting himself linger on these feelings wouldn't fix anything. It wouldn't mend the damage he'd done the night before. It wouldn't do anything to repair the trust she'd lost in him. And before he could even feel indignation over the way she'd very nearly forfeited *his* trust in *her*, he thought back to Ephesians 5.

Seriously. Was this what life in Christ would be like for the rest of his life? Scripture coming to mind, convicting, rebuking, encouraging, correcting, strengthening, challenging all that he naturally felt inclined to do, calling him to more?

What a scary thought. What an empowering thought. For all that Scott was certain he couldn't do, for all that he knew he would find impossible in God's will and calling in his life, and for all that he still didn't understand, he found immense comfort in knowing that God would remind him, would guide him, would call him out of what he was allowed to feel, was justified to feel, was wanting to feel... and call him to grace.

"I'm sorry," he said to Marie, shocked to hear the words come from his mouth, floored by the way they came from his heart.

"What?," she asked, staring at him through her tears.

"I'm sorry that I set you up for that, acting the way I did last night."

"Scott," she said, raising up to look at him. "You didn't do this. I did. I'm the one who let it happen."

"But," he said, "when I married you, I knew I was taking responsibility for your heart as much as my own. And you can do what you want to do, of course, but I have to answer for my part in leading you. Closer to Christ, farther away from Him. I have to answer for it either way."

She regarded him with shock. "Scott..."

"Is that what everyone was talking about?," he asked. "Is that why Ana Marie was crying? You ending things forever with Piet?"

"No, shame, Ana Marie was crying because I lost my temper with him and *yelled* obscenities at him."

He was glad he missed the kiss. But he kind of wished that he had seen this. "Really?"

"All in Afrikaans, too," she sobbed, "so I know I hurt him as deeply as I could. Shame, man. Why am I hurting everyone so much? And they just… they were trying to cheer me up because it hurt… Scott, it *hurt*, to hurt Piet like that. To hurt them all like that. To know that I had hurt you as well. So all the singing and dancing? Just trying to make it all better, when I'm the one who's messed it all up."

Scott watched her quietly, realizing that for all he knew about her, he didn't know much at all, honestly.

"Perfect Marietjie," she cried, "so good and so right and so wonderful now that she's gone off to the States and found herself in Christ. But, Scott, I'm not even who I was three months ago, because I let him get to me… and who am I now, huh? What good am I to anyone now, if I don't even know who I am anymore?"

And with only a moment of hesitation, he reached out and pulled her into his arms.

"I'm such a loser," she whispered, crying against him.

"You're a lot of things," he murmured. "But a loser isn't one of them."

"How do you know that?," she asked.

"Because," he said, very simply, "when we're in Christ, we're not losers anymore, are we? I don't think Jesus would waste the effort on people who couldn't be someone in Him."

"But I'm not new at this, Scott," she said. "Grace is nothing new to me."

"Except it seems like it is," he noted. "Or that you don't believe you'll get it wrong. That you'll need grace all the time." He shrugged. "I'm relieved, quite honestly, to know that we're on even ground in this. Because it means that I won't be the only one screwing things up."

She watched him sadly. "You're relieved that he kissed me?"

"No," he sighed. "And if I think about that too much, I'll probably stop being so spiritual about the whole thing and react the way that I want to… which will put me in need of some grace."

She sighed at this. "Scott…"

He said nothing for a moment. "Do you want to be with him?"

"No," she said, looking at him. "I meant it when I sent him away. I don't want him. I want you." Her lip quivered. "I hope you still want me."

"Yes, Marie," he breathed. "Forever."

"Are you sorry?," she asked, fresh tears falling from her eyes.

"About the way I acted last night?"

"No," she said, her voice trembling, "about being with me. Are you sorry that you're with me?"

"Good grief, no," Scott said, touching her face. "I'm sorry about how I went about it all, but, no, being with you, marrying you… even having a baby with you… no, I'm not sorry about that at all."

"Me neither," she said.

"Hey," Scott whispered, leaning over her, kissing the tears away one by one, until she finally put her hands to his face. "I love you," he said. "And I'm going to take care of you. Of both of you. You can trust me. I've made a lot of bad decisions in my life, Marie. But I swear… you weren't one of them."

And as she eventually fell asleep peacefully in his arms, he thought through all that would have to change as soon as they got home. And how changing everything was more than worth it for Marie.

Scott had a plan. And unlike his foolproof plan to get her to go out with him, then his foolproof plan to get her to marry him in Vegas… well, this one was going to work out just fine.

And the reason why was because he had his super-scary father-in-law in on the plan with him. And fate itself? Wouldn't cross Daniel Boyd. He was sure of it.

He had explained what he wanted to do. Daniel had listened to him, and his expression had gone from grim, lethal, and terrifying to... well, grim, slightly sentimental, and at least agreeable.

From terrifying to agreeable. It was a start.

The two of them set to work immediately, making calls and getting plans together. And before long, they brought Sara in on the whole thing. She burst into tears, hugged them both for a good long while, and swore to them, as she shooed them out the door, that they'd be ready on the beach right at sunset.

Marie

"Marie? Marie, you need to wake up, sweetheart."

Marie opened her eyes to her mother, forgetting for a moment that she was all grown up... then remembering all too well when the wave of nausea hit her.

"Shame," her mother cooed, handing her a glass of Ana Marie's mommy tonic. "Just lie there until it passes."

"Where did Scott go?," Marie asked, thinking of the way he'd held her earlier, the way he'd forgiven everything, the way he'd spoken such grace.

Was it possible to love someone more because you'd walked through hardship with him? She certainly felt a more intense love for him now and wondered at what the years ahead would bring. Hardship, struggles, frail humanness... more grace, more understanding, more refining, more and more genuine love every single day.

"He's with your father," Sara smiled. "They're working."

"Up north? Again? Dad should be paying Scott for his trouble," Marie groaned.

Sara shook her head. "Oh, no, not up north. They went to the beach."

"The beach?" A vision of her father drowning Scott in the ocean crossed through her thoughts –

"All Scott's idea," Sara smiled, relieving that concern at least a little. "And you don't need to know all the details right now," she said standing up and making her way to the closet.

"What's going on?," Marie smiled at the gleeful way her mother pushed aside the clothes in the spare closet, searching.

"Well, a surprise. Which you'll probably figure out if... well..." She looked to Marie with tears in her eyes.

"Mom, what's wrong?"

"I thought you might want to see if... well, if this fits you." She held up a familiar dress.

"Your wedding dress?"

Her mother nodded. "Didn't you say you –"

"Always wanted to be married in it," Marie finished.

"Shame," Sara smiled. "As soon as your stomach settles, let's try it on. I think you're going to need it tonight."

Several hours later, Marie made her way across the Namibian sand, just as the sun tucked itself into the ocean.

The family was gathered there. Riaan and Ana Marie, seated next to Sophie and Willem. Then her mother, already dabbing her eyes with a tissue. Her father, coming to her side with a smile. And all their eyes were on her, as she stepped forward, a small bouquet in one hand, her father's arm clutched in the other.

And Marie's eyes? Were on Scott.

Scott

Scott hadn't slowed down all day.

There hadn't been much to do to get the ceremony ready, thanks to the beautiful backdrop that the sunset and waves naturally created for them. His work had been in setting up everything for a small family reception at Marie's favorite restaurant overlooking the sea, preparing for a celebration that was long overdue. He and Daniel had gone through all the details together, reaching an amicable agreement on this new chapter of everyone's lives. It hadn't been easy, but watching Marie walk down the aisle now, beaming at him? It was all worth it.

And so they were married... again. By Marie's father, on a beach, overlooking the ocean... just like Marie had always dreamt she would be. Daniel used the very same scriptures she'd said to him in anger, about leaving and cleaving, about becoming one with someone else, about moving on from the past and moving forward in Christ, a new creation.

And Marie said goodbye to what home had been... and found her home in Scott, in who they were together in Christ, in this new tune that they were both learning to play together.

CHAPTER NINE

Scott

She was playing the piano when he snuck in through the garage.

He wasn't in the habit of sneaking home in the middle of the day. Business was good, and there was a long list of projects that he was overseeing all over town. He rarely allowed himself the freedom of just leaving it in someone else's hands so that he could do what he really wanted to do.

But today was an exception. Because today was a big day.

He moved over to where she sat, still playing, still oblivious to his presence, and whispered in her ear...

"Happy anniversary."

She grinned and kept on playing. "Heard you come in," she whispered.

"Really?," he asked. "And I was being quiet. Half expected you to stand up and kick me in the eye, as you've been known to do when you're startled."

"Maybe next time," she laughed softly, leaning over to kiss him. "Happy anniversary. I was so tired when you left this morning that I didn't even remember."

"Yeah, but I did," he said, pulling the bouquet of flowers out from behind his back. "Present number two."

She grinned at this. "Two anniversaries. Two anniversary gifts. I could get used to this."

The big gift had been the piano, brought in a month earlier, and placed in the living room for her. Scott had made Sam carry the heavy side, of course. But it had been worth his brother's pain and effort, as their home had been filled with one new tune after another ever since.

"Mmmm," she sighed, leaning over to smell the flowers and smiling, her hands still moving over the piano keys. "Beautiful."

"Exactly what I was thinking," he said, putting them to the side and attempting to gather her into his arms, finding it difficult as she kept playing.

"Scott," she giggled.

"I don't think the world will stop turning if you take a break from the music," he said. "Just long enough to –"

"Oh, but it will," she said. Then, with a very serious look, "If I stop playing, Nathan will wake up." She raised her eyebrows and kept right on with her tune.

He remembered how hard it had been when the baby was born, how she'd sat on the floor of the nursery and cried, telling him that she'd never get to sleep again nor have enough milk to satisfy this monster of a child, who stayed up and ate *All. The. Time.* Scott had stayed up with her, wisely choosing to keep his suggestions to himself when she'd thrown his new book, *The Definitive Guide on Breastfeeding,* at him when he'd told her she wasn't doing it right. He figured out quickly enough that the best thing to do was to sit there, supportively, getting no sleep right along with her, and telling her at every opportunity that she was doing awesome and that she was, in fact, beautiful.

"You're beautiful," he said, landing a kiss on her forehead. (See? So smart.)

"He's got to start sleeping regularly at some point, right?," she asked, through her yawn. "I mean, he's up all night nursing and most of the day, too, so eventually, he's going to have to wear himself out enough to finally sleep more than two hours at a time, right? I mean, hopefully before he leaves for college, right?"

"You should sleep while he sleeps," Scott noted, congratulating himself on giving such great advice. (He'd gotten that from another book. He was full of gems, just like these.)

She regarded him with a smile, shaking her head. "Oh, I would... but every time I take my hands off the piano, I can hear him start to stir. And I'd rather sit here playing in peace than have him awake and nursing. Again. For what feels like the hundredth time since you left the house this morning."

"Poor Marie," Scott murmured, moving his kisses to her neck.

"Oh, poor Marie my butt," she said with a smile. "If it's not him keeping me up, it's you. I swear, you both want my body twenty-four seven but for entirely different reasons."

"Speaking of," Scott said, pulling her into his lap, her hands finally leaving the keys, "it's my turn with you now while the little prince sleeps."

"He's going to wake up, any second now –"

"He wouldn't dare."

She grinned at this, raising her eyebrows at him.

"Okay, so he totally will. Which is why we'll need to be quick."

"I'm game," she said against his lips. "But Sam –"

"He's out for the rest of the afternoon," he said, returning her kiss. "Sent him on a wild goose chase with a remodel at some medical clinic."

"Score."

"I'm about to," he said, pulling her close.

And then, they heard the baby.

"Shame, man, that's my cue," she groaned, pulling her mouth from his reluctantly. "I told you."

"Take a number, Nate!," Scott yelled over her shoulder. "Seriously, he's the worst wing man ever, Marie."

"I think he's actually helping you," she murmured, "because all these delays and distractions are making me want you even more."

"Then, just ignore the crying, and let's –"

"Scott, my milk is letting down the longer we let him cry," she sighed.

"Wow," he laughed. "Sexy moment averted."

"For now," she said, kissing him soundly.

"Yeah," he murmured back. "Go ahead and settle in on the couch. I'll bring him to you."

"I love you, Scott," she whispered.

And he smiled to hear it, even as he jogged to the little blue room, where manly, masculine rubber duckies were painted on the walls.

What? They were much manlier than the bunnies Marie had originally wanted. He could thank Daniel for being his advocate in refusing to subject his man-child to bunnies, at least, when they had come back to the US just in time for the birth. The two men had spent more than a few days getting everything just exactly like Marie wanted for the baby's room, and it had been manly men work, with little talking but plenty of camaraderie, something that Scott had appreciated now that Daniel seemed to hate him less.

And then? Well, Nathan had arrived, and they became the most unmanly of men, sitting as close as they could together on the couch so that both of them had a hand on the tiny infant at the same time, neither of them willing to miss a movement, a tiny little yawn, or even a simple heartbeat.

Nathan was just that awesome, clearly.

Scott opened the door and peeked in, a set of precious little feet and little hands flailing about and peeking just above the rails of the crib.

The sight of those little feet and hands made Scott's heart swell up in a way that he had never known possible. Who knew life could get any better than just him and Marie together? He hadn't been able to fathom the truth of it until the moment the doctor put his tiny son in his arms. Who knew that adding just one person could make things exponentially sweeter?

"Hey, buddy," Scott whispered as he approached the crib, noting that Nathan began to kick more at the sound of his voice and that his impatient cries turned to content coos. And when his little eyes met Scott's, he actually squealed out his approval.

Well, those eyes were his father-in-law's, but Scott suspected that the delighted personality was all Marie. Or maybe all him, as he had more reason to be delighted than ever before these days.

"Tell me about it," Scott cooed along, pulling his little man up out of the crib and kissing him on the forehead before cradling him close. "We've got to talk, man. I know you're really into Mommy and all, but she was mine first. And it's not like I'm asking for the moon, Nate. Just five minutes. Well, maybe more than that, if you know what I'm sayin' and all, and –"

Nathan looked at him with wide eyes. "Oh, well, I'll explain it to you when you're older, when you marry a knockout girl like your mom. Actually, I probably won't need to explain it then, will I? Because you'll totally get it on your own, friend." Nathan squealed in response.

"So," Scott said, walking him over to the changing table and starting the now natural process of diapering, dressing, and delivering him to his mother, "it was a hard day at work. Your Uncle Sam is a real pinhead and contracted out all these jobs that he should have just left for me to take care of myself. The wiring is all messed up, the plumbing is all wonky, and the plans for the duct work? It's a mess." He whistled under his breath. "Not unlike what's happening here in your pants, my man. How are you able to do this when all you drink is milk?"

Nathan chewed his fist in response, his brow furrowing for a moment. "My mistake, mentioning milk and all," Scott said. "I'm hurrying, I'm hurrying. Hey, and don't you point that thing at me either. I'm onto your tricks, and I don't want pee in my eye. Again."

He cleaned up the mess, threw away the offending diaper, and slid a new one up under his son, all with one hand, all under five seconds. He was getting good at this.

"Anyway, it's going to take another week to get the work done now. And correcting what's already been done incorrectly? Is a headache and a half. Can't blame Sam for trying to make things easier on me so I could spend more time here with *you*, but... well, yeah, I can blame Sam. And I do."

He finished the diaper, snapped up the little bodysuit, and picked Nathan back up again, kissing him on the cheeks. "But he does fine. And I'm glad he's there, honestly. But you know what? I can't wait until *you're* out there with us, working alongside us, showing up Sam with what I know will be your completely advanced and totally gifted knowledge of all things relating to or pertaining to engineering and architecture. Just like me with my own dad."

Nathan pushed a wet fist into Scott's shoulder as he let out a delighted laugh.

"I know, I know, I'm excited about it, too," Scott smiled at him. "But first things first. Manly men have to eat dinner before talking work, right? Taking you that way right now, my man. And then? Then we can talk about all that's up ahead."

And he left the nursery with Nathan in his arms, ready to see what was up ahead for all of them...

A SNEAK PEEK AT
"PURE FICTION"
COMING OUT IN AUGUST 2014!

Madison

It was, quite possibly, the worst book she'd ever written.

Madison held the advance print copy in her hands and regarded it as though it was a prodigal child. Born of natural and right means, nurtured and grown over many sleepless days and nights, believed in, hoped for... then, before she could grasp what had happened, it had gone the way of its prodigal siblings. Trash. Such filthy trash.

But it wasn't like a child. It was her work, her thoughts, her very words. And she'd let it happen. The stories started out sweet and innocent, but she could hear her publicist in her head, her editors whispering in her ears, and her agent, Kaci, in her very dreams. *This won't sell.*

It wouldn't. And so, she sent her characters off into situations they didn't need to be in and made them lewd, crude, and for the majority of the book, completely nude.

She'd never even known that this was an actual legitimate literary genre back when she'd first started writing.

Madison bit her lip as she ran her hand over the cover. It was well done. It would catch eyes, would look pretty on store shelves, and would entice readers to buy it. Once inside, they'd discover that as far as literary efforts went, this was her best by far. As far as skill went, she was at the top of her game. As far as entertaining plots went, this was better than she'd ever done.

But it was trash. And raunchier than all the ones before it. It was, most definitely, the worst book she'd ever written.

Number 12, she called it, because she refused to call it "Read My Lips." Or just "Lips" as Kaci insisted on calling it. She only acknowledged its place in a long line of books just like it. Number 12.

She glanced over at her laptop, where Number 13 was already halfway written. There was money in being prolific in this genre, and because there was nothing else in all the world that demanded her time and attention, she was able to keep the words coming. The money was shocking to her at first, the very idea that people would pay to read something she'd made up, but this far into the game, advance payments on books and royalty checks were more subdued affairs.

Likely because the guilt had become greater lately.

She put Number 12 down quietly and looked out her window. She managed a faint smile looking over the neat, tidy lawn and the quiet street beyond her doorstep. Kaci had balked at the small house back when Madison had bought it, saying that she could certainly afford something bigger and in a much more affluent neighborhood.

And she could have. But this street, this place, had so many wonderful memories attached to it, and because there were precious few pleasant memories from her childhood, the ones that she did have in this particular place were even sweeter. She'd been a kid here, going to visit her friend, Faith, who lived just down the road. They went to church and school together from elementary school to junior high then on to high school. And when things had gone from bad to really, really bad at home, Faith's house was the one place where Madison had felt some stability, some warmth, and some normalcy. Faith's father was the pastor of their church, and Madison had assumed that his family put on a show for church like her family did, that they pretended life was okay when they walked into the sanctuary, that they tore one another to pieces as soon as they got home.

But Faith's family wasn't like that. They were the same no matter where they were. And they really believed what they said about Jesus.

Faith's own mother had led Madison to Christ in the pastor's house, on this very same street, so many years ago. And when her parents did divorce, when her dad left them, and when her mother left the church, Madison had come back to this same place so many times, so distraught, so hurt, and so completely messed up.

It was a strange thing, knowing the security of Christ and believing in His Lordship... and discovering that still, she held part of herself back from Him. This pain, the feeling that abandonment was part of life, was what she'd held back.

And in the end, long after she'd gone away to college and figured out that she could write, it was that part that was so easily given over to something so completely set apart from Him.

It had only moderately bothered her before. With her bank account full and promising, she had made her way back here to settle down, to hole herself up and write, to make a home for herself. She'd been swept up in nostalgia when the realtor had showed her this place, saying, like Kaci, that it was really less than what she could afford. Madison had hardly heard her as her mind rushed through memories of this neighborhood, of how her heart had felt, of how she had known love here.

She honestly assumed that Faith's family had long since moved on from the church and from this neighborhood. It had been years, after all. That's why she'd been caught so off guard when the first neighbor at her door was none other than Chloe Hayes, Faith's mother.

There had been surprise, just a moment of it, and then, instant recognition.

Madison hadn't been prepared to have been remembered. And so fondly remembered, as Mrs. Hayes, nearly forgetting the basket of homemade desserts in her arms, had reached right out to Madison, gathered her close and murmured, "Maddie... Maddie Smith... I've been praying for you."

Even now, tears pooled in Madison's eyes as she remembered. To know that she'd been prayed for, all these years, as life had taken some strange turns... it was a lot. It was so much, in fact, that Madison immediately agreed to go to her old church now that she was back in town. And she'd been going for months now, where everyone knew her, where everyone loved her, where she was learning again about who Christ was, and where no one ever asked what it was that she was doing with her life.

Perhaps they knew. Perhaps that's why Mrs. Hayes had been praying for her.

Madison looked back over at Number 12. Scripture began to pop up in her mind. Irritating. This conviction that came up at the worst times. It was church. It was being back in a community where people lived what they believed, where they said what Jesus said, where she could feel Him speaking to her heart, and —

Her phone rang, and she snapped her eyes from Number 12. Crossing the living room and walking into the kitchen, she reached out for her cell phone and glanced at the screen.

Clark.

Clark of Ye Giant Publishing House of Smutty Books. How thrilled Madison had been to have gotten that first call from him, never guessing how far the hole she was stepping into was, so many years ago. How great the dread was now when his number lit up the phone.

She took a deep breath and reminded herself just exactly who she was now.

"Vivian Chase," she said in that breathy, sultry, completely ridiculous voice that Kaci had made her perfect after she'd first hit the bestseller list. She'd have never consented to acting like this or even adopting the pen name to begin with, but it had been a point not worth arguing as Kaci had sold the book with the pen name already on it. *Too confusing*, she'd said, waving Madison's concerns off.

Maybe it was better this way. It certainly made acting like Clark was expecting her to act a little easier. It was just Vivian Chase, after all. Not Madison Smith.

"Viv," Clark murmured. "I have some huge news."

"Me, too, Clark," she murmured right back. "I've been meaning to call you ever since I got the advance copy of 'Read My Lips.'"

"Do you like it?," he asked. "The cover turned out great. And the reviews read just as well as I thought they would."

"Oh, that's great," she said, not giving two flying flips about any of it. "But what I really meant was... well, the good news is about the story, Clark."

He paused. Then, "The story?" She could practically hear him grin.

She forced a flirtatious laugh. "It's been soooo loooong, Clark," she said. "So long since I've read that book, you know. And I swear, last night as I was reading it in the bubble bath, I blushed at that scene twenty pages in." She knew it by heart. Could probably recite every nasty word by memory.

"Did you now?," he asked. The skeeve was probably imagining her in the bath now. Great.

"I sure did," she said, forcing another giggle. "Clark, if it's making *me* blush, it's going to be a best seller."

"Well, we already knew that, Vivian," he said confidently. "So I have the bigger news still."

"And what's that?," she asked, with just the right measure of coyness in her voice.

"We're changing up your press tour for this one," he said.

So, she wouldn't be doing her standard jaunt from city-to-city, selling books, speaking at events, teaching the odd writer workshop here and there, smiling, and making sexy jokes. Hallelujah. Playing Vivian Chase for the crowds was the worst part of writing, honestly.

"Oh!," she fake-gasped and moaned, ever so slightly. "But, Clark, I *love* the press tour!" Not hardly.

"You'll love the changes even more, though," he said. "We've been focusing on the East Coast and the South, of course, since your fan base is strongest there."

"Mmmm," she murmured, wondering what he was getting at.

"But your last book... Vivian, you were selling *more* copies in Texas alone than in all the southern states combined."

Well, this was unexpected. "I'm sorry... what?," she asked simply, hearing Madison Smith in the question.

"Women in Texas love you!," he exclaimed. "I don't know what it is, but we're going to hit that while we can. And with you in Texas, it'll be simpler to fly you out to the West Coast, where we're projecting even better sales and an entirely new fan base out there."

"But how do you know —"

And then, she focused in on what he'd really said. "With me in... Texas?"

"That's what I said," he said, a smile evident in his voice.

"But I live in Florida," she managed.

"I know," he said, "but for the next six months, you're going to be in Texas, promoting yourself. And we're going to keep you to one place for the most part, let you settle in there, and teach a class."

"Teach a class?," she asked. "On writing?"

"Yeah, and we've already gotten all the details set up with Kaci. She said you'd prefer Fort Worth — smaller than Houston and Dallas both, you know. Has already gotten your living arrangements squared away and your flights booked. She also told us that you'd prefer teaching in a more intimate setting. A restaurant. A non-chain kind of place. We found the perfect place, worked it out with the owner, and have you on schedule to be there in a couple of weeks."

"But I live in Florida!," she repeated.

"Kaci's got the details," he said, not even hearing her anymore. "It's gonna be great, Viv."

And he hung up before she could even think of a sexy comeback.

Grant

Sunday morning.

It was the one day of the week that Grant kept the restaurant closed.

He set every day of the week apart for Christ in his heart, living for the Lord and His glory with all of his life, but he took special care on Sunday to keep from work.

The restaurant was work. But cooking wasn't. He couldn't sleep in after all these years of running his place, so he usually headed over to Rachel's house for breakfast, and he almost always was the one to do the cooking.

He pulled up to her house at seven and grabbed the bag of groceries out of his backseat before he made his way down the sidewalk. He'd just picked her up at the airport yesterday after two weeks abroad, so he figured the odds were bad that she'd even have eggs or milk in the fridge.

She'd be glad to see him.

He thought on this as he knocked on the door... and waited. He leaned on the doorbell... and waited. Finally, just as he was taking a breath to yell towards the direction of her bedroom window, the door opened.

And there was Micah, wearing a towel.

He looked at Grant for a long moment. "Hmm," he said, very simply.

"Good morning to you, too," Grant said. "Did I catch you while you were in the shower?"

Micah opened his mouth to ask a question, then frowned again. "No, actually."

"Then, why the towel?," he asked.

"First thing I could find to throw on when the pounding on the door started," he said.

"Why exactly weren't you wearing clothes?," Grant asked.

Micah sighed. "Do you really want to have this conversation with me?"

They watched one another for a few more seconds. "Aren't you going to ask me in?," Grant said.

Micah looked over his shoulder... then looked back. "Should I, Grant?"

"Rachel usually does," he said. "Sunday morning breakfast and all." Then, to sweeten the deal, "I'll make you an omelet."

Micah considered this for a minute. "Come on in, then," he said, moving aside as Grant came in and headed straight towards the kitchen. "I should probably go tell Rachel that —"

But his words were cut short as the door to Rachel's bedroom opened and her voice rang out. "Micah, who was that at the — *Grant!*"

The door slammed shut again. Micah sighed at this. Grant shrugged and started making himself at home in the kitchen.

Five seconds later, the door slammed opened again. And Rachel, tugging on a bathrobe, came into the kitchen.

"Grant, what are you doing here?," she screeched.

"It's Sunday," he said by way of explanation. "Thought you'd still want breakfast."

She stared at him, her mouth open, wordless.

"What?," he asked. "Married people don't eat?"

Oh, yeah. The two weeks abroad? Had been her honeymoon. And the half dressed man who'd opened the door for him? Was his brother-in-law, Micah.

Who was, by all appearances, no longer bothered by Grant's presence as evidenced by the way he was now sitting at the dining room table, towel and all, peeking at the ingredients Grant had laid out.

"We just got back from our honeymoon!," Rachel continued on. "Did you stop and think that maybe, just maybe, we might want some privacy?"

He shrugged. "I don't know. Maybe. Not really."

"Last night was our first night in this house!," she yelled.

"Then, this meal is my housewarming gift," he said.

"Micah?" She looked to her husband for affirmation.

"He told me he'd make an omelet," Micah shrugged.

She looked at both of them for a long moment. "Unbelievable."

"Rachel," Micah murmured, pulling her over to sit on his lap. "If it doesn't bother him, it doesn't bother me."

"It bothers me," she cooed, putting her arms around his neck. Then, to Grant, "How do you know you weren't interrupting something?"

He glanced over at her. "Apparently, I was, since Micah is still naked —"

"I have a towel on," he said, kissing Rachel.

"Good enough for me," Grant said. "And before you say it, Rachel, I know that things have changed. And I won't be here every Sunday. Unless Micah requests an omelet."

"I can make him an omelet," she argued.

"I'm sure you do a lot of really great things for Micah that I don't want to know anything about," Grant noted. "But you can't possibly make a better omelet than me. Give the man what he needs, Rachel."

She frowned at this, then looked back at Micah. "He's right," he muttered. "I've had his omelets before. They're the best."

Rachel opened her mouth to argue this, but Grant put a cup of coffee in front of her and said, with great enthusiasm, "I've got some awesome news."

"You're getting a life outside of the restaurant and hanging out here? Finally?," she muttered.

"Ouch," he said. "I have a life, Rachel. But actually, this new is about the restaurant —"

"Big surprise there," she said, picking up her coffee.

He ignored this jab. "When are our profits the lowest, Rachel?," he asked.

"Tuesday and Thursday evenings," she said, knowing the business almost as well as he did, given how involved she'd been in it all, from the very start of his business a few years back until now. "But they're not all that low then."

"Always room for improvement," he said. "And I've figured out a way to improve those particular evenings."

"How so?," Micah asked. "Promotions? Deals?"

"Didn't have to change anything," he said. "Just secured new clientele."

"New clientele?," Rachel asked.

Grant grinned over at her. "Sealed a deal," he said. "Some book club thing. Fifty women. Romance writers... or wannabes, I don't know. In the restaurant two times a week, Tuesday and Thursday, every week for the rest of the semester."

Rachel frowned. "Well, that doesn't mean that they'll all show every week. Or that they'll spend anything —"

"Twenty dollar charge per head, with or without food," he said. "Part of the deal. And they only have part of the restaurant. The lady who booked it told me that the rest of the place will be filled with overflow people, trying to hear the lectures."

"Well, then," she murmured. "Lectures?"

"Yeah," he said. "Big name writer coming in. They're on a waiting list to have this lady teach them or read out loud to them or... well, whatever she's going to do. The roster for the class filled up in ten minutes, and I've got people already calling who didn't make it onto the list, trying to reserve tables for weeks and weeks on out so they can hear the lectures as well." He slid in across from Micah, passing the omelet over to him.

"Wow, really big name, apparently. Who is it?," Rachel asked, taking a sip of coffee.

"Some lady named Vivian Chase."

And with that, Rachel spit all of her coffee out, practically in Grant's face.

"Good grief, Rachel," he said, picking up a napkin and wiping what had splattered onto his forehead. "Could you at least try to be a lady?"

"Vivian Chase?!," she shouted. "Grant! Do you know who she is?!"

"Yeah," he said, "some romance writer. Chick lit. The woman who's about to up my business substantially, and –"

"Grant, she writes *dirty* books," Rachel whispered. "Bestsellers, of course, but... well, you know."

"Actually, I don't," he said flippantly. "And I don't care either way. She didn't want to teach in a stuffy classroom or academic setting, and her agent said the restaurant was just right."

"Seems like a conflict of conscience, though," Micah noted, mid-bite. "Assisting this lady with promoting her work when, like Rachel says, it doesn't honor God."

Grant sat back and sighed. "I'm just cooking food."

"You do more than that," Rachel said. "And you know it. By allowing this in your restaurant, aren't you giving clearance to what she does? Aren't you affirming it?"

"I'm cooking," he said simply, not wanting to think about it, honestly. His life was the restaurant, and he did everything in his power to make it succeed. This book club was a good thing, no matter how these two were spinning it. "Not unlike I'm doing right here, right now. Rachel, you want something?"

"Sure, since you're already here," she said. Then, "Grant?"

"Yeah?," he said, already back at the stove, pushing aside any negative thoughts his family had put into his head.

"Just be careful," Rachel said softly, as he watched her exchange a concerned look with Micah.

ABOUT THE AUTHOR

Jenn Faulk is a full time mom and pastor's wife in Pasadena, Texas. She has a BA in English-Creative Writing from the University of Houston and an MA in Missiology from Southwestern Baptist Theological Seminary. She loves talking about Jesus, running marathons, listening to her daughters' stories, and serving alongside her husband in ministry. You can contact her through her blog www.jennfaulk.com